A CATERED BIRTHDAY PARTY

Books by Isis Crawford

A CATERED MURDER

A CATERED WEDDING

A CATERED CHRISTMAS

A CATERED VALENTINE'S DAY

A CATERED HALLOWEEN

A CATERED BIRTHDAY PARTY

Published by Kensington Publishing Corporation

A Mystery with Recipes

A CATERED BIRTHDAY PARTY

ISIS CRAWFORD

KENSINGTON BOOKS
www.kensingtonbooks.com

KENSINGTON BOOKS are published by

Kensington Publishing Corp.
119 West 40th Street
New York, NY 10018

All Kensington titles, imprints and distributed lines are available at special quantity discounts for bulk purchases for sales promotion, premiums, fund-raising, educational or institutional use.

Special book excerpts or customized printings can also be created to fit specific needs. For details, write or phone the office of the Kensington Special Sales Manager: Kensington Publishing Corp., 119 West 40th Street, New York, NY, 10018. Attn. Special Sales Department. Phone: 1-800-221-2647.

Kensington and the K logo Reg. U.S. Pat. & TM Off.

Library of Congress Card Catalogue Number: 2009934754

ISBN-13: 978-0-7582-2194-0
ISBN-10: 0-7582-2194-0

First Hardcover Printing: December 2009

10   9   8   7   6   5   4   3   2   1

Printed in the United States of America

To Dan for surviving.
And to my Aunt Pearl, an inspiration to us all.

Chapter 1

Libby dried her hands on the edge of her apron. She put the spatula covered with brownie batter in the sink before turning to face her younger sister. Then she took a deep breath. When that didn't calm her down she took a second and a third. Maybe her boyfriend Marvin was right. Maybe she did need to mellow out.

"You like dogs," Bernie said to her in her most soothing voice.

"Not to the point of making dinner parties for them," Libby told her sister.

"Birthday party," Bernie corrected. "We're making a birthday party."

Libby frowned and waved her hand in the air. "Same thing."

"No, it's not."

"It's close enough."

"Let's not get overly semantic."

"You do," Libby told her.

Bernie decided to ignore the comment and stick to the matter at hand. "This isn't for 'any' dog," Bernie said. "This is for Trudy, Annabel Colbert's dog."

"I know who Trudy is," Libby replied as she studied the

toothpick she'd just plunged into the first batch of brownies in the oven. "Everyone in the world knows who Trudy is."

Okay, that was an exaggeration, but not by much, Libby thought. There might be some obscure tribe living in the Brazilian jungle who didn't know about Trudy, but that was about it. Trudy was the model for the Puggables, a group of stuffed toys that were the lynchpin of the Colbert toy empire.

The collection was composed of Eenie and Minnie, the mom and the dad, plus the three pups, Paggie, Poogie, and Twinkles, as well as numerous other family members with names too disgustingly cute to mention. Not only that, but they came in a range of annoyingly saccharine pastel colors. However, they had made Annabel and her husband a fortune. Before the Puggables, Colbert Toys had been just another company struggling to survive.

Libby sighed as she turned her thoughts back to the brownies. They were almost done. Five more minutes at the most. That was the trouble with brownies: They were easy to make, but difficult to make well. If you added the chocolate and butter mixture to the flour before it cooled, the bars came out heavy. If you baked them too long they came out dry.

Bernie nodded at the brownies. "Are these the ones you made out of seventy percent dark chocolate with chili powder?"

Libby nodded. "It'll be interesting to see how they sell."

"We need to call them something cool." Bernie was a firm believer in the power of names.

Libby shrugged. She wasn't.

"Dogs can't eat chocolate, you know," Bernie told her, getting back to the matter at hand. "It gives them heart attacks."

"Then I'm glad I'm not a dog," Libby retorted as she watched her sister smooth her shirt down around her waist.

It was twenty-five degrees out, but Bernie was wearing a

long, black cotton sweater, a white and gray striped scarf, a silk shirt, twill pants, and suede boots. How she did it Libby didn't know. She herself was wearing a flannel shirt, a hoodie, jeans, and wool socks and she was still cold.

"It's really for Annabel Colbert's friends and family," Bernie continued. She took up the conversation where she'd left it a moment ago.

Libby slammed the oven door shut. "And dogs."

"Pugs," Bernie corrected. "Six pugs."

"Wonderful."

"Well, you wouldn't want Trudy to have a birthday party without her friends. That would just be mean."

Libby threw the toothpick into the garbage can, stalked over to the cutting board, and began shredding ginger for their special gingered chicken. As Bernie followed her, she reflected that she probably should have talked to her sister about the dinner later in the day. She might have been more receptive then. The fact that they were behind because their counter girl, Amber, had called and told them she was going to be three hours late this morning hadn't put Libby in a good mood.

As Bernie peered over her sister's shoulder she once again marveled at the speed with which her sister's hands moved. "I'm going to Sam's Club to get napkins, plates, sugar, and salt. Do we need anything else?"

Libby kept chopping. "I don't like pugs," she informed Bernie.

"Neither do I," Bernie said as she snagged a piece of carrot off the table. "They wheeze."

Libby stopped chopping and turned to face her. "So why are we doing this?"

Bernie snorted. "You can't be serious?"

Libby wasn't. Not really. She knew exactly why they were doing this. They were doing this because you don't say no to the wealthiest person in town. At least you don't if you want to stay in business. Libby chewed on the inside of her lip as she extracted a piece of chocolate from the pocket of her shirt, unwrapped it, and popped it into her mouth.

That wasn't the issue. Not really. The issue was respect. Bernie was always running off and committing them to engagements without asking her first, leaving her to run around like a chicken without its head, as her mother used to say. Frankly she was sick and tired of it.

"You should have discussed it with me first," Libby told her.

"I was going to," Bernie protested. "But you were asleep when I got home."

Libby grunted. "You could have left a note."

"I wanted to talk to you."

Libby felt her resolve weakening. This was the problem. She could never stay annoyed with her sister for long. "When is this event supposed to take place?"

Bernie hemmed and hawed. Libby started tapping her foot.

Bernie plastered a grin on her face. "Friday." She gave the word an upward swing.

"Which Friday?"

"Er . . . this Friday."

"That's two days away!" Libby yelped.

Bernie looked unhappy. "Well, you know how impulsive Annabel Colbert is. But on the bright side, the Fieldses canceled their dinner party, so that leaves an opening."

Libby's eyes narrowed. "You didn't tell me that either."

"It was on the answering machine last night. I figured you'd listen to the messages."

Libby cursed silently as she strode toward the calendar hanging on the wall. At least they hadn't butterflied the lamb yet or ordered the scallops for the Coquille St. Jacques, so that was good. And she had to admit that what Bernie had just said was true: Annabel Colbert was impulsive. And insistent. She never took no for an answer. She had that sense of entitlement the superrich have. Just saying something made it so.

Libby clicked her tongue against the roof of her mouth while she studied the calendar. They were pretty well booked, what with dinner parties, benefits, and bar mitzvahs. But Bernie was correct. The Fieldses' party was the only event they had going for Friday night.

"She's going to want a deal," Libby said. "She always does."

"No, I'm not," a voice behind them trumpeted. "Nothing is too good for my Trudy."

Libby and Bernie spun around. Annabel Colbert was standing in the doorway between the kitchen and the counter area with her pug in her arms. She'd recently gotten a short, spiky hairdo, but instead of making her look punk, it made her appear even gaunter. Scrutinizing her, Bernie decided that the "too thin" part of the adage "You can never be too rich or too thin" had definite limits and Annabel Colbert was on the verge of transgressing them. There was thin and then there was just plain bony. Bernie was thinking about what the tipping point was when she noticed that their counter guy Googie, aka George Nathan III, was right behind her.

"I'm sorry," he stammered as he wiped his hands on his apron. "I couldn't stop her. She just barged in."

Libby nodded. "It's okay."

"I . . ."

"Seriously. Go back behind the counter," Libby said, and she shooed Googie away before turning her attention to Annabel. A Little Taste of Heaven wasn't packed, but there were ten people out front waiting to be served. Aside from which it didn't do to leave the cash register unguarded. Longely wasn't the type of place where you had to worry about stuff like that, but why take chances? "I'm sorry but Trudy can't be in the kitchen," Libby told Annabel. It would just be their luck to have the health inspector walk in on them.

"But I'm holding her," Annabel protested.

Bernie shrugged. "Health code rules are health code rules."

Annabel scowled. "She's cleaner than most people."

"I'm sure she is," Bernie said as she escorted Annabel out of the kitchen and up the stairs to the Simmons's living quarters.

Luckily her dad was out at the moment; he wasn't a big fan of the Colbert family.

"Morons," was the kindest comment he made whenever their name came up.

"I like Trudy's collar," Bernie said on the way up the stairs. It was thick braided leather with a large gold buckle.

"Hermes," Annabel trilled.

Bernie managed to restrain herself from asking how much. But it had to be at least five hundred dollars. Probably more.

"This flat is so . . . so . . . cozy," Annabel commented in that annoyingly arch way she had when she and Bernie walked into the Simmons's living room.

Translation: *small*. But then Bernie supposed that when you lived in a place that boasted its own solarium, library, gym, media room, bowling alley, and beauty parlor, as well as a canine fitness center complete with treadmill, the Simmons's flat *was* small. Annabel plopped herself down on the sofa, put the pug on her lap, and began fingering one of her diamond studs.

In case I missed them, Bernie thought as she took the armchair opposite her customer. Like that was possible. Missing them would be like missing a flashlight beam in the dark. Despite Annabel's make-up, Bernie noted the dark circles under Annabel's eyes and the fine lines around her mouth. The haircut was definitely not kind to her. Bernie bet it had been expensive too. Probably six hundred dollars. Maybe even eight. She was just about to ask Annabel who did her hair when Annabel started talking.

"We have to revamp the menu," she announced.

Bernie barely managed to suppress a groan. It had taken them three hours yesterday to agree on the one they had.

"I've decided I want the same menu for the dogs and their humans," Annabel continued. "It'll be much more of a bonding experience that way. And I want the food served on my good Limoges. Naturally the dogs will be seated at the table."

"Naturally," Bernie murmured.

Annabel shot her a look. "They do it in Paris all the time."

But we're not in Paris. We're in Westchester County, Bernie wanted to say. But didn't.

"Yes," Bernie added. "It's wonderful. So humane. When I was in Brussels I sat next to an extremely well-behaved standard poodle riding on the bus with his owner. There was me, the poodle, and the owner all sitting in a row, all staring straight ahead."

For a moment Annabel looked miffed at having been outdone in the story department, but she rallied. She waved her hand in the air. "And you don't have to take care of the decorations. I'll do those. I'm thinking of using the whole Puggable family. That will work, don't you think?"

Bernie didn't think it would work at all. She wasn't a fan of huge stuffed animals. On the other hand, she wouldn't have to deal with them. That was a plus. Also in situations like this, despite what her sister thought, Bernie always went with the client's wishes. Therefore, she lied and told Annabel she thought it would be great.

"Absolutely," Libby added. She'd come up after finishing the chicken and was now standing in the doorway with her arms crossed over her chest. She felt that it behooved her to be in on the planning due to Bernie's well-documented tendency to commit them to things without thinking them through. Witness today. "Do you have any ideas about what you'd like to serve?"

"Ideas? Ideas?" Annabel repeated. She wrinkled her nose, giving the impression that she found the question puzzling. "That's why I came to you."

Libby flicked a tiny piece of ginger off the sleeve of her hoodie. "Well, what's your price range?"

"Price is no object," Annabel snapped. "I already told you that in the kitchen, isn't that right, Trudy?"

Trudy yawned, curled her tongue, stretched, and licked Annabel's hand in a desultory manner.

"See. She agrees," Annabel said.

Bernie and Libby both managed to not roll their eyes.

"What about the wine?" Bernie asked, changing the subject.

"What about it?" Annabel said.

"What are your thoughts? California? Long Island? They've gotten a lot better recently. French? Italian? Australian? Do you want us to get it or . . ."

"No," Annabel replied before Bernie could finish her sentence. "Forget about the wine. Richard will take care of that. He orders it from The Grape, that little shop over by Henley Drive."

"I know where it is," Bernie said. Not that she ever bought anything there. They only carried high-end stuff.

"They get my wine for me there. I'm particularly fond of an estate-bottled Spanish Rioja that's quite hard to come by, but somehow the owners manage. It's my special wine. In fact, it's the only thing I'm drinking now. In any case, we'll just have wine with the meal; otherwise we'll stick to bubbling water and soda. Richard will take care of that as well. After all, it's Trudy's party, so I think it would be nice if there's nothing there she can't have."

"Understood," Libby said.

Annabel went back to fingering her diamond earring.

"And needless to say, I want all the ingredients in this meal to be organic. We don't tolerate anything else in our house. My husband won't allow it. Local would be even better. The less of a carbon footprint we leave the happier all of us will be. Also, I don't want any black pepper in anything, because Trudy's allergic to it. Naturally I want both of you to set up and serve. It'll be more intimate that way. You won't have to worry about my staff getting in your way. In fact, I've given them the time off."

"Is that it?" Bernie asked.

"For the moment," Annabel replied as she got up. "If I think of anything else I'll let you know."

Bernie stood up as well. "We'll call you with the menu."

"That won't be necessary," Annabel replied. "You can fax it to my personal assistant, who will show it to me. If I have any quibbles I will relay them to her and she will fax you back. Unfortunately, I'm terribly busy with my new projects at the moment. I'm trying to get them squared away, so I can announce them at the birthday party, but I'm sure you girls will do a marvelous job. After all, that's why I hired you." She glanced at her watch. "Can I tell my assistant to be looking for your fax in an hour or so?"

Bernie looked at Libby. Libby looked back at Bernie.

"That'll be fine," Libby said as she saw her plans for the day disappearing over the horizon. Now she'd be even farther behind.

"Good." Annabel smiled. "And by the way, Bernie," Annabel added as she got to the doorway, "you should cut down on the carbs. You're getting a little chubby around the derrière." And she patted her rear end. "I hope you don't mind my saying something, but if the positions were reversed I'd certainly want to know."

Bernie managed to get out a strangled "thanks" as Annabel walked through the door.

"Am I?" Bernie asked her sister as soon as she was sure Annabel had left the building. She wasn't going to give

Annabel the added satisfaction of overhearing her comments if she could help it.

"Don't be ridiculous," Libby replied.

"Really?"

"Really. Of course, in comparison with her rear end, *everyone's* is big."

Big was not the word Bernie wanted to hear at the moment. "Thanks a heap."

"Oh, come on. Annabel just can't stand to see anyone looking good. I would kill to have your body," Libby told Bernie as she watched her sister study herself in the mirror hanging on the wall. And she wasn't just being nice. She meant it.

"Maybe I shouldn't wear these pants anymore."

"Bernie!"

"You're right." Bernie brushed a lock of hair off of her face. "Why am I listening to someone who could be a stand-in for a famine victim?" The corners of Bernie's mouth worked themselves into a smile. "And we *are* charging her a lot of money."

Libby smiled. "Pots of it. And we're getting three-quarters of it up front or we're not doing it."

"Good," Bernie said. If there was one thing she'd learned over her years of catering it was that the rich don't like to settle their bills. "And now for the menu. I think we should start with a liver pate on toast points, some cheese stuff, maybe some bacon and peanut butter on slices of bread. . . ."

Libby wrinkled her nose.

"Hey, I know they're not haute cuisine, but dogs and kids like them," Bernie said a little defensively.

Libby nodded. It was true. They did.

"And then," Bernie continued, "we move on to steak and potatoes."

"What about the cake?"

"Something vanilla. Maybe an old-fashioned layer cake, light on the frosting, in the shape of a dog bone?"

Libby pursed her lips. That would do. "Ice cream?"

Bernie thought for a moment. "Probably not. That might be overkill in the sugar and dairy departments."

"This should work," Libby observed after she'd written down the menu and faxed it over.

"Of course it's going to work," Bernie said indignantly. "We designed it, didn't we? Although I'm sure Annabel will have some quibbles." Bernie bracketed the word *quibbles* with her fingers.

"I'm sure she will," Bree Nottingham, real estate agent extraordinaire and social arbiter of Longely, said as she swept into the living room with Rudolph, her six-month-old pug puppy, trailing behind her. They were both wearing pink coats and rhinestone collars. "Annabel always has quibbles. Of course, when you have that kind of money you can afford to."

"It's not the quibbles I'm worried about," Libby replied as she pictured six dogs running up and down the table. "It's everything else."

"It'll be an interesting event," Bree commented as she watched Rudolph sniff the sofa leg. "I just came by to tell you that Rudolph is allergic to chicken, so don't put chicken on the menu. He's a sensitive soul, the poor dear."

Bernie looked down at Rudolph, who was currently trying to dig a hole in the carpet. He didn't look sensitive to her. He looked like a miniature Sherman tank.

"Interesting in what way?" Bernie asked. She decided to sidestep the whole dog food-allergy issue. Bad enough she had to deal with people with food allergies let alone their canines.

Bree smiled brightly. "In the way that married couples frequently are, dear."

"And that is?" Libby asked. She'd expected the conversation to go in another direction.

Bernie leaned forward slightly. "Yes. Elucidate for us. Inquiring minds want to know."

But instead of answering, Bree gave the Simmons sisters another of her smiles and said, "I'm sure you two will do an excellent job. You always do." After which she left. Just like the Grand Duchess, Bernie thought.

"Now what do you think she meant by that?" Libby asked Bernie as soon as she heard the downstairs door closing.

"I think she means that the Colberts are getting a divorce. Or one of them is having an affair."

"Seriously?"

Bernie gave her a look. Honestly, sometimes her sister was so naïve. "What else could it be?"

Libby shook her head. "I don't have a clue. All I know is that whatever it is, it's none of our business."

"I suppose," Bernie said, feigning agreement even though she really didn't believe that, and she didn't think Libby believed it either. After all, they'd been raised in a house with a mother who had elevated minding other people's business into an art form.

"I think we should concentrate on planning," Libby said.

"I think you're right," Bernie agreed.

This was not debatable. They had lots to do and not much time to do it.

Chapter 2

As Bernie would tell her dad on Friday evening after the furor had died down, things at the Colbert household got off to a crummy start and went downhill from there. Although she couldn't fault Annabel for her decorating efforts. Those were great. Normally, seeing the Puggables engendered an acute case of nausea in Bernie, but this time, for some reason, the six-foot-high pink, blue, and purple stuffed pugs worked. Maybe because they balanced out the chintz draperies, the ersatz Louis IV furniture, and the knights in armor standing sentinel in the hall. She wasn't sure.

In any case, there were several Puggables draped over the knights in the entranceway, and then the whole family, all fourteen of them, was perched on the dining room window seat, which lent a festive air to the proceedings. Large helium balloons in the shape of bones, dog biscuits, and various chew toys hung from the ceiling.

Richard Colbert, Annabel's husband, met Bernie and Libby at the kitchen door and ushered them in. Bernie noticed that although he was dressed in casual clothes, his jeans were pressed, his salmon-colored cashmere crewneck matched his salmon-colored socks, and he was wearing the Patek Phillipe watch she'd seen advertised in the Sunday edition of the *New York Times* for ten thousand dollars.

The first words out of his mouth when he opened the door were, "How long is this going to last?"

Bernie raised an eyebrow. "This?" She'd thought he was attractive in a preppy kind of way on first sight, but that impression was instantly dispelled when he opened his mouth.

Richard tapped his fingers on his thighs. "This event. What else would I be referring to, for heaven's sake?"

"Excuse me, I didn't get your name. Who did you say you were?" Bernie asked, even though she already knew who he was. "I thought Annabel said the staff would be gone."

One for our side, Bernie thought as Richard glared at her, then pointedly glanced at his watch. "I have an appointment at five so I want the cake served by four at the latest," he replied, taking the high road and ignoring her comment.

"Well . . ." Bernie began, but Libby jumped into the conversation before her sister could finish her sentence.

Because if there was one thing that Libby knew it was that whatever Bernie was going to say wasn't going to be nice. This, of course, was another type of situation where she and her sister deviated in their responses. She didn't see any point in making things worse, while Bernie seemed to revel in it.

Libby cleared her throat. "That shouldn't be a problem," Libby told him, not meeting her sister's gaze. "We're planning on being out of here by four-thirty."

Richard grunted. "My *wife,*" he said, making the word sound as if he were talking about a particularly nasty substance, "has a way of dragging things out." He looked down at Libby, something that was easy enough for him to do since he was six feet four inches tall. "All I can say is that I hope you two are worth the money."

"We are," Bernie assured him.

But Richard didn't seem reassured. He shook his head in disgust and started speaking again. "All this hoopdedoo for a dog. Ridiculous. Absolutely absurd." And he stalked off.

Libby and Bernie exchanged glances.

"I guess he wasn't in favor of the party," Libby said. Even though she agreed in principle with what Richard Colbert had just said, she didn't like the way he'd said it.

"I guess not. Trudy just a dog?" Bernie raised an eyebrow again. "Hardly. I bet Annabel would have something to say about that. Trudy's the foundation of their company, for heaven's sake. Colbert Toys was nothing before they started marketing her."

"Maybe Richard just doesn't like eating at the table with canines," Libby suggested.

Bernie snorted. "Why do I think that's so not the issue. But I do have to say this definitely gives new meaning to the phrase, 'going to the dogs.' "

"Dad would freak."

"He wouldn't be happy, but he'd have done it if that's what Mom had wanted," Bernie said as she plunked the carton she'd been holding down on the countertop.

"Not that Mom ever would." Libby had begged for a cat or a dog or even a hamster for years to no avail.

"That's true, but that's not what I was saying. In any case, let's hope the other guests don't feel the same way."

"We know that Bree doesn't," Libby pointed out.

"Fortunately," Bernie said.

She couldn't believe that she was happy that Bree was going to be in attendance, but she was. Nitpicky as Bree was, she was at least a friendly face. Bernie had just brought in another carton when a tall blonde with a set of conical breasts that reminded Bernie of war missiles bounded into the kitchen and introduced herself.

"Hi," she said, extending her hand. "I'm Joanna Trubottom, Richard's personal assistant."

Bernie managed to avoid making eye contact with Libby. Otherwise she would have burst into an uncontrollable giggling fit. They'd sent their fax to a Joanna. The name Trubottom had not appeared on the return sheets.

Libby was also having trouble keeping a straight face, not to mention keeping her eyes off of Joanna Trubottom's chest. Libby decided her boobs looked as if they were about to launch themselves into the stratosphere. She was trying not to picture that in her head when Joanna spoke.

"You look puzzled," Joanna said to Libby.

"Not at all," Libby lied. She was puzzled, but she was puzzled by why someone would do that to herself. How could anyone think that was attractive? "I just thought Mrs. Colbert told me you were *her* personal assistant."

Joanna laughed in a mirthless kind of way. "No. No. I work for Richard now. I was merely helping Mrs. Colbert for a few days."

Bernie reflected that Joanna's expression indicated that this had not been a particularly pleasant experience.

"That was nice of her husband to lend you out, as it were," Bernie observed.

Joanna managed to suggest by her body language that he hadn't had any choice in the matter. "Mrs. Colbert tends to . . . tends to . . . misspeak," Joanna ventured, after starting and stopping speaking several times.

As in lie, Bernie thought. "That must be . . . difficult," she continued, trying for neutral conversational ground.

Joanna gave a shrug. "Things are what they are. Mrs. Colbert and Trudy will be down as soon as possible. Trudy is in the middle of her appointment with the dental hygienist," Joanna explained.

"Dental hygienist," Libby echoed.

"Yes. Well. Groomer really. She comes twice a week to brush Trudy's teeth. Trudy's back teeth have a tendency to develop cavities."

"What does the tooth brusher use?" Bernie couldn't resist asking. "Crest or Colgate?"

Joanna Trubottom offered a thin smile. "Actually the toothpaste Anna uses is chicken and bacon flavored," she informed them as she walked out of the room.

Libby rummaged around in her bag, found a piece of chocolate, and popped it into her mouth. "Do you think that Trubottom is Joanna's real last name?" she asked Bernie.

"No one would make something like that up unless they were a porn star," her sister replied. "I can't imagine what elementary school must have been like for her. Trubottom indeed. Give me a break. And did you notice how she called Annabel Mrs. Colbert and Richard, Richard?"

Libby began taking the pâté out of the carton. "I bet Joanna started off working for the wife. Note the word *now* in the phrase 'I work for Richard now.' "

Bernie brushed a wisp of hair out of her eyes. "I gotta tell you if I were married I'd never hire someone that looked like that to work for me as a personal assistant."

"Maybe she didn't look like that when Annabel hired her. Maybe Richard bought her her boobs," Libby opined.

"Well, someone did."

Libby laughed.

"I have to say you're getting jaded in your old age," Bernie told her.

Libby ate another piece of chocolate. "Learned it from you."

Bernie was quiet for a moment. Then she said, "Or maybe Annabel doesn't care what Richard's personal assistant looks like. Maybe she doesn't want to have sex with her husband. Maybe she's happy to be relieved of the responsibility."

"I can't imagine that," Libby said.

"I can," said Bernie. "There are a couple of women at the gym like that." And she proceeded to fill Libby in on the details.

"Still. If he leaves her . . ."

"Maybe she has all the money," Bernie said as she started chewing on a carrot stick. "Richard doesn't look like someone who would leave his meal ticket."

"You just don't like him because he was wearing salmon socks," Libby said.

"No. I don't like him because he was rude and obnoxious *and* he was wearing salmon-colored socks," Bernie replied. "Of course," she reflected, "Annabel is no prize either. They're equally matched." She went back to unloading the carton. "I guess this is what Bree meant when she called Richard and Annabel Colbert an interesting couple." She held up her hand, forestalling Libby's comment. "Or words to that effect. Fortunately, we'll be out of here in two and a half hours so they're not our problem. I just hope that the other people who are coming are a little more enthusiastic."

"Well, even if they're not, their dogs will be," Libby said. She began laying bread slices out on the counter in preparation for cutting them into bonelike shapes. Not just any bread, mind you. This was bread made with 100 percent organic flour and baked in-house. As Annabel had said, nothing was too good for Trudy. "I just had this terrible thought," Libby went on. "It would be really bad if the dogs didn't like what we were serving."

"That's one of the virtues of the canine species. They eat virtually anything," Bernie observed. "Well, almost anything," she amended as she picked up a half-eaten dog biscuit still in its wrapper and threw it in the trash. "I don't think most dogs like citrus fruit."

"Maybe we should have taste tested the menu first?"

"For the species that eats from garbage cans," said Bernie as she thought of the neighbor's dog that had gotten into their trash last week. "Anyway, what's not to like? All the dogs will like the liver toast points, the peanut butter and bacon canapés, the steak and mashed potatoes. I'm not too sure about the carrot coins with ginger and the tossed salad, but under the circumstances I don't think it matters all that much."

"Well, I hope you're right," Libby said as she finished cutting out the bread.

Then while Bernie was putting peanut butter on the cutouts, Libby took the silver serving pieces that Annabel had laid out and filled the dishes up with the Kalamata and Nicoise olives, the spiced pecans she'd made yesterday, and the salted almonds she'd roasted this morning. Then she took everything into the room Annabel had indicated they'd be serving the hors d'oeuvres in.

The Eaton room, as Annabel called it, was painted a dark hunter green with white molding and had a white ceiling made of molded plaster. The walls were covered with pictures of dogs and horses in the British style, while the sofa and the armchairs were upholstered in chintz fabric. There were Oriental rugs over the dark wood flooring. The only thing missing, Libby decided, was a coat of arms.

In line with Annabel's wishes to limit wine to the main meal, the highboy along the left wall had already been set up with bottles of sparkling water, sparkling cider, and various kinds of soda. What had she said? Libby tried to remember her exact words. Something to the effect of trying to limit the things that the animals couldn't partake in so both species could have a more communal experience. Which was the rationale for not serving coffee or tea with dessert. Not that Libby was complaining. That just made things easier for her, since nowadays you had to serve both regular and decaffeinated coffees, as well as a variety of teas.

Libby looked around and decided to put the nuts and olives on the end tables where the dogs couldn't get at them, rather than on the coffee table, which was snout level. After she'd placed them to her satisfaction, she walked into the pantry to make sure that all the serving pieces she and Joanna had faxed each other about were out. Which they were. She'd give Annabel and Joanna kudos for that. They were efficient. Unpleasant, but efficient.

Out of force of habit, Libby moved the Limoges china platters and bowls slightly so they were all perfectly aligned, then checked on the glasses—Waterford—to make sure there were no smudge marks, which there weren't, and then she inspected the wine.

Three bottles of Lafitte plus one bottle of Annabel's wine, an obscure Spanish red, had been set out. She carefully moved them all a little farther down the counter so she'd have room to bring in the salad and the vegetables. Then she made sure that the corkscrew, although this was a way fancier device, was next to the bottles.

She was glad that Richard was opening and decanting the wine, because she always had visions of having the cork break off in a two hundred–dollar bottle of the stuff. She gave the pantry one last look to make sure everything was in place—in catering it was all about the details—and left.

On her way back to the kitchen she could hear Richard and Annabel screaming at each other out in the main hallway. Richard was calling Annabel a stupid cow and she was calling him a turd. Not a good sign, Libby decided as she quietly tiptoed behind them so they wouldn't turn around and see her. But she needn't have worried. They were too engrossed in their hostilities to be aware of anybody else.

Great, Libby thought. Host and hostess fighting. Dogs running all over the place. Probably on the table. Despite what Bernie said, in Libby's humble opinion the prognosis for this event was not good. She wondered how bad things were going to be as she watched a woman she presumed to be Trudy's tooth brusher come down the stairs and go out the side door. If she was done, that meant that Annabel and Trudy would be in the kitchen soon.

Libby could wait. But as she looked on the bright side,

they'd already been paid enough to cover their materials and time. Even if worse came to worse and they didn't get their 20 percent, they'd still be ahead of the game. It would just be a trying couple of hours. Libby would remember that thought frequently in the days ahead.

Chapter 3

Three-quarters of an hour later, Bernie and Libby heard the doorbell in the mansion chime, "How much is that doggie in the window?" That in turn was followed by footsteps, voices, barks, and squeals of laughter.

"The guests have arrived," Bernie said as she put slivers of tomato on the plate containing the goat cheese toast points, a last minute addition.

"At least they're on time," Libby noted.

It was especially bad when they were serving something like a roast, and guests were half an hour or more late. You could keep things warm, but the taste really suffered. At least here they were serving steaks, which were a lot less tricky. Libby was thinking about the timing when the kitchen door was flung open and Annabel and Trudy strode in followed by three women and a knot of snuffling, snorting pugs.

Trudy was dressed in a mink stole and pearl choker, while the other three pugs had on a tux and top hat, a pink tutu and tiara, and a fireman's coat and hat. Clearly, Bernie thought, Trudy was the grande dame of the group. As the sisters watched, the pug in the tux and the top hat ran over to the kitchen table, lifted his hind leg, and peed on one of the legs.

"Conklin," the tall, thin lady in frayed Chanel and black slacks shrieked as she scooped him up. "That was very, very naughty of you." She turned to Annabel. "I'm just mortified."

"Joyce, it's perfectly fine," Annabel said, even though her expression said that it wasn't. "Conklin is just a tad overexcited."

"If you ask me, he's a tad undertrained," an overly made-up woman dressed in jeans and a clean white T-shirt declared.

"Melissa, that is not true," the fireplug of a woman standing next to her snapped.

"That certainly is, Ramona. As well you know."

Ramona sniffed. "I know nothing of the kind. Conklin is one of my star pupils. I'm very proud of him. We've worked extremely hard to overcome his deficits."

Melissa rolled her eyes. "Deficits. Deficits?" she repeated in a louder voice. "That's a good one. My dogs don't have deficits. Every single one is a paragon of its breed. As my record attests to."

"Really," Ramona said, picking up the pug in the pink tutu and yanking its tiara back in place.

"Yes. Really," Melissa replied.

"What about the disqualification at the Hartford dog show last year for poor dentition?" Ramona asked. "That was your pug, wasn't it?"

Two spots of color appeared on Melissa's cheeks, but before she could answer Annabel stepped in and clapped her hands. "Ladies, ladies," she said. "Please. This is a special day. Let's maintain a festive mood."

Melissa swallowed. "By all means let's," she said with a notable lack of enthusiasm.

"Wouldn't have it any other way," Ramona added.

Were those notes of sarcasm Bernie detected? Yes indeedy. The two women looked as if they'd prefer to be having a root canal. The third one didn't look much happier, Bernie decided. Her mouth was smiling but her eyes weren't going along with the program. But if Annabel noticed her guests' reactions she gave no indication of that fact.

Instead she pointed to Libby and Bernie and said, "These are the wonderful people who are catering this little soiree for me. And they've made sure that everything being served today is both dog and human friendly, because as everyone here knows, I make it a point of pride to never feed Trudy anything that I wouldn't eat myself."

Then Annabel made the introductions. The woman whose pug had peed on the kitchen table was her best friend, Joyce; Melissa Geist owned Precious Pug, the kennel the redoubtable Trudy had come from; and Ramona was Trudy's trainer.

Everyone murmured polite, uninterested hellos, while the pugs ran around the kitchen looking to lick up any odd bits of food that had fallen on the floor. Trudy was in the middle of trying to hump the dog in the pink tutu when Annabel announced they'd start with the hors d'oeuvres in the Eaton room.

"Now there's a jolly little group," Bernie said when everyone was out of earshot.

"Add Richard, Joanna, and Bree and it's going to be a long two hours," Libby observed.

Bernie put a sprig of parsley on one of the plates. "I think it's going to be an interesting two hours."

"But not in a good way," Libby countered.

Bernie picked a speck of cheese off of her blouse sleeve. "I'm wagering there's going to be lots of drama."

"And it's not going to be the baked Alaska supplying it," Libby replied, not that they were serving that particular dish. It had just seemed like a good thing to say.

However, despite the sisters' misgivings, the appetizers went smoothly. Everyone seemed to like the toast points, the pugs particularly liking the bacon and peanut butter canapés.

Libby started to relax a little. Things were going to be all right after all.

Then they served the first course and everything went to hell.

Libby and Bernie had just put the soup on the table. As per Annabel's instructions, they were serving the beef bouillon in the Limoges soup bowls. The bouillon was decorated with egg custard cutouts in the shape of half-moons and a sprinkling of chopped sorrel.

Both sisters were silently congratulating themselves on how well everything was going. Everyone, human and canine, was sitting in his or her chair. Everyone, human and canine, seemed to appreciate the soup. The humans were using their spoons, and the pugs, perched on baby booster seats, were using their tongues. Interestingly, Bernie noted that the rate of consumption for both groups seemed to be the same. She and Libby were turning to go back into the kitchen when Annabel stood up and lifted her wineglass.

"I have two announcements I'd like to make today. Firstly, I'd like to propose a toast to my new product, Trudy's Treats," she said. "It's the first organic, venison and veggie–based, nongrain dog treat on the market."

Everyone stopped talking, although the dogs kept lapping.

Annabel lifted her glass higher. "To my new product. Trudy's Treats."

"Trudy's Treats," Annabel's best friend, Joyce, cried. "I can't believe you didn't tell me."

"I wanted this to be a surprise," said Annabel.

Libby and Bernie agreed later that judging by everyone's expression it was.

"I am hoping that, as befits Trudy, they are truly the best dog biscuit in the world," Annabel continued.

Joyce glared at Annabel. Later, both Bernie and Libby

agreed that if looks could kill, Annabel would have dropped dead then.

"You're kidding, right?" Joyce growled.

Annabel lowered her glass slightly. "What a thing to say."

Joyce's eyes narrowed. "You're not kidding."

"Obviously," Annabel retorted.

"What recipe are you using?" Joyce asked.

"A good one," Annabel said.

"Is it mine?" Joyce demanded.

"Of course not. I would never do something like that," Annabel shot back, but Bernie didn't think that Joyce looked convinced. "First of all," Annabel went on, "I want to thank all of you for taking time out of your busy, busy schedules"—here she glared at Richard—"to honor me with your presence this afternoon. Secondly, I want to thank everyone here for accompanying me on this leg of the journey. I couldn't have done it without you. You've made me stronger. You've made me the person I've become."

There were some unenthusiastic expressions of "hear, hear" as Libby leaned in to Bernie, covered her mouth with her hand, and whispered, "It doesn't sound as if she means that in a good way, does it?"

"Nope. It sure doesn't," Bernie whispered back.

Annabel grimaced although Bernie was sure she meant the grimace to be a smile. "I've learned a lot from you. I've learned the meaning of backstabbing, for example."

Everyone froze. Ramona dropped her spoon, Joanna's eyes flitted from one person to the next, while Bree stifled a yawn.

"It's true," Annabel continued. "It's true for every single one of you. You thought I wouldn't find out about everything. But I have. And I'm making changes. Lots and lots of changes. Yes. Indeed."

Annabel turned a shade paler and ran her tongue over her lips. Her eyes glowed with hate. She raised her glass still higher. A drop of wine slipped over the side and slid down her arm. She didn't appear to notice. "Here's to treachery in all its many forms. What did Mach . . . Mach . . . whatever his name was say? Keep your friends close and your enemies even closer. I'm tired of doing that. It's a waste of my time." No one at the table moved, except for Trudy, who'd decided to climb up on the table and investigate the butter dish. Annabel burped. "Oops," she said and giggled. "What? No one wants to drink with me?"

"Annabel," Bree said, "I think you've had enough."

"For your information I haven't had anything to drink yet. I'm drunk from watching the expression on your faces."

"I don't believe that," Melissa said.

"Too bad for you," Annabel retorted, making a slight curtsey. "Here's to me and my new ventures and to hell with all of you. I don't know where any of you are going, but if I had to guess I'd have to say to the bad place, and don't pretend you don't know what I'm talking about." Annabel raised her glass to her lips and drank the wine down. A strange expression came over her face. Her eyes widened. Her hand went to her throat. "I've been poisoned!" she cried. "Someone has put something in this wine!"

"Now, dear," Richard said. "I'm sure you're fine. You know how you tend to exaggerate."

"Are you calling me a liar?!" Annabel screamed. "Are you telling me I don't know what my wine should taste like? For God's sake, call a doctor."

Trudy started barking. The other dogs joined in. The noise was deafening.

Richard made no move to get up. Instead he yelled, "No, darling, I'm not saying that you're lying! I'm simply saying that you tend to over dramatize certain events. Witness the little scenario you just pulled."

"It's true," Annabel's best friend, Joyce, said. "Remember when you thought that someone had put salmonella in your tomatoes and it turned out you had a bad case of the stomach flu?"

"Yes," Melissa chimed in. "How can you say what you just did after all the time I've put in on Trudy? If that isn't being paranoid what is?"

Annabel clawed at her throat. "Call the doctor," she whispered.

"I will," Bernie and Libby both said together.

"No. No. Not you." She waved her hand at them. "Don't leave. I want you to promise me . . ." She paused to gather her strength. "I want you to promise me you'll find out who murdered me."

"Annabel!" Richard cried. "Now, you've gone too far."

"Promise me," Annabel said.

"You're probably having a heart attack," Bernie suggested. "Let me call the ambulance."

"She does have arrhythmias," Ramona said as she moved to round up the dogs and take them into the other room. "Bad ones."

"Promise me!" Annabel cried, ignoring what Ramona had just said.

"But," Libby said as Ramona chased the dogs around the dining room table.

The color was draining from Annabel's face. "I won't let you call the ambulance till I have your solemn promise."

"Fine," Bernie said. "I swear to find your killer if you die."

"Me too," Libby added. "But you're not going to die. You're going to be fine."

"Put up your hands and say you swear to do this before God," Annabel said.

Bernie and Libby looked at each other. Bernie wanted to say, *We get it. You've made your point*. But she didn't. Obviously Annabel was in some sort of distress and needed to be seen by a doc. Pronto. So she and Libby would do whatever it took to get Annabel there. Bernie put her hand up and swore. Libby followed.

"Now can we call an ambulance?" Libby asked when they were done.

"Yes. Now you can call the ambulance," Annabel replied.

Bernie was reaching for her cell when Annabel's eyes rolled back in their sockets and she fell face forward into her soup.

"I told her she needed to eat more," Joanna observed.

"So did I," Joyce said.

"Why wasn't she eating?" Libby asked.

There was an awkward pause and then Melissa said, "She thought someone was trying to poison her. I told her she was crazy and she needed to get to a doctor. I wish I had been more insistent about it. She needed to be on serious meds."

"Maybe," Bernie told her as she dialed 911, "she wasn't so crazy after all."

"No. She's nuts," Richard said as he stared down at the top of his wife's head.

On reflection, Bernie thought it was interesting that no one rushed in to help. It was Libby who rushed over and picked Annabel's head up so she wouldn't drown.

Unfortunately, Annabel Colbert had nothing to say about anything. She was unconscious and she remained so until the moment of her death two days later.

Chapter 4

The day after Annabel's death Bernie, Libby, and their dad were sitting around the kitchen table having a late breakfast. The noise from the shop, A Little Taste of Heaven, bubbled up from below, making a faint reassuring hum.

Sean was tucking into his pancakes and drinking his third cup of coffee of the morning, even though, according to his daughters, he wasn't supposed to have anything with caffeine. It was bad for his condition, they said. But then so was a lack of caffeine. He'd been drinking the stuff since he was ten years old and had no intention of quitting now, despite what anyone said. As far as he was concerned, when you got to his age you should be able to do anything you gosh darn pleased.

"Well," he said as he pushed the *Longely Bugle*, the local morning paper, off to the side and turned to survey his oldest daughter. "Libby, you asked my opinion and I'm telling you. Yes. You have to investigate. A promise is a promise."

"But . . ." Libby objected.

"See," Bernie said. "I told you."

Sean turned his attention back to his pancakes for a moment. The trick was to have the proper ratio of butter to syrup in every bite, which was harder to do than it sounded.

"Seriously," he said to Libby when he was done configuring. "If you don't like the answer I gave you, why bother asking the question?"

Ever since the girls were little they seemed to feel that if they kept on asking a question, eventually he would give them a different answer. And it wasn't as if he didn't want to in this case. He wasn't exactly thrilled with the idea of his daughters getting involved in yet another murder investigation, especially one involving the Colberts. Not that he'd ever say it, but they didn't seem worth the bother. On the other hand, the case did sound interesting. And given the circumstances, what was the choice?

"It's not that," Libby said after she reread the article about Annabel Colbert's death out loud for the third time.

Sean poured a little more maple syrup on his last two buckwheat pancakes. "Then what is it?"

"The article doesn't say she was murdered. It says she died under suspicious circumstances and an autopsy has been conducted, although the results have not been released yet."

Bernie reached for the homemade strawberry preserves. "Duh. Same thing," she observed as she spread some on her pancake and took a bite. Delicious. They definitely had to make some more preserves next spring.

Libby put the paper down. "Don't duh me. That's just rude. They'll probably find she died of an arrhythmia. . . ."

"Brought on by whatever was in the wine," Bernie added.

"Hey, girls," Sean said in an effort to change the subject. "Did you see that Annabel was going to buy up that big tract of land down by Forrester's Way and make it into Puggables' Paradise, a charitable camp for disabled boys and girls? She was supposed to sign the final papers today. Guess that's not happening now."

"Sorry, Libby," Bernie said, putting the top back on the preserves. "But you're being willfully stupid."

"That is so unfair. She was having a heart attack," Libby persisted.

Sean dabbed at his mouth with his napkin before he took another sip of his coffee. As far as he was concerned his daughters made the best brew in the world.

"Doubtful," Bernie said. "You were there. You saw."

"You're not a doctor," Libby pointed out. "You don't know."

Sean put down his coffee cup. "People who have heart attacks don't clutch at their throats." As the ex–police chief of Longely he'd seen more than enough cardiac incidents in his time to have an opinion. "They clutch their chests."

Libby thought for a moment. Then she said, "Women display different symptoms from men. There was a big article about that in the paper last month."

Bernie rolled her eyes. "Give it up, Libby."

"It's a fact," Libby insisted. "Go Google it."

Bernie snorted. "I'm not Googling anything. Annabel did not have a heart attack. Contrary to what Joanna said, Annabel did not collapse from hunger. She was poisoned. She drank the wine, grabbed her throat, and cried that someone had poisoned her wine. Then she keeled over and two days later died in the hospital, never having regained consciousness. How much more obvious can you get?"

"The police didn't see it that way. They didn't treat the dining room as a crime scene," Libby pointed out.

"Of course they didn't. Not when one of the richest men in Longely tells them his wife has had a heart attack," Bernie retorted. "And anyway, Annabel wasn't dead when they arrived, so it wasn't a crime scene, then."

"If the police even had the remotest suspicion that it was they wouldn't have taken our statements and let us go," Libby argued. "What do you think, Dad?"

Sean just sighed. Ever since he'd lost his top-cop job and Lucas Broadbent, aka Lucy, had taken over the department, law enforcement, as he knew the concept, had gone out the window. The department had become a handmaiden to Longely's political folderol.

"Clyde will call me with the postmortem results," Sean said as he went back to eating his pancakes. "That should tell us something."

"That's nice of Clyde," Bernie observed.

"Yes, it is," Sean agreed.

More than nice actually. Because if he was caught, his old friend could lose his job. But, as Clyde had said, that presupposed that someone over there was paying attention. Which no one ever was. And even if they did catch him, Clyde declared that he could talk his way out of the situation. If he couldn't at this stage of his life, he deserved to be caught. In this case, though, Clyde did better than call Sean with the results. He brought them over in person ten minutes later. Bernie suspected that this was because he never lost an opportunity to eat there.

"Hot off the presses," he cried as he brandished a manila folder in front of Sean.

"Does Lucy know you have these?" Sean asked as he opened the folder and began leafing through the pages.

"Ha, ha," Clyde said as he seated himself at the table. "Very funny. No one knows. Thank heavens for copiers. Anyway, he and Mrs. Lucy are off at a conference in Vail. Something about the transitional role of the chief of police in small towns."

Sean looked up. "Transitional? Does this mean that local law enforcement is on its way out?"

"There's a lot of melding and blending going on," Clyde replied. "You're lucky you got out when you did. I wish I had."

"I didn't get out. I was thrown out, if you remember correctly."

Clyde waved his hand. "I was being polite. You're still

lucky." He pointed to his friend's empty plate. "Got any more of those?"

Libby smiled as she got up. "I was just going to ask if you wanted any."

Fortunately, they had just enough batter for one more batch.

"Have I ever turned down any offer of food?" Clyde asked.

Bernie laughed. "Never," she said. "That's one of the things we love about you." And she got him a coffee mug, filled it up, and set it down before him, while her dad read the report.

Clyde took a sip. "This is heaven. What kind of coffee is this anyway? I'll have to tell the wife."

Bernie told him. Not that it would make any difference, she reflected. His wife was one of those unfortunate people who couldn't even brew a cup of drinkable tea or boil an egg without burning it.

"That's interesting," Sean said when he got done reading. "The M.E. is calling the death accidental."

"Accidental?" Bernie said. "Be serious."

Her dad tapped the report with his hand. He was pleased to see the tremors in his fingers were hardly noticeable at all. "I am. Mike is saying Annabel Colbert's death resulted from an overdose of Malathion and flea and tick spray."

"She drank the stuff. It wasn't accidental," Bernie retorted.

"Maybe. But you can't prove it," Clyde said.

Bernie frowned. "What do you mean? It was in the wine. We saw it. She drank the wine and clutched her throat."

"You should have saved the bottle," Clyde told her. "In the confusion someone threw the wine bottle out. We have nothing to test. And the stuff that's in her is all stuff commonly used around animals. She could have absorbed it through her skin. While it's not deadly to most people, evidently she had a heart condition."

Bernie bit her lip. She felt awful. But saving the bottle had never occurred to her. Her attention had been totally fixed on Annabel.

"It's okay," her father said, intuiting her thoughts. "Given the circumstances I would have done the same thing."

"No, you wouldn't have," Bernie replied.

Her father didn't answer, because what Bernie said was true. But he was a professional and his daughter was a civilian. He told her that and it seemed to help a little.

"What about the witnesses?" she demanded. "Everyone was there. Everyone saw what happened."

Clyde added a tad more heavy cream to his coffee and stirred. "Evidently their statements don't add up to anything definitive. The only point everyone seems to agree on is that Annabel Colbert was given to exaggerating things. The best friend, the husband, and the dog trainer thought she was being overly dramatic. The husband's personal assistant and the kennel owner thought she'd collapsed because she hadn't been eating enough."

"And Bree Nottingham. What did she think?" Libby asked.

"That Annabel was having a bout of hysterics."

"But what about our statements?" Bernie demanded.

Clyde shrugged. "Your viewpoint is outweighed by everyone else's."

Libby put a stack of pancakes down in front of Clyde. "But we saw it."

Clyde reached for the syrup and poured. "So did everyone else."

"How can you misinterpret something like that?" Libby demanded.

"Why do you care?" Bernie asked her.

Libby sniffed. "Of course I care."

"Well, you sure sounded as if you didn't a moment ago."

"This is just so . . . so . . ." Libby stopped and tried to think of the word she wanted.

"Egregious," Bernie supplied.

"Exactly," Libby said.

"So you've changed your mind?" Bernie asked.

Libby considered for a moment. "I suppose I have. I just don't understand Mike's findings," she said, taking her seat.

Sean closed the folder and pushed it toward Clyde. "Then I'll explain," he said. "The results of postmortems are not always as clear-cut as people think. There are primary, secondary, and tertiary causes of death listed on the reports. For example, someone could be stabbed and die of a heart attack brought on by blood loss. Obviously this man died of a knife wound, but if there were reasons—if the knife wound was minor and the incident brought on a fatal coronary event, or if the son of an important personage was the one who did the stabbing—then perhaps the primary cause of death would be listed as a heart attack, and the secondary cause of death would be listed as the stab wound instead of the other way around."

Libby frowned. "So what are you saying?"

Her dad replied, "I'm saying that the M.E. has chosen to emphasize different facts. There could be other explanations as well. Annabel Colbert might have used Malathion to kill fleas. For all we know, she could have been ingesting small amounts of Malathion over the past few months and it finally caught up with her. She may have been taking it to kill her appetite."

"That's absurd," Bernie cried. "No one would do something like that."

"Not true," her father said. "Back in the early nineteen hundreds women used to swallow arsenic to make their skin glow."

"But they don't do things like that now," Bernie objected.

Clyde shifted position. "Ellen Tarbrush did it five years ago. Of course, she was trying to frame her husband for murder."

"Well, in this case Annabel's husband probably is guilty. Her husband probably put the Malathion and flee and tick spray in her wine. He was the one who was opening the bottles," Libby said. Then she added, "Or it could have been one of her friends. Although 'friends' is a misnomer. Everyone at the party seemed to have a real grudge against her. And she knew it, because she was getting ready to kiss them all off."

Bernie nodded her agreement. "Maybe that's why they felt that way. Maybe they knew or at least suspected what she was going to say."

Sean shrugged. "That's all very well. What you say may be true, but you have to prove it. That's a bit more difficult."

Libby raised her coffee mug to her lips and put it down again without having any. "What is Malathion anyway?"

"It's a pesticide," Clyde informed her. "People don't use it that much anymore, because it's so toxic."

"Evidently," Bernie observed.

Clyde continued, "But it used to be fairly common and people still have bottles of it around their houses."

"So," Libby mused, thinking aloud, "a ruling of accidental death means no homicide investigation."

"Exactly," Sean and Clyde said simultaneously.

"And they're cremating the body tomorrow," Clyde said.

"That was quick," Sean said.

Clyde nodded. "That's my thinking too."

Sean paused for a moment to eat the last bit of his pancake. Then he said, "Almost too hasty, unless you're an orthodox Jew, if you ask me."

"It's downright unseemly, to my mind," Clyde agreed.

"Well," Sean rejoined, "I hate to state the obvious, but it is hard to run a tox screen on ashes."

"Yup. Can't exhume a body when there's no body to exhume," Clyde said.

"Can't someone stop Richard?" Libby asked.

"On what grounds?" Clyde responded. "There's no legal basis. We need a reason."

"But that's going to end the possibility of any investigation," Bernie observed.

"Not necessarily," Sean said.

Clyde nodded. "Back in the day we used to get a fair number of convictions without any of that fancy equipment they have now."

"Yes," Sean agreed. "It's amazing what one's powers of observation and a little common sense can produce." He looked at Bernie and Libby. "I've found that funerals can be especially interesting places to people watch. Deaths do not necessarily bring out the best in everyone."

Bernie nodded. "That's what I was just thinking."

"Me too," Libby agreed. "We should probably offer to take a plate of something over to the grieving widower as well."

"If he's not too busy to eat because he's being consoled by another member of the fairer sex," Bernie replied. "I've been told by reliable sources that on occasion sex is seen as the antidote to grief."

Libby threw up her hands in feigned horror. "Why, Bernie," she cried. "What a wicked thing to say."

Bernie grinned. "I know. I'm truly repentant."

Libby turned to her dad. "You were right. A promise is a promise. We swore to Annabel that we'd find her killer and we will."

Sean beamed. He felt blessed to have two such wonderful daughters. Not that he would ever say that to them. At least not in those words. But he suspected they knew how he felt anyway.

"Mom would have had a fit," Libby said suddenly.

"This is true," Sean agreed. His wife had never approved

of his career in law enforcement and would certainly never have sanctioned her daughters' involvement in such activities. But they loved it, so what could he do?

"Of course, she had a fit when you put cumin in the beef stew," Bernie pointed out.

Sean rose to her defense. "She was a good woman."

"We never said she wasn't," Libby and Bernie said simultaneously.

"She loved you both."

"We know," Libby said.

"She was just a little bit conservative," Sean observed.

Everyone fell silent. But a moment later Clyde brought up Annabel Colbert's funeral and they were off and running again.

Chapter 5

Libby reflected that given Annabel Colbert's social standing her funeral was extremely modest by any standards. Marvin had told her that last night when he'd dropped by to retrieve his gloves. He'd said he'd heard that her husband had chosen the cheapest route possible. But it was one thing to hear it and another thing to see it.

The service itself was a graveside affair that took place in the Oakwood Cemetery, which was over in the old part of the town. Even though it had once been the final resting site of the Longely elite, these days anyone who was anyone was buried in the Mission Cemetery over in Pine Haven.

Although it was never explicitly stated, it was common knowledge that the Oakwood Cemetery was now reserved for the middle and lower-middle classes. It seemed to Libby that Annabel Colbert, a woman who practiced the art of social climbing in all its myriad forms, would have been extremely unhappy if she had known where she was being laid to rest. In fact, she would have considered it a direct slap in the face by her husband, which was probably what he had intended.

There had been no obituary in either the local paper or the *New York Times*, another glaring omission by her husband. This was probably why there were a small number of people attending her funeral—that and the fact that she was an unpleasant person, although that never stopped people from showing up if the unpleasant person was sufficiently financially well endowed. In any case, Annabel would have been furious.

She would have wanted hordes of people pouring out of black limos, she would have wanted hundreds of roses covering her coffin, she would have wanted to be the center of attention at her last biggest event, but that's not what she got. No indeedy. The only people in attendance were the minister, the people who had been at the dinner Bernie and Libby had catered, their dogs, and Bernie and Libby themselves.

Richard had dressed Trudy in a little black shrug and a matching black leather collar for the occasion. Melissa's and Joyce's dogs were also wearing black, while Bree's dog, Rudolph, was wearing sunglasses, a biker's hat, and a small black leather jacket with chains. Bree, on the other hand, was dressed in her usual pink Chanel except for the addition of the huge fuchsia Prada bag slung over her shoulder, which Bernie decided was almost worth killing for.

"I know Rudolph looks a little distingué in his leathers, but Annabel loved this outfit, so I thought seeing it would give her a lift wherever she is," Bree confided to Bernie and Libby as they trooped up to the grave site together.

She'd looked slightly surprised to see them when she'd pulled up behind Libby and Bernie's van, but so far she hadn't commented on their being there, which Bernie thought was a good thing. It meant that she didn't disapprove of their presence at the funeral. There was really no reason that she should, but with Bree you never knew.

The day was overcast. Even though this February had been atypically mild up till now, it was more than cold enough for Libby, who wound her scarf more tightly around her neck to ward off the chill. During the spring, summer, and

fall, the old oaks and trembling aspens that dotted the land-
scape lent shade and color to the cemetery, but in mid-
winter their bare branches gave the place a melancholy air.
But then maybe that was the point.

"I didn't know you were coming," Bree said as she paused
to button the blond, full-length shearling coat she had on.
"You should have called. We could have ridden together."

So you could have pumped us for information, Libby
thought uncharitably as she apologized for their oversight.

Bernie pulled the heel of her boot out of the semifrozen
ground before replying. She kept forgetting that stilettos
were not a good shoe to wear in this weather. "Well, since
we were there when it happened," she explained, leaving
the "it happened" conveniently vague, "we thought we
should be there at the end."

Bree didn't look convinced. "How did you find out?
This is a private affair. There's going to be a memorial service for everyone in a couple of months."

"Really," Bernie said. "How odd."

She didn't mention that she and Libby had gotten all the
details from Marvin last night. His dad may not have been
handling the funeral, but that didn't stop him from knowing everything.

"Not really," Bree replied. "It's the way it's done these
days. Especially when the mourners are prostrate with grief.
At least that's what Richard tells me."

Had Bree actually rolled her eyes when she'd uttered
that sentence? Bernie wasn't sure. She'd have to ask her
sister later.

Bree turned to Libby. "Who knew?"

"Not me for sure," her sister replied.

"Speaking of which," Bree said, "does Richard know?"

"That we're coming?" asked Bernie.

"No, Rudolph, that's rude," Bree said to her dog as he
stopped to pee on a grave marker before turning her attention back to Bernie. "What else would I be talking about?"

Libby put a gloved hand to her mouth and feigned wide-eyed innocence. "Oh dear. Do you think he'll mind?"

Bree swallowed. Libby knew Bree wanted to say something on the order of *Tell me you're kidding me.* But she didn't. Instead she cast her gimlet eyes on her and said, "You girls aren't thinking of investigating, are you? After all, you did promise Annabel that you would."

"Oh no," Libby said. "Perish the thought. We just said that so we could call the ambulance."

"What's to investigate?" Bernie added. "Annabel's death was declared an accident."

"Yes, it was," Bree agreed. She paused for a moment while she considered her conversational options. Libby could see that she was having trouble finding a way to say what she wanted to. Finally, she came out with, "I know Annabel could be a bit overbearing from time to time, a bit hysterical, but I always admired her spirit." She paused again and fiddled with the brown leather buttons on her coat. "She was a go-getter and I can relate to that." She looked down at the ground for a moment before fixing her gaze on Bernie and Libby. "I understand that investigations can be . . . reopened . . . from time to time if sufficient reasons are found."

"So we've been told," Bernie said.

"Good reasons," Bree reiterated.

"Very good ones," Bernie repeated.

Bree nodded. "Of course one has to tread carefully where the superrich are concerned."

"Especially when they're one's bread and butter," Bernie said.

"There is that," Bree said.

Bernie nodded. "Makes sense to me."

Bree bent down and picked up Rudolph. "I thought you would understand," she replied. "What does your dad say?"

Bernie scratched Rudolph under his chin. He snorted in

pleasure. "He says that mistakes have been known to happen. They're not anyone's fault. It's just the way things occur."

The three women exchanged looks.

"Good," Bree said briskly. "Let's join everyone, shall we? I believe the service is about to start."

Bernie could tell from the scowl on Richard Colbert's face that he was not pleased to see them. Not pleased to see them was probably an understatement. And really, why should he be? she reflected. Essentially, they were crashing the funeral.

But before he could say anything, Bree chirped, "Look who I met walking up. Isn't it sweet of the girls to come and pay their respects?"

"I hope you don't mind," Libby said.

"Mind?" Richard's laugh at the absurdity of the notion was less than convincing. Bernie wondered if anyone there believed him as he continued. "Why should I mind? What a silly notion. It just never occurred to me that you'd be interested in coming."

"When we heard we just decided to come over," Bernie told him. "If you'd like we can leave."

"No. No," Richard said in an insincere-sounding voice. "Don't be ridiculous. We're having a bite after the service. I know you girls are terribly busy and probably don't have the time, but I know Annabel would have adored it if you could join us."

"We'd love to," Libby and Bernie said in unison.

"We brought some food," Bernie said.

Richard looked even unhappier, if that was possible.

Libby took up the conversational baton. "It's nothing much. Just some homemade bread, a couple of roast chickens, and a tossed salad. No one should have to cook at a time like this."

It was with great difficulty that Richard managed to get out the words "Great" and "You shouldn't have" as he turned to the minister.

"He was definitely not pleased," Libby told her dad later.

"Yeah," Bernie said. "He expected us to take the hint and leave."

Sean smiled. "Well, given the circumstances, of course he wasn't pleased to see you. If I were him, I wouldn't be pleased to see you either."

"Neither were the other guests," Libby recalled. "I got the feeling we were as welcome as a . . . a . . ."

"Weevil in a cotton field?" Bernie suggested.

Libby nodded. "Exactly."

"And no doubt for the same reason," Sean said.

"Which is?" Bernie asked.

Sean smiled. "That you're going to cause a lot of trouble and be hard to get rid of."

Chapter 6

Libby and Bernie both agreed that the funeral itself was extremely brief. The phrase "pro forma" occurred to Bernie frequently. A small hole in the ground had already been dug by the time everyone had arrived. It was covered with a green mat, which reminded Bernie of cheap indoor/outdoor carpet.

The only thing cheaper than going this route, according to Marvin, was not having a service at all and scattering the ashes, a practice he pointed out that was both illegal and unsanitary. Libby was thinking about that when the funeral director and his assistant arrived bearing Annabel's ashes in a dull-looking metal container.

"Annabel would have wanted an urn from Tiffany at the very least," Bernie whispered in Libby's ear.

"I don't think Tiffany's makes urns," Libby whispered back.

Bernie indicated the urn with a nod of her head. "Maybe not, but I think someone makes something better than that."

"According to Marvin, that urn is the bottom of the line," Libby replied sotto voce.

Then she fell quiet because the minister began to speak. The service consisted of the Lord's Prayer and a few generic words out of Funeral 101 along the lines of "Annabel was a fine lady who will be missed, and she is no doubt going to a better place." When he was done Joyce stepped forward and recited "Trees," which she claimed was Annabel's favorite poem—a claim Bernie was sure Annabel would have been mortified to hear if she had been there.

Throughout the proceeding Libby watched Richard, who was fidgeting and could hardly hide his impatience with the whole thing. One thing was clear to both Bernie and Libby: he was definitely not prostrate with grief. In fact, Bernie said later that she'd seen people show more emotion over the loss of a favorite pen.

No one else said anything after Joyce was finished except for Trudy, who barked at a passing squirrel. The people seemed disinterested and the dogs seemed restless and anxious to leave.

Libby was reflecting that she hoped she had a better send-off when Melissa's dog squatted and pooped on Annabel's grave.

Joanna glared at Melissa. "Have some decency," she cried, pointing to what Melissa's dog had done.

"What is that supposed to mean?" Melissa demanded.

Joanna's white skin looked almost translucent in the thin winter light. "It means that I'd like to think you'd have some respect."

"Respect? What does respect have to do with it? Of course I have respect. My pugkins has been having stomach problems recently."

Joanna snorted.

Melissa pointed to the little pile of poop. "Are you saying *I* made her do this?"

"No, although I wouldn't put it past you. I'm saying you should clean it up."

"I will clean it up. I always clean up my own messes, which is more than I can say for you."

"Meaning?" Joanna demanded.

"Meaning you're one to talk. If anyone around here should be cleaning up their own messes it's you."

"I already have, thank you very much. At least I don't go around shoving things in people's faces."

Melissa took a step toward her. "And you're saying I do?"

"Judge not lest you be judged."

"Oh, *puh-leze*," Melissa said. "Spare us that nonsense."

Joanna put her hands on her hips. "Now let me get this straight. Are you saying the Bible is nonsense?"

"No. I'm just saying your quoting the scriptures is laughable." By now Melissa was nose to nose with Joanna.

The irises of Joanna's eyes went from brown to black. She stuck out her chest, which, Bernie reflected, looked even larger than it had the day before—if that was possible. Joanna opened her mouth to say something, but before she could, Richard grabbed her by the sleeve and pulled her away. Bernie watched as she and Richard talked. Or maybe *talked* wasn't the right word. It was like watching a handler calm down a nervous filly.

Joyce coughed and everyone turned to her. "I'm sure Annabel wouldn't have wanted this," she said. "She would have hated to see her nearest and dearest fighting."

"I don't think that's how she thought of us," Ramona pointed out.

She had on sensible shoes, jeans, and a hoodie. She definitely hadn't dressed for the occasion, Bernie thought.

"You know how she got when she was upset," Joyce persisted. "She said things she didn't mean."

"If you say so," Ramona said. Her expression showed that this clearly wasn't the case at all.

Trudy started to whine.

"And you've got Trudy all upset," Joyce continued. "She doesn't like discord, you know. Richard, why don't you pick her up? She's cold."

Richard pretended he hadn't heard.

"I would," Joyce said, "but I'm afraid Conklin will get upset." Conklin didn't look as if anything would upset him—besides not being fed—but that was just Libby's view.

Finally Bernie went over and lifted Trudy up. Despite the cashmere sweater Trudy had on, the pug was shivering from the cold.

"I think it's time we went back to the house," Richard said.

It was a sentiment that Bernie and Libby heartily agreed with.

Chapter 7

The first thing that Bernie and Libby noticed when they entered the Colbert household was that the Puggables were no longer there. Evidently, they'd been returned to wherever they'd come from in the past two days. Without them the house seemed larger and colder, more like a museum than a place where people actually lived.

Bernie and Libby went into the kitchen to drop off the food they'd brought, while the other guests trooped off to the sunroom, dogs in tow, except for Trudy, who tagged along with Bernie and Libby.

Bernie noted yet again that Richard seemed to have no regard for the animal, which struck her as odd considering the position that Trudy occupied. Or maybe it was *because of* the position she occupied, Bernie thought. Maybe he didn't like anyone or anything being the center of attention except himself.

"I wonder what's going to happen to her?" Libby asked, nodding to the little dog trotting at their feet as they entered the kitchen.

A girl with long, prematurely gray hair was standing by the sink scrubbing a pot. "Have you read *Poor Little Rich Girl*?" the girl asked them.

"No," Libby replied. "Why?"

"Because that's the fate that's awaiting Trudy."

"She's not Gloria Vanderbilt," Bernie pointed out as she bent down and scratched Trudy under her chin.

"Barbara Hutton," the girl said.

"Whoever," Bernie replied.

The girl tossed her head. "It doesn't matter. The principle is the same. My point is that no one here likes her. Except me. And I don't live here." She turned to the dog. "Isn't that right, pokums?" she crooned.

Trudy wagged her little tail as hard as she could.

"Do you work here?" Libby asked, because she certainly didn't look like your typical domestic.

"Would I be doing this if I didn't?" the girl asked. "Mr. Colbert hired me to help serve the mourners when they returned from the funeral." She eyed the package Libby was holding. "So you've brought the funeral meats," she observed. "That's good, because there isn't a friggin' thing in this house to eat. Lots of booze but no food."

"Actually, it's roast chicken," Libby replied.

The girl briefly considered Libby's statement. Then she said, "I guess roast chicken could fall under the funeral meat description in a broad, generic kind of way. They're both protein."

Bernie fed a piece of bread that was on the counter to Trudy.

"You know," the girl said to her, "Joyce and Melissa are gonna kill you if they see you feeding that dog anything but her special diet."

Bernie looked down at Trudy, who had dragged the slice of bread under the table and was proceeding to devour it.

"She seems okay to me. Anyway, if it's all right for her to eat a piece of birthday cake, surely it's okay for her to eat a piece of bread."

The girl's eyes widened. "I thought you guys were the caterers. You were here when the missus died."

"Yes, we were," Bernie said, wondering at the word *missus*, which seemed to come from some old movie.

"Wow."

"You could say that," Bernie replied. "Although I'd use the words *scary* and *stressful* myself."

The girl gave the pot she was working on one last vigorous scrub before taking the sprayer and washing the soap off. "I read in the paper they're saying it was an accident."

"You don't think it was?" Bernie asked.

"I didn't say that."

"It sure sounded that way," Libby observed.

"Hey," the girl cried. "I just help out here from time to time."

"Okay. But that doesn't mean you can't have an opinion," Bernie noted.

The girl hitched her jeans up. "Well, I don't."

"What did you tell the police?" Libby asked.

The girl took a towel and began drying the pot. "I didn't tell the police anything. They didn't ask me."

"Really?" Bernie said.

"Yes, really," the girl said. She wiped her hands on the towel and carefully replaced it on the rack next to the sink. "And even if they had there's nothing I could have contributed. I wasn't here then. As you know."

"I do know," Bernie agreed. "I just thought they might have wanted to talk to you anyway to get background material, impressions of people, stuff like that."

"Well, they didn't," the girl said decisively.

"And if they had, what would you have said?" Bernie asked, out of curiosity.

The girl curled her lip. "I couldn't have said anything. I already told you that. Besides I signed a letter of confidentially, which means I can't talk about what happens in this house."

Somehow Bernie didn't think that counted when it came to police investigations, but she let that pass. "But if you could?" she persisted.

The girl frowned. "That's not going to happen. Richard . . . Mr. Colbert won't allow it."

Interesting sentence on two levels, Bernie thought. First there was the "Richard, Mr. Colbert" thing, and then there was the implication that Richard was running the investigation. Maybe *running* wasn't the right word. Maybe *influencing* was. Which squared with what Clyde had said previously.

"I didn't say it was going to happen," Bernie continued. "I'm just asking, if you could talk what would you say? Hypothetically speaking."

"I wouldn't say anything," the girl repeated. "I signed this paper. Mr. Richard says bad things will happen to me if I do."

"He doesn't have to know," Bernie told her.

"He know," the girl replied, a hint of a Spanish accent creeping into her voice.

"Are you afraid you're going to lose your job?" Libby asked.

The girl shook her head. "He told me he ain't gonna need me no more since the missus done died, so I'm leaving."

"Great," Bernie said. In the last two replies the girl had changed her accent and her speech patterns. What was up with that?

"What are you going to do?" Libby asked.

The girl thought for a moment before answering, then said in a voice that sounded like your standard East Coast suburban college girl, "I'm going to Buffalo to visit some friends."

"Is there any way we can get in touch with you?" Bernie asked.

The girl shrugged.

"Just in case," Libby said.

"Just in case what?"

"Just in case we need to talk to you," Libby told her.

"I already told you I don't know anything."

Au contraire, mon ami, Bernie thought. *I think you know a great deal. Otherwise why would you be pulling the shtick you're pulling?*

"At least give us your name," Libby urged.

The girl remained mute.

"I mean, it's obvious that you liked Annabel," Bernie observed.

"Is that supposed to be a joke?" the girl asked.

The girl touched the gold pendant hanging around her neck. "She was difficult. Very difficult. But she like the things I make for her. She say I make the best hot chocolate."

Here we go with the Spanish accent again, Bernie thought.

"And what kind was that?" Libby asked, who had an abiding interest in all things chocolate.

"Some Mexican brand. She also like my *ropa vieja*. I make this for her too."

Bernie interrupted. "Enough with the food."

The girl folded her arms over her chest. "I can't believe you of all people would say something like that."

"Believe it," Bernie said. She took a deep breath. This girl was definitely into playing games, but Bernie losing her temper was not going to help matters. She tried another approach. "Annabel asked us to help her. We're just doing what she wanted."

The girl's mouth formed itself into a narrow line. "Towards the end she was very sick. Always yelling at Mr. Richard. Calling him awful names. He said she was not well. He said she was crazy." And she took her finger and made a twirling motion near her head. *"Loca."*

"Do you think that's true?" Libby asked. The last time she'd seen Annabel, *crazy* was not the word she would have used.

The girl shrugged. "All rich people are crazy. They want this. They want that. They are never happy."

"Please help us," Libby pleaded.

The girl shrugged again. "What's done can't be undone."

"If there's enough evidence it can be," Bernie told her.

The girl laughed. Bernie observed that in some subtle way her body language had shifted again.

"All I know is that rich folks got different rules than you or me."

You are so full of shit, Bernie wanted to say, but she held her tongue. "At least give me your name," she said instead.

"It's Rita. Rita Moreno."

"Seriously," Bernie told her.

"I am serious. My momma was a huge fan."

Bernie kept her hands at her sides so she wouldn't strangle the girl. She tried one last time. "Can you tell us anything at all that would be helpful?"

"Yeah," Rita said, her Spanish accent now miraculously gone again. "I can tell you that people around here act like cats in heat. If I did what they're doing my momma would have had me tarred and feathered. And now if you'll excuse me . . ."

"You're not going to stay?" Libby asked.

"Nope."

"Who else works here?" Bernie demanded.

"No one right now. Mr. Richard let everyone go. He said he wanted to be alone with his grief. I'm the last one here."

"He didn't really say that?" Libby asked.

Rita put her hand up. "Swear to God that he did. And even if they were here it wouldn't do you no good anyway. Everyone had to sign the same agreement I did."

Bernie stared at Rita for a moment. The look. The shifts in speech patterns. The different accents. The body language. She should have gotten it before. "You're quite the little actress, aren't you?"

The girl grinned.

"Do you have a SAG card?" Bernie asked.

The girl's grin broadened. "I'm working on it."

"Is anything you told us the truth?" Bernie demanded.

The girl's grin grew even bigger. "What do you think?"

"I think I'd like to strangle you, that's what I think," Bernie said. "Where did Richard get you from?"

"A mutual friend. I was between jobs and I needed a gig." And with that she reached up and pulled off the wig she was wearing.

"Does the wig work?" she asked as she fluffed out her spiky bright green hair.

"No," Bernie said. "It's too distracting."

The girl shrugged. "That's what I told Angel." And she stuffed the wig in the backpack that was on the counter before she turned and started out the door.

Trudy, who had been silent up till now, let out a loud belch.

"Told you not to feed her bread," the girl said. "If she poops on the floor Richard is going to be wicked pissed."

"I'll bear that in mind," Bernie said.

"In case you're interested, I'm the Spanish maid in *Seems Like Old Times* by Neil Simon at Syracuse Stage."

"Well, it seems like something, but it isn't old times," Bernie cracked.

Libby gave her sister an interrogatory look as the girl formerly known as Rita flipped them both the bird and walked out the door.

"*Seems Like Old Times* is a movie," Bernie called after her. "It never was a play. If you're going to lie, at least get your facts straight."

The girl popped her head back in. "Whatever. Play. Movie. Who cares?"

"Neil Simon would probably care, for one, and so should you if you're serious about your craft," Bernie told her.

"You're saying I'm not?"

"I'm saying I don't know what you are," Bernie said.

The girl put her hands on her hips. "I'll tell you. I'm going to be a great actress one day. That's what I'm going to be." The girl squared up her shoulders. "And for your information, I have a bit part in *Cat on a Hot Tin Roof* at the Longely Playhouse." She wiggled her fingers. "Ta ta," she trilled. "I'm off."

"I don't think there are any bit parts in *Cat on a Hot Tin Roof*," Bernie mused after the girl left. "She certainly can't play one of the children."

"All I know," Libby opined, "is that she is a truly exasperating person."

"Yup," Bernie said as Trudy puked on the floor. Maybe feeding her the bread hadn't been such a good idea after all.

"Do you think anything the girl said was true?" Libby asked as Bernie went to get some paper towels off the counter.

"Dad always says there's a kernel of truth in every lie."

Libby tapped her fingers on the counter. "I wonder if Richard did let everyone go. That would certainly be interesting if it's true."

Bernie grinned. "I was thinking of the cats in heat part myself."

"Well," Libby said, thinking back to their other cases, "it always seems to come down to sex or money, doesn't it?"

"Or revenge," Bernie said. "Don't forget revenge as a motive for murder."

"I wonder which one it's going to turn out to be in this case?" Libby said.

"I guess we're going to have to wait to find out, aren't we?" Bernie replied. "Although what about fashion as a motive? There are shoes I would die for."

Libby opened her mouth and closed it again. On this subject she had nothing to say.

Chapter 8

Trudy watched Bernie with a great deal of interest as Bernie cleaned the floor.

"You're a bad girl," Bernie told her.

Trudy wagged her tail. Bernie laughed. She really was hard to resist.

"You know what I'm betting?" Libby said as Bernie straightened up and dropped the towels in the wastepaper basket. "I'm betting that Rita, or whatever her name is, is referring to Joanna and Richard. It's the classic man meets secretary, man falls for secretary, man kills wife so he can have the money and the secretary."

"Personal assistant," Bernie interjected. "People don't have secretaries anymore. They have personal assistants."

"Whatever," Libby said. "We could ask Bree."

Bernie shook her head. "I don't think she knows. I think if she did, she would have told us."

Libby nodded. Her sister was right. "She must be losing her touch."

"It would seem so," Bernie continued. "However, we could ask Kevin O'Malley. He might know."

Kevin O'Malley was the owner of Smithfield and O'Malley, an upscale grocery store that most of the wealthy households in Longely patronized. He pretty much knew everything about everybody in those circles. Even better, Libby and Bernie knew just where to find him.

"What would Kevin know?" a man's voice behind them demanded.

Libby and Bernie spun around. Richard was standing behind them. They'd been so intent on their conversation they hadn't heard him come in. Trudy scratched Libby's leg and she bent down and picked her up.

"He'd know whether we could get peaches that are decent tasting this time of year," Bernie ad-libbed, wondering as she did how much of their conversation Richard had heard.

Evidently judging from his expression he'd heard only the last part, which, given the circumstances, was a good thing. Richard grunted. Then a puzzled expression crept over his face as he looked around the kitchen.

"Where's Sam?" he asked.

"Sam?" Libby and Bernie repeated.

Richard gave an impatient wave of his hand. "Sam. Samantha. She was supposed to help with the dishes and the serving. I know she was here a moment ago."

"She left," Libby said.

"Left?" Richard echoed.

"Yes, left. As in walked out the door. She said you didn't have any food," Bernie said.

Richard gave a sigh indicating suffering on a par with Job. "Of course I have food. O'Malley delivered the platters this morning."

Good call, Bernie, Libby silently thought.

"It serves me right for hiring her," Richard grumbled. "By now I should know better. She's a total nut job. Comes from living with that mother of hers. No basis in reality whatsoever. No. If you want something done professionally, hire a professional."

"Who is she?" Libby asked.

"Sam's one of my friend's kids. She's living at home while she studies acting. Her father is trying to teach her the value of work, but he's not having much success."

"Seems to be going around," Bernie said as she recalled the array of college kids they'd employed over the years at A Little Taste of Heaven. "So where's the rest of the staff?" she asked, thinking that it would be interesting to be able to talk to them and hear what they had to say. "I would think that a house like this would require six live-in help— at least."

Richard favored her with a wintry smile. "Perhaps in the nineteenth century that was the case, but since we're in the twenty-first, and there are a multitude of labor-saving devices at one's disposal, that is not true. Surely even you recognize that?"

"That's funny," Bernie said. "Because I distinctly remember Annabel telling me she'd given the staff the day off for Trudy's birthday party."

Richard gave a snort of disgust. "Annabel likes . . . liked to play the part of the English country lady. She was fixated on the idea actually. Not that it's any of your business, but we don't have any staff. We have people coming in as needed."

"Like the tooth brusher for Trudy," Libby said.

Richard frowned and rubbed his hands together. It was obvious from the expression on his face that he found the topic of Trudy and the tooth brusher distasteful.

"I came in to see whether you two are all right. I thought maybe you were having trouble finding your way back," he told the girls, ignoring Libby's last comment.

"You have such a magnificent house," Bernie gushed. "I'd love to see it."

Richard gave her a look that suggested she had a better chance of seeing the inside of the private vault of the queen of England. Instead of replying he just grunted and stood there with his arms crossed over his chest while Libby and

Bernie unwrapped the food they'd brought and set it up on platters. When they were done he escorted them into the sunroom, where everyone else was sitting.

Interesting, Bernie thought. Most people would have taken five minutes and given them a quick house tour. Clearly he found the idea distasteful. Why? Was it them? Was there something he wanted to hide? Or did he just have an overdeveloped sense of privacy? Or all three?

"I found them," he announced to the room as the other pugs ran over to sniff Bernie's and Libby's feet.

Libby put Trudy down. She expected her to run over to the other dogs, but she stayed at Libby's side.

"Good," Joyce said. "We were afraid you'd lost your way."

"Spiritually or spatially?" Bernie quipped.

No one replied, which, Libby reflected, might be a good thing, considering the possibilities. Then she lost her train of thought as she contemplated the room she was standing in. It was truly spectacular. The walls and the ceiling were made of glass panels joined together with copper strips. It was like being outside, only better because the center of the room was filled with five extremely large potted palms that towered over everything.

Various types of ferns lined the periphery. The floor was ornately laid in a complex pattern of blue and white mosaic tiles, while the furniture was wicker with sky blue cushions. She felt as if she'd been transported to a solarium in an English country estate.

"This is wonderful," Libby commented as she thought of all the English mysteries she'd read as a girl. All that was missing was a white-gloved butler serving tea and scones with clotted cream and strawberry jam.

Richard shrugged. "Annabel insisted we build this after we came back from England. I don't know why. She called it her folly, and it certainly is. It takes an enormous amount of gas to heat this thing."

Bree picked up Rudolph. "She certainly had a vision of how she wanted things to be."

Bernie unbuttoned her cardigan. It was almost oppressively warm in here, but she supposed it had to be for the palms.

"I wouldn't know I was in Longely being here," Bernie said.

"I believe that was the general idea," Joyce said dryly. "Anyway, you're here and that's the important thing."

"Yes," Joanna agreed. "It's easy to lose your way in a house like this."

"Not if you're careful," Ramona chimed in.

Joyce lifted an eyebrow.

"What's that supposed to mean?" Melissa demanded.

"Nothing," Ramona said. "Absolutely nothing."

I'm missing something here, Bernie thought as she listened to the conversation. She didn't know what these people were talking about, but it definitely wasn't about the house's floor plan. She could see from the expressions on Bree's and Libby's faces that they didn't think so either.

"Now that you're both here," Richard said, "and since Sam's departed, I wonder if I could possibly impose on you to serve some tea."

"Not at all," Bernie said, thinking that that would allow her a little time for a quick examination of the house.

But that didn't happen. For all intents and purposes, Richard never let them out of his sight all the time they were there.

And neither did Trudy, who followed the girls around as if she were glued to them.

Maybe Sam was right, Bernie thought. Maybe she shouldn't have fed her the piece of bread after all, but not for the reasons that Sam thought.

Chapter 9

Libby took a sip of her Guinness and settled in on her bar stool. She didn't know why she was drinking this— she really didn't like beer, and she wasn't keen on being here either. She'd rather be home baking bread and watching television. It had been a long day and she wanted to go to bed early, an unlikely possibility the way things were turning out.

It was nine o'clock on a Wednesday night at R.J.'s and she, Bernie, Brandon, and Kevin O'Malley, the person they'd come to talk to, were the only souls in the place. Usually the place was packed, even during the week, but a winter storm advisory had kept anyone with any sense snugged up in his or her house. She and Bernie would be at home watching TV with their dad if Brandon hadn't alerted them to Kevin O'Malley's presence.

Kevin O'Malley was a man of regular habits. Even the promise of a nor'easter wasn't enough to interrupt his midweek stint at R.J.'s. At first Libby hadn't minded going because Marvin was going to meet up with them. She hadn't seen him in three days. Unfortunately, on the way over he'd called, said he had an emergency, and would be there later if he could. Which, in a word, sucked. Libby took another sip of beer and pondered how a funeral director could have an emergency, but then she decided she didn't want to think about that and ate a peanut instead.

For the life of her she could never understand how people, specifically Brandon, could say stout had a chocolate undertaste. Beer tasted like beer, and chocolate had nothing, absolutely nothing in common with beer whatsoever.

"Try it," Brandon said for the third time as he pushed a bottle of the stout across the bar with the tips of his fingers. "If you like chocolate you'll like this."

"I already told you I won't."

"How do you know if you don't try it?"

"I just know," Libby snapped.

Brandon shrugged and left the bottle where it was. "In case you change your mind," he said.

"God, you're persistent," Bernie told him.

Brandon smiled. "That's how I got where I am."

"Which is?" Bernie prompted.

"Being the sexy red-haired bartender every girl wants, but you are lucky enough to have."

Bernie laughed. "I believe sexy men are described as tall, dark, and handsome, not tall, redheaded, freckled, and handsome."

Brandon pounded his chest with his fist. "You have cut me to the quick."

"I figured."

"Fortunately, I have a robust ego."

"That's one way of putting it."

Brandon leaned over and gave Bernie a quick kiss. "I can get off early tonight. Mick's coming in to close. Unless the storm gets here first. Then *I* get to close early."

"He would actually close because of a storm. He's getting soft in his old age."

Brandon patted his gut. "It happens to all of us."

"What time were you thinking?" Bernie asked.

"Eleven o'clock."

Bernie checked her watch. That was a little under two hours from now. "That's the veritable shank of the evening."

Brandon picked up a glass and started wiping it. "What does that mean?"

"Haven't got a clue," Bernie admitted. "I just like the way it sounds."

Brandon put the glass down and picked up another one. "So eleven is good?"

"Eleven is perfect," Bernie allowed. "Unless the storm blows in."

"Where's your sense of adventure?"

"I must be getting old too. Getting in at three and getting up at five to shovel a path to the store just doesn't excite me as much as it used to."

"You mean I'm not worth it?"

Bernie gave him The Look.

"How about if I helped shovel?"

"That might be feasible," Bernie conceded. "Not that you will."

Brandon wiggled his eyebrows up and down. Bernie couldn't help it. She burst out laughing.

Brandon plunked his elbows on the bar. "See, Libby," he said. "I'm just an irresistible force of nature."

"You're something," Bernie told him. "That's for sure."

Libby smiled, but her heart wasn't in it. Marvin could at least call.

"Don't you worry," Brandon said, reading her mind. "He'll be here soon. Go on and have a sip of the stout. It's the sovereign cure for what ails you."

"I thought that was chocolate."

Brandon pushed the bottle closer to her.

This time Libby took a sip.

"Not bad," she said grudgingly.

"Not bad?" Brandon yelped.

"Okay," Libby conceded. "It's good. But it still doesn't taste like chocolate."

"How can you say that?" Brandon protested.

Before Libby could answer, Bernie held up her hand. "Enough," she said. "It's time to do what we came here for—talk to Kevin O'Malley."

Brandon shrugged. "You can try, but as I told you on the phone, he likes to drink alone."

Bernie fluttered her eyelashes. "I'm hoping to change his mind."

"I don't think that's going to work, babe," Brandon said. "Not that you don't have . . . um . . . great lashes, but Kevin used to run a strip club and has become immune to feminine wiles. Unlike me."

"Hmm," Bernie replied. "Strip club to a fancy food store. That's an interesting leap. I wonder how he did it."

Brandon shrugged. "I heard that his dad died and left him some money and he did this because it was as far away from a strip club as he could possibly get. But I don't know for sure. He isn't a real chatty kind of guy. He likes to be left alone and have his three shots of Black Label. So that's what I do. I don't think you're going to have much luck getting him to talk about the Colbert household."

Bernie shrugged. "I know it's a long shot, but I figure anything that we learn is better than nothing. Right now we don't have much."

"We don't have anything," Libby interjected.

Bernie cracked open a peanut. "Except for what Annabel said."

"To which no one is paying any attention," Libby observed.

"And they may be right," Bernie said. "Who knows? She might have staged this whole thing herself. According to Dad, that's the latest theory going around—no doubt suggested by her husband."

"He suggested what?" Libby practically yelped.

Bernie took a sip of her Brooklyn Brown. "Didn't I tell you? The new scenario is that Annabel poisoned herself out of spite, so Richard would then get arrested for her murder."

"I gotta say, that would be quite a grudge she was carrying," Brandon said. "Talk about not being clear on the concept."

Libby turned to her sister. "You don't actually believe that, do you?"

"Obviously not," Bernie told her.

"Me neither," Libby said. "But it's a very . . ."

"Seductive explanation," Bernie supplied.

Libby nodded. "Exactly."

Brandon refilled the plastic bowl in front of Libby and Bernie with shelled peanuts. The peanuts were R.J.'s trademark. Usually the floor was littered with the shells, which crunched when people stepped on them, but tonight the only piles were around Bernie's and Libby's feet. Not only did the peanuts add a little local color, but they were cheap, and they absorbed the alcohol so people could drink more.

"I thought you guys weren't going to take this on?" he said. "How come you changed your minds?"

Bernie lifted up her hands and brought them down. "What can I say? Our consciences got the better of us."

"I hate when that happens," Brandon said. "But deathbed promises are hard to ignore."

"It wasn't a deathbed promise," Libby said. "It was more like a dining room table promise."

"You don't have to be so literal," Bernie retorted.

"I was just being accurate," Libby rejoined. "You always tell me my speech is sloppy."

Bernie rolled her eyes. "Let's just get on with it, shall we?" She picked up her drink and walked over to where Kevin O'Malley was sitting.

He didn't look up. Not promising, Bernie thought as she sat down next to him.

"The answer is no," he said, before taking another sip of his drink.

"No to what? I haven't even said anything yet," Bernie protested.

"No. I'm talking about Annabel Colbert's business."

"How do you know that's what I want?"

He gave her a look. "I'm not stupid. This is a small town. What else could you want?"

"Well, I could want to know how much you're selling your mangoes for."

Kevin raised an eyebrow.

"Or your hothouse peaches. Or how you price your platters. Richard Colbert was especially pleased with the feta, grape leaves, and olives. The garnish was quite nice. I'll have to try the three different types of radishes myself."

"By all means do," Kevin said.

"I was thinking of doing more veggie things. What do you think?"

"I think that you're perfectly capable of adding some new items to your menu without my help, so you can can the charm."

"That's rather rude," Bernie said.

Kevin took a sip of his Scotch. "It was meant to be."

"So," Bernie said, trying again. "When did Richard Colbert order the platters to be sent to his house?"

Instead of answering, Kevin laughed and rubbed his finger around the top of his glass. "Do you know why I'm successful?" he asked.

"Good hygiene?"

"Seriously."

"Okay. Because you stock good products. Because you offer good service. Because you have good suppliers."

"Besides that."

Bernie thought for a moment. "Good word of mouth."

Kevin nodded. "Exactly."

"I'm still not seeing where this is leading," Bernie said.

"It's really simple. I've targeted my business to the rich, the superrich, and the merely well-off."

Bernie nodded.

"And one of the things people like that appreciate is discretion."

"You run a grocery store, for heaven's sake."

"Then why are you talking to me now?"

Bernie fell silent.

"Exactly. You're talking to me because you want to know all the latest gossip that I've heard. Well, I don't do that. I don't do that because it would lose me customers. I have keys to my customers' houses so I can go in and put their orders away before they come home from vacations. That way there will be food in the house when they get in.

"I wouldn't have that level of trust if they didn't know I was discreet. That is the foundation I've built my business on. There are lots of fancy grocery stores. My discretion is my ace in the hole. And in any case there's nothing to say about Annabel Colbert. Her death was an accident. Everyone says so."

"Especially her husband."

Kevin inclined his head but said nothing.

Bernie thought for a second. Then she said, "But if you were going to tell me something, what would you say?"

Kevin laughed again. Bernie noted that his teeth were small and pointed and very white.

"I would say you should go see *Cat on a Hot Tin Roof* at the Longely Playhouse. I think you'll like Brick."

"That's it?" Bernie said.

"That's it," Kevin replied. "And now, if you'll pardon me, I'd like to finish the rest of my drink in peace and quiet."

"By all means," Bernie said, and she returned to her stool.

"But what does that mean?" Libby asked when Bernie told her what Kevin had said.

"I have no idea, but I think we'd better check it out," Bernie told her.

Libby groaned. "Like I have time to go to a play."

Brandon grinned. "There's always time for culture."

Libby laughed. "Like what? Fantasy Football?"

"Exactly." He cocked his lead. "Listen," he said.

"Listen to what?" Bernie asked.

Then she heard it. Something was flapping outside. A moment later there was the unmistakable sound of hail hitting the roof.

"I do believe the nor'easter has arrived," Brandon loudly announced.

Down at the other end of the bar Kevin O'Malley lifted his glass. "Then I'd better have another quick one before I go."

"I'm just glad we got new tires on the van last week," Libby said. The old ones had been so threadbare the van probably would have slid all the way home.

Bernie was just about to tell her that she worried too much when the front door banged open and Marvin came stumbling in. He shook his head and brushed off his coat. Little snowflakes danced to the floor. He gave Libby a hug and a kiss.

"Boy it's really starting to come down," he said. "It's not much fun out there. It's not much fun at all."

Which turned out to be an understatement.

Chapter 10

The storm blew itself out around four in the morning, leaving lampposts capped in little hats of snow and cars buried halfway up their tires. For a short while, until people got up, everything was sparkling white.

"You have to admit it's pretty," Bernie said, looking out the window as she sipped her coffee.

"It's beautiful," Libby allowed as she dug her snow boots and mittens out of the closet. "And if we didn't have to shovel it would be even prettier."

It was a little after six, but Libby figured they'd better get started clearing the sidewalk. At least that way they wouldn't be too far behind with the other stuff they had to do.

"I wonder if Trudy goes out in the snow?" Bernie mused while slipping into her Uggs and ski parka.

"She probably has custom-made boots and a matching jacket," Libby said as they started down the stairs.

Bernie dug her mittens out of her parka's pockets. "It wouldn't surprise me at all."

It took the sisters a little over an hour to salt and shovel. They were totally exhausted by the time they were done, but as their dad said when they got back upstairs, people might not be able to drive down Main Street yet, but when they were able to A Little Taste of Heaven would be ready to receive them. Which was a good thing, because the number of people who started trickling in as soon as they opened the doors wanting to buy coffee and a pastry or two surprised Libby.

By nine o'clock the shop had already sold out of their apple, apple cranberry, and prune and apricot pies, as well as their corn, pumpkin, and chocolate chip muffins, in addition to their apricot and oatmeal cookies. Googie and Amber, who had fortunately made it in, were a blur of activity behind the counter.

Libby and Bernie were in the kitchen drinking coffee, eating slices of two-day-old apple pie that hadn't sold, and getting ready to make some more muffins.

"Pie in the morning," Bernie observed. "Nothing better."

"For sure," Libby said as she mashed the last crumbs of the crust onto her finger and conveyed them to her mouth. "You know," she said, "I was thinking. Maybe we should try half whole wheat and half white flour in the pie dough."

"I don't know." Bernie added a little more heavy cream to her coffee. "I think I go with Mom's adage: If it ain't broke don't fix it."

Libby cut herself another little sliver. "She never said anything like that."

"She didn't have to. That's the way she lived."

"Maybe," Libby conceded. "But there's always room for improvement."

"Not with our pie dough. Our pie dough is perfect."

"We could sell this as a healthier alternative."

"Then we'd have to have too many different types. We'd end up throwing too much out."

"We could only do it by special order."

Bernie frowned. "I don't know. It's one more thing to keep track of and we don't do such a good job keeping track of what we already have, as it is. Basically, I think it's going to be too much work and not enough profit."

"Boy you're in a bad mood," Libby noted. Normally she was the negative one, not Bernie. Bernie was always up for trying something new.

Bernie shrugged. It was true. She was. Mostly because she hadn't gone home with Brandon. She'd been afraid she'd get stuck at his place and not be able to get back in time to help open the shop. Sometimes, she wished she'd stayed in California and hadn't come back to work here. This place ran her life. Then she shook the thought off. She was just in a funk brought on by too much work and not enough sex.

"Okay. Try the crust out," Bernie said. Then she added hastily, "But not today."

Today they wouldn't have time to do anything but keep baking so they could restock the display cases. That was the problem with making everything fresh: It was a balancing act. Too much and they had to throw stuff out. Not enough and they had unhappy customers.

Libby was just about to tell Bernie that she agreed that today wasn't the day to start experimenting with anything, that they'd be lucky if they had time to pee the way things were going, when Googie came in with an envelope and handed it to Bernie.

"This guy said to give this to you."

"What guy?"

"Don't know." Googie straightened his hat. "He gave it to me when I was waiting on Mrs. Ruffo," he told Bernie.

Libby peered over Bernie's shoulder while she opened the envelope. There were three tickets to *Cat on a Hot Tin Roof* inside.

"Kevin O'Malley," Bernie and Libby said together. Then they took the tickets up to show to their dad.

"I guess he really wants to tell us something," Libby said.

"I guess so," Sean agreed, putting his coffee cup down. "He's obviously sticking to the letter of the law."

Libby gave her dad a puzzled look. "Law? What law?"

"His law," Sean explained. "Last night he told you. . . ."

"He told Bernie. . . ."

"Then Bernie—that he couldn't tell you anything directly. In his mind that would be gossiping, but if he points you in the right direction and you make the connections you need to make, you find out whatever it is that he deems important, well then, that's not his doing. He's in the clear. I wonder what made him change his mind?" Sean mused as he picked up yesterday's paper and scanned the headlines. He liked his news a day old. It put everything in perspective.

"Maybe his conscience?" Bernie said.

"He ran a strip club," Libby protested.

"So? What's that have to do with anything?" Bernie demanded.

"Oh, come on," Libby said. "You can't be serious."

"You're becoming very judgmental in your old age."

"No. I'm not," Libby told her.

"Ladies," Sean growled, glaring at both his daughters. "Sometimes I don't know what's wrong with you people," he declared. "All you do is bicker. It gets very trying."

"Sorry," Libby and Bernie murmured, although from where Sean was sitting they didn't look at all repent.

"It's an interesting question, isn't it?" Bernie said, getting back to the matter at hand.

"What?"

"Why Kevin sent us the tickets. It would be so much easier if Kevin just came out and said what he wanted to, but at this point I guess we'll have to take what we can get."

"When are they for?" Sean asked.

"Tonight," Bernie told him. "Unfortunately."

Libby stifled a yawn. "I just hope I don't fall asleep in

the middle of it," she said. There was something else about the play that was important, but Libby couldn't remember what it was. The trick was to stop thinking about it. Then it would come to her. Probably when she was rolling out dough for the pies. That's when things always seemed to pop into her head.

Bernie patted her on the back. "Don't worry. If you start snoring, I'll wake you up."

"I don't snore," Libby protested.

Bernie crossed her arms over her chest. "You most certainly do."

Libby appealed to her dad. "I don't, do I?"

Sean decided to concentrate on the paper. Replying would be a lose-lose situation for him. He'd learned from years of living with his wife and daughters that there were some questions you never answered, the archetypical one being, *Does this make me look fat? Do I snore?* might not be as laden as that one, but it was close enough.

"Would you like to go?" Libby asked.

Sean refolded the paper. "Go where?" he asked as if he didn't know.

Libby sighed. She hated when her father did this. "To the play, of course."

"I'd love to," Sean lied. "But Clyde is coming over."

Bernie put her hands on her hips. "Dad," she said.

"It's true," Sean blustered. Clyde wasn't really coming over for a visit, but he was sure he could lure the big guy to the flat with the promise of some lemon squares and pecan bars.

In Sean's opinion there were some things that went beyond the call of duty and this was one of them. Why sit through an inferior version of one of his all-time favorite movies? After all, who could replace Elizabeth Taylor as Maggie? No one. That's who.

Chapter 11

The Longely Playhouse was based in the Longely Community Center, an old firehouse on Warren Street. The town had done a very nice job of remodeling the building several years ago after the fire department had moved into more modern quarters. Now the two-story building housed a variety of activities, up to and including yoga classes, story times for toddlers, lunches for senior citizens, figure-drawing classes, as well as local theatrical efforts, or amateur theater as Sean insisted on calling it.

Superior Productions, the company that was mounting *Cat on a Hot Tin Roof,* had been in business for the last three years. Sometimes it benefitted from Longely's closeness to New York City, by getting a number of out-of-work actors who were looking to build up their resumes to perform in its plays. But mostly it relied on local talent.

The theater, which accommodated a respectable seventy-five people, was practically empty when Bernie, Libby, and Marvin arrived, a fact that didn't surprise Bernie, Libby, or Marvin. Even though all the roads were clear, people were tired from their round of early morning shoveling and were opting to stay in and watch TV, a course of action Libby kept telling everyone she would have liked to have followed as well. And Bernie had to admit that she wouldn't have minded too much either. Between the baking, the shoveling, and clearing the van off so they could get to the store and buy more butter and vanilla, the day had just worn her out.

The three of them had just walked through the door and were standing in the entranceway studying their tickets to find their seat assignments when Libby gave Bernie a sharp nudge in the ribs.

"What?" Bernie asked, rubbing her side. "That hurt."

Libby pointed. "That's what I was trying to remember," she said.

"You want to take a figure-drawing class?" From what Bernie could see, Libby was pointing at the schedule for art classes.

"No, dummy. I'm talking about Sam."

Bernie hit her forehead with the flat of her hand. "I can't believe I forgot. That's right. She said she had a bit part in the play." She continued, "Well, she does. In a broad sense. She's acting as an usher."

Sam came toward them. "What are you doing here?" she demanded.

"We're going to see the play," Libby said.

Sam practically shoved their programs in their hands, then hurried off.

"I think she's embarrassed," Libby observed as they took their seats.

Kevin had gotten them center-row seats.

"I don't think anything would embarrass her," Bernie said as she put her coat over the back of her seat.

"She used to work at the Coffee Grounds," Marvin told them.

"Really?" Libby said.

"Yup. I remember her because she tripped and spilled the coffee she was carrying all over my shirt. She had purple hair then."

Somehow Bernie wasn't surprised. "Well, she was wearing a gray wig the last time I ran into her. She probably changes her hair color the way some people change their shoes. Do you know anything else about her?"

Marvin thought for a moment. Then he said, "I heard her mom died last year down in the city. She was involved in some sort of accident, so Samantha came up here to live with her dad, Robert Barron."

Bernie raised an eyebrow. Robert Barron was a developer, although what he developed no one seemed to know. About six months ago, she'd read an item in the business section of the local paper about a deal Robert Barron was finalizing with Colbert Toys. That might explain why he didn't want his daughter even peripherally involved in anything that had anything to do with any sort of scandal that would affect his business.

Marvin bent down and pulled up his socks. "Supposedly, she's his kid from his first marriage."

Libby put her program down on her lap. "I didn't know he had a first marriage."

Marvin straightened up. "It didn't last too long."

Libby took a chocolate bar out of her bag, broke off a piece, and passed the rest to Marvin. "Now I feel bad for the kid," she said as the chocolate melted in her mouth.

"Why?" Bernie asked as she got out of her seat. "Just because her father is an egotistical, self-absorbed moron?"

"Something like that," Libby replied.

"Wow," Marvin said. "That's quite a mouthful."

"We did a dinner party for him a couple of years ago and never got paid," Libby explained. "He's very cheap. Not to mention the fact that he has these disgusting hunting trophies all over his house." She looked up at her sister. "Where are you going?"

"To find Sam."

"She didn't say anything before," Libby said. "Why do you think she'll say anything now?"

Bernie reached up and repinned her hair. One of these days she was going to cut it all off. "As Dad says, 'persistence is the cornerstone of good police work.' "

"You're not a policeman," Libby retorted. "You're a caterer."

"I never would have known," Bernie said as she walked up the aisle.

The building housing the Longely Community Center was a small place composed of a large entranceway, the performance space, four rooms on the bottom floor and three on the top floor. Therefore, it didn't take Bernie long to locate what passed for a green room. It was the second room on the left-hand side of the hall. Sam was sprawled out on a mustard yellow sofa that looked as if it had been dragged in off the street, listening to her iPhone and licking the vanilla cream from the middle of an Oreo cookie. Evidently she was taking her ushering duties as seriously as she took her cleaning ones, Bernie thought as she stepped inside.

It took a moment for Sam to notice her. When she did, she lifted herself into a sitting position.

"You can't come in here," she told Bernie, not bothering to take her earphones off. "This is for cast members only."

"I had a part in *The Wizard of Oz* once."

"I'm serious."

"So am I. I was Glinda. And I was very good. You can ask Miss Grover, my fourth-grade teacher. No? You're not going to? Fine. If it bothers you that I'm in here, we can step outside."

Sam ate the last of her cookie and brushed the crumbs off her hands. "I don't have to talk to you and I'm not going to."

"Okay. I'll just sit here till you do," Bernie said. "That sofa looks awfully comfortable."

Sam pointed to her ears. "I can't hear you."

Bernie took two quick steps toward Samantha, reached

down, and yanked Sam's headset off. "There," she said, holding it up. "Problem solved."

"You can't do that!" Sam squawked.

"I just did."

"Give them to me," Sam demanded as she grabbed for her earphones.

Bernie took a step back. "I will after we're finished talking."

"They're Bose. They're really, really expensive."

Bernie smiled. "I know. I have a pair."

Sam glared at her. Bernie returned the favor.

"Well," Bernie said after a couple of moments had gone by. "It looks like we're at a stalemate."

"What's a stalemate?"

"An impasse."

Sam put her hands on her hips. "My dad says I don't have to say anything to you, so I'm not going to."

"Who is your dad?" Bernie asked, wanting to hear what Sam was going to say.

"What do you care?"

"Maybe I want to call up this paragon of silence and talk to him. See if I can change his mind."

An expression of alarm flickered across Sam's face. "You wouldn't do that, would you?"

"I might," Bernie said, thinking as she did how young and vulnerable Sam looked.

Sam thought for a moment before shaking her head. A triumphant expression replaced the one of alarm. "Like, duh. You must think I'm really dumb. You can't call him. You don't know who he is."

"Actually, I do."

"No. You don't. Otherwise you wouldn't have asked me."

"I asked you because I was curious to hear what you would say."

"How would you know?"

"This is a small town. People know things. Your dad is Robert Barron."

The alarmed look on Sam's face returned. She scrunched her eyes together as if she didn't want to see what was going on in front of her.

Bernie pointed to the package of Oreos sitting on the table. "Mind if I have one?"

"You know something? You suck," Sam cried.

"So I've been told," Bernie replied as she went over and helped herself to one of the cookies. She twisted off the top, ate the cream filling, and then ate the cookie. God, she loved these. "Now then, why did your dad tell you to keep away from me?" she asked Sam when she was done eating. "If he did."

Sam dragged the toe of her foot across the floor. "I don't know."

"I think you do." Bernie watched Sam. It was obvious she wanted to talk. She just needed a nudge.

"You might feel better if you tell me," Bernie suggested gently.

Sam mulled that idea over for a while. "I don't really know anything," she finally said. "It's not like I saw anyone putting poison in Annabel's wine, or anything like that."

"Then what's the big deal?"

"It's just that Richard is a friend of my dad's. My dad says it wouldn't look good if I got"—she made quote marks with her fingers—"involved."

"But you don't think that's the case?"

"My dad doesn't have friends. He has business acquaintances. I mean he actually sleeps with his Blackberry. That's why my mom left him. She said he spent all his time doing boring business stuff. She never saw him."

"I'm sorry for what happened to your mom," Bernie said to Sam as she watched the girl's eyes mist over.

Sam looked down at the floor. "Stuff happens." When she looked back up she had a smile plastered on her face, but her eyes remained hooded. "But me and some friends are getting an apartment in Fort Green in a couple of months," she said brightly. "So that should be cool."

"No doubt," Bernie said.

"My dad doesn't think so. My dad wants me to go into finance." Sam made a face. "How lame is that?"

"Pretty lame," Bernie conceded as she glanced at the clock on the wall.

"And he hunts. That's even lamer. He has these disgusting heads on the wall."

"I've seen them," Bernie said.

"He's really proud of them, but I think they're really yucky."

"Me too," Bernie said. And she meant it. Ten minutes to showtime. It was time to wrap this up.

"Okay, Samantha," Bernie continued. "I just have one more question for you and then I'll let you get back to work."

If Sam caught the irony of Bernie's statement, she gave no notice of it. Instead she cocked her head and waited.

"The guy who plays Brick," Bernie continued.

"That's Rick Crouse."

"Well, I was just wondering, where does he hang out after the play?" Bernie asked.

"Why?"

"You saw the guy I came in with?"

Sam nodded.

"He's from ICM," Bernie amazed herself by saying. "He wants to talk to Rick." Bernie touched her finger to her lips. "But don't tell anyone, okay?"

Sam's eyes widened. "Wow," she said. "That's huge. Aren't they the biggest talent agency in the country?"

"One of the biggest," Bernie said.

"I hope that happens to me one day."

"It will," Bernie assured her. She felt ridiculously guilty about the lie she'd just told. Why did she do things like this? Especially at times like now when it had been totally unnecessary.

Sam went over to the table and took another Oreo cookie. "Rick will be at Leon's. That's where everyone goes after the show."

Leon's. Bernie had forgotten all about that place. It had been years since she'd been in it. Bernie nodded her thanks and turned to go.

"That's it?" Sam asked.

Bernie turned back. She could tell from Sam's voice that there was something else she wanted to say. "Yes?"

Sam scratched her head. "It's nothing. It's just that I'm surprised . . . you don't want to talk about the other thing."

"Well, you told me you don't want to."

Sam corrected her. "I told you I *can't* talk about it. That's different. My dad told me he doesn't want me getting involved."

"So you said. I can understand that," Bernie answered. "It wouldn't be very good for him."

"No, it wouldn't," Sam said. "But, on the other hand, what happened to Annabel wasn't very good either."

"No, it wasn't," Bernie declared.

Sam ran her hands through her hair. "Have you ever been someplace where things just didn't feel right?" she asked.

Bernie nodded.

"Well, that's what the Colbert household was like. Everything was business. It was all dollars and cents. Poor Trudy. They spend all this money on her, and no one likes her. She's an accessory to them. I was going to smuggle Trudy into our house, but my dad said he'd kick me out if I ever did anything like that." Sam sighed. "I mean, when people get married they should stick together, right? They shouldn't go off sleeping with everyone they feel like. I'm not gonna do that when I get married . . . not that I will."

"You'll get married," Bernie assured her.

"Are you married?" Sam asked.

"Not yet," Bernie admitted.

"How come?"

"I guess I haven't found anyone yet." Then Bernie thought of Brandon and said, "Although that may be changing."

Sam smiled. "That's nice."

"I hope so," Bernie replied, surprising herself by what she'd just said.

While she was still thinking about it Sam beckoned her closer.

"What?" Bernie asked.

Sam leaned over, cupped her hand over her mouth, and whispered in Bernie's ear.

Chapter 12

"I'm going to be what?" Marvin yelped, turning his head to better hear Bernie from the backseat.

"A talent scout," Bernie repeated.

She was glad that she'd remembered to save this bit of information for when they'd arrived at their destination. Unfortunately, Marvin was one of those people who seemed to need to make eye contact when conversing. This was an admirable trait most of the time, except when one was behind the wheel. And while her dad had made great progress extinguishing this habit, it was the consensus of opinion in the Simmons family that it was better to impart information to Marvin when he was stationary, if at all possible. Why take chances when you didn't have to? Bernie reckoned.

It was eleven o'clock at night and they were parked in front of Leon's, a dive bar on Catham Street. The place looked exactly as Bernie remembered it. The "e" in Leon's was still out, the burnt panel on the lower part of the door where three drunk college kids had set a fire hadn't been replaced, and the parking lot was still a deeply pitted obstacle course. It was nice to know that some things never change. They probably still had the same duct tape–patched uncomfortable booths in there and the same watered-down beer, Bernie thought.

Marvin turned the car off. He turned back to Bernie. "Did you say a talent scout?" he asked, hoping he hadn't heard correctly.

"No. I said a goldfish bowl."

"There's no need to get snippy," Libby told her sister.

"I'm not getting snippy," Bernie said even though she knew she was. She always did when she felt uncomfortable with what she'd done. Her therapist had called it a defense mechanism. Her mother had called it pure pigheadedness.

Marvin shifted around until he found a slightly more comfortable spot. He just hoped that no one in the cast had used the funeral home recently, thereby increasing the odds of his being recognized. If his dad heard about this he would kill Marvin. He was always stressing that funeral directors had to be dignified. This was not dignified.

"And you want me to do this why?"

"Ah. Because I told Sam that you were."

"And you told Sam that why?"

"Yes," Libby interjected. "Why did you? You know what Marvin's dad is like when it comes to this kind of stuff. He already thinks we're crazy."

Bernie sighed. "I know." Unfortunately she'd forgotten about Marvin's dad. What could she say? He was a forgettable person. Not that that was an excuse. Okay, so maybe this hadn't been one of her best ideas, but they were stuck with it. "Frankly, I don't know why I did it," she admitted. "It was one of those seemed-like-a-good-idea-at-the-time type of things."

"Not to me," Marvin observed.

"It'll be fine," Bernie assured him.

Marvin just stared at her with those big soulful eyes of his.

"I just thought it would make it easier to talk to Rick

Crouse," she explained, feeling slightly guilty at what she'd done. "And I don't think Sam would have told me where we could find Rick Crouse if I hadn't said that."

Marvin reached into his pocket, extracted a wadded-up tissue, and blew his nose. "Who is Rick Crouse?" he asked after he was done.

"Brick, of course. Didn't you read the program?"

"I read it. I just don't remember it," Marvin said. "He was awful. He sounded like a New Jersey truck driver."

"But gorgeous," Libby observed.

"Movie star gorgeous," Bernie agreed.

Marvin blinked. He turned to Libby. "You really think so?"

Libby squeezed his cheeks. "But not as gorgeous as you."

"I'm not gorgeous."

"No. You're sexy."

Marvin looked down at himself. His shirt was slightly stained, his pants were wrinkled, and he had the beginnings of a potbelly. And then there was his hair. Or rather the beginning loss thereof.

"Hardly,"he said.

"Well, you're sexy to me."

Bernie coughed. Marvin and Libby turned and looked at her.

"Folks, this is all very heartwarming," Bernie said. "But let's go over our plan."

"We don't have a plan," Marvin pointed out.

"I have a plan," Bernie said.

"Like what?" Libby demanded.

Bernie remained silent. Nothing was coming to her. Finally, she said, "Well, we'll just have to go in there and see what happens, won't we?"

"We?" Libby said. "What *we?* You don't have a plan. Let's go home. I'm exhausted."

"Me too," Marvin said plaintively. "We have two funerals tomorrow. Why do we want to talk to this Brick . . . Rick Crouse guy anyway?"

"Because Kevin O'Malley said we should," Bernie replied.

"He didn't say anything of the kind," Libby reminded her sister. "He just gave us tickets. He could have been talking about anyone."

"Not so. If you remember, he told us to watch Brick. And there's something else as well." And Bernie shared what Sam had whispered in her ear in the green room. "Sam thinks that Rick Crouse was having an affair with Annabel."

"You're kidding," Libby said.

Bernie shook her head.

"That's huge. Why didn't you tell me when you sat down?"

"Hey, I'm not even sure it's true. Sam said she just got the feeling when she saw them together."

"Where did she see them together?" Libby asked.

"At Denny's having breakfast."

"When?"

"Eleven o'clock."

Libby sucked air in through the space in her front teeth. "That's not really indicative of anything," she said.

"No, it isn't," Bernie agreed. "On the other hand, I don't see Annabel at Denny's eating The Grand Slam without a really good reason."

"Maybe they were conducting some sort of business deal," Libby hypothesized.

"You don't conduct business deals at Denny's," Marvin interjected.

"I was just being the devil's advocate," Libby replied.

"Sam was pretty sure they were holding hands," Bernie said.

"There goes that theory," Marvin said.

"Pretty sure?" Libby asked. "What does that mean?"

Bernie unwrapped her scarf. "Sam thought they were holding hands under the table."

"Excuse me," Marvin said. "This is all very interesting, but what does my being a talent agent have to do with this?"

Libby turned to Bernie. "Well?" she asked in turn.

"Because then maybe—no, make that definitely—Rick Crouse will want to talk to you," Bernie told Marvin.

"He'll want to talk about his acting career," Marvin said. "That's what he's going to want to talk to me about."

Bernie grinned. "Right. And then you can ask him about some personal background. You know, get him talking about himself."

Marvin took a deep breath and let it out. "What if he recognizes me?"

"He won't," Bernie assured him. "According to the program, he lives in the city. So if he's buried anyone recently, it hasn't been through your place."

Marvin was not persuaded. "Maybe he's come up for a friend's funeral," he said.

Libby patted Marvin's hand. "Don't worry. Sam may not even have told Rick Crouse."

Bernie thought back to Sam's expression when she'd told her about the agent in the audience. "No," she replied. "She told him. I'd bet anything on it."

"Great," Marvin muttered.

"Just think Tom Cruise in *Jerry Maguire* and you'll do fine," Bernie told him.

Marvin barely managed to keep himself from laughing out loud at the absurdity of Bernie's suggestion. He was many things, but Tom Cruise wasn't one of them.

"Okay," he said as he opened his vehicle's door. He was now resigned to his fate. "If we're going to do this let's go."

The sooner he got this done the sooner he could go home. He just really, really hoped that no one in the play had had cause to use the funeral home in the recent past. He should have paid more attention to the cast names. In hindsight, keeping the program wouldn't have been a bad idea either.

But perhaps he was being overly cautious, he reminded himself as he slammed the car door shut. He did have a tendency to do that. After all, most people in times of bereavement didn't notice him standing there. He was like the beige wallpaper: necessary, but unobtrusive.

A blast of stale beer and old cigarette smoke hit Bernie as she opened the door to Leon's. The place was as dark as ever. Two televisions, one set to a sports station, the other to the news, were going full blast. It was so loud it was difficult to talk unless you were very close to the person you were talking to, but, Bernie reflected, maybe that was the general idea.

Bernie noticed that the same pool table with a tear in the green felt was shoved up against the back wall. The same matched set of deer antlers hung on either side of the dusty mirror in back of the bar. Crookedly hung pictures of local soccer and baseball teams dotted the walls in no particular order. The outside had looked the same and so did the inside. Nothing seemed to have changed. Except the bartender. When Bernie had come here, he'd been a short, fat, bearded guy called Carl. Now the bartender was a tall, fat, bearded guy whose name Bernie didn't know.

"Didn't you come here back in the day?" Libby shouted at her sister as the three of them walked toward the bar.

"With Dwight," Bernie yelled back.

"Whatever happened to him?"

Bernie shrugged. "Last I heard he was in jail for robbing a convenience store," she told Libby as she looked around.

There were four guys at the bar drinking, none of them cast members. She looked at her watch. They were early. If Sam was right, the cast members of *Cat* would start trickling in in another twenty minutes or so.

"Mom hated him," Libby said.

Bernie switched her shoulder bag from her left to her right side. "For once, she was right," she mouthed.

"Of course," Libby reflected, "she hated pretty much everyone you went out with."

"The same could be said of you," Bernie commented. "I mean, Mom wasn't exactly fond of Orion."

"No, she wasn't," Libby allowed. "She was right about that too."

"She was right about most things," Bernie conceded, not that she had thought so when she was younger. This, she thought, must be a sign of her age.

Bernie pointed with her chin to the line of booths over by the far wall. You could see everyone at the bar from there and the people at the bar couldn't see you, she told her sister. And it was quieter there because it was away from the televisions. No small thing, considering.

The noise had never bothered Bernie before. That it did now was just another indication of her advancing age. Well, she was getting old. Everyone got old. But old, old. In a few months she was going to be thirty-three. That was only two years away from thirty-five, and after that—well, she didn't want to think about forty. It was too scary. She really did have to start thinking about Botox. And soon.

"How about we get some beers and sit over there," she suggested, forcing herself to think about something other than the crow's feet she was developing.

"I think I'll have a soda," Libby replied as they walked over and put their order in at the bar.

Ten minutes later the three of them were seated in a booth debating the merits of using Splenda in baking when Richard's assistant, Joanna, walked through the door.

Libby tugged on Bernie's sleeve. "Is that who I think it is?" she whispered.

"Looks like it to me," Bernie whispered back as she slouched down in her seat before she remembered there was no need to.

It wouldn't be the worst thing in the world if Joanna

saw them, Bernie reflected. But it would be better if she didn't. More educational. For them. When Bernie turned her head she noticed that Libby and Marvin had followed her lead and were slouched down in their seats as well.

Joanna turned and looked in their direction. Bernie held her breath. For a moment, she could have sworn there was an awareness in Joanna's eyes that she was being watched. But then that vanished and she turned back to the bar. Bernie, Libby, and Marvin let out a sigh of relief. Obviously she hadn't seen them. As long as they didn't do anything that attracted attention to themselves she wouldn't.

"Guess you were right about the seeing-but-not-being-seen thing," Libby told her sister.

"Of course I'm right," Bernie said indignantly.

She knew this from experience. She'd been here with one of her friends and watched Dwight making out with one of his new chickies, as he had liked to call them. To her infinite satisfaction she'd gotten both of them with the beer she'd thrown in their faces. Sometimes the old moves are still the best.

Libby turned to Marvin. "What do you think?" she asked.

But Marvin didn't answer. Libby didn't think he even heard her. He was too busy staring at Joanna.

"Quite a set of boobs she has on her," Libby observed dryly.

Marvin startled. Then he blushed and turned his head away.

"It's okay," Libby reassured him. "It's hard to stop looking at them."

"They're not real, are they?"

Bernie laughed. "Not unless women are born with the potential to grow rocket cones."

"That's what I thought," Marvin said as he ran a finger around the collar band of his shirt. "I wonder why someone would do something like that to themselves?"

Libby smiled sweetly. "So people like you can stare at them."

Marvin looked even more uncomfortable, if that was possible.

"Do you think I should get a pair like that?" Libby continued. "I mean, I could if I saved up enough money."

Marvin hemmed and hawed.

"Listen," Bernie went on. "The hell with her boobs. The bigger question is: What is Joanna doing here? I mean, this isn't exactly her type of place. The Four Seasons, yes. Leon's, no."

Libby took a sip of her soda. "It's another fish-out-of-water deal. Like Denny's."

"That's certainly so," Bernie commented. "And what is it Dad always says about broken patterns?"

"That they're significant," Libby said. "A change is a signifier. Whether it's a signifier of something large or small is what a detective has to find out," she said, paraphrasing her dad as she fiddled with her straw. "If I had to guess, I'd say that Joanna is here to see Rick Crouse."

"Why Crouse?" Marvin asked. "I don't get the connection."

"It's a little tenuous," Libby admitted.

"Yeah," Bernie chimed in. "And I have a feeling that the relationship you're referring to in this case isn't the incorporeal kind, if you get my meaning."

"You mean you think they're sleeping with each other?" Marvin asked Bernie. He wished that she'd stick to five-cent words instead of the dollar ones.

"It wouldn't surprise me," Libby replied for her sister. "Of course, I thought Richard and Joanna were an item."

"They probably are. One thing doesn't negate the other," Bernie observed.

"True," Libby said. She was slightly ashamed to admit she hadn't even thought of that possibility.

Marvin looked from sister to sister. "Well, if Rick Crouse

and Annabel had something going on, that would give Joanna a good reason to kill Annabel, wouldn't it?" he asked.

"One of the oldest reasons in the book," Bernie said. She ticked them off on her fingers as she said, "There's money, sex, and revenge. Take your choice."

"So which one do you think is operating here?" Marvin asked.

"Good question," Bernie replied. "Don't know. Could be any of the three."

"Or none," Libby said. "Maybe Joanna being here really is totally random. We could be absolutely wrong."

"Maybe," Bernie conceded. But she didn't really believe that and she was pretty sure that Libby didn't either, that she'd just said it for the sake of argument.

She and her sister weren't big believers in coincidence or random events. Neither was her dad. He subscribed to the old theory that if it looks like a duck and quacks like a duck, then it is a duck.

"Maybe Rick Crouse was involved in Annabel's death," Marvin suggested.

Bernie brushed her bangs out of her eyes with the tips of her fingers while she thought about Marvin's suggestion. "Could be," she conceded. "Although I don't see how. He wasn't there when Annabel got poisoned."

"True. But he could have come in earlier and put the poison in the wine," Marvin said.

"Anyone could have, for that matter," Libby said. "The wine was sitting out," she observed. "Anyone could have come along, put something in the bottle, and then resealed it."

"How could they have resealed it?" Bernie asked.

"I don't think it's that difficult," Libby said. "But you do need special equipment and time to do it." She mused, "Of course, most actors do spend most of their working lives as waiters or bartenders. Still, I think it's a long shot."

"Maybe Rick and Richard were in cahoots," Marvin said.

Bernie wrinkled her nose. "Rick and Richard? Sounds like a bad TV show. Why would they be in cahoots?"

"I don't know," Marvin said. "I guess Richard could have paid him."

"Why? Especially because Richard could have done it himself," Bernie said. "In my humble opinion, this is not the kind of task you want to turf out if you don't have to. At least, I wouldn't want to."

"True," Marvin agreed.

Libby rubbed her hands. There was a draft blowing in on her feet and it was making her cold all over. She picked a spot of pumpkin pie filling off her sweater. How she'd gotten it on there she didn't know.

"I agree with Bernie," Libby said. "First of all, Richard just doesn't strike me as the delegating type. Second of all, I don't see Richard and Rick Crouse doing anything together. They're both way too egotistical. On the other hand, I can see Rick Crouse and Joanna getting together."

"Now, I'm totally confused," Marvin complained. "That makes no sense."

"Yes, it does," Libby argued. "Think about it. Let's suppose Bernie is right and Rick Crouse is sleeping with both women. . . ."

"I didn't say he was," Bernie objected. "I suggested it."

Libby waved her objection away. "Fine. Let's say hypothetically speaking, if that makes you happy. As I was saying, Joanna wants to get rid of Annabel because she's jealous, so she gets Rick to help."

"That's certainly a plausible scenario. The problem is that there are too many plausible scenarios, way too many," Bernie said. She took a sip of her beer and made a face. How she had drunk this swill when she was in college was beyond her. "In any case, we should still definitely talk to Rick Crouse. One way or another I'm betting he's involved."

"Because of what that girl Sam said she saw?" Marvin asked.

Bernie nodded. "That and the fact that Kevin O'Malley pointed us in his direction."

And they settled down to wait for the cast to come in.

Chapter 13

At eleven-thirty the cast and some of the crew of *Cat on a Hot Tin Roof* straggled through Leon's door. There were Brick and Maggie, Big Momma and Big Daddy, the brother and sister-in-law, and some of the running crew. The doctor, the "no-neck monsters," and Samantha were missing from the group.

As Bernie watched them come in, she reflected that she was glad her father hadn't gone to the play. The performances the actors had given were mediocre at best, the staging was clumsy, and the miking made it difficult to understand what the actors were saying in several key scenes. For the next several months, her dad would have been complaining about being made to sit through the play.

By now Joanna had been sitting at the bar for a little over ten minutes alternately looking at her watch, tapping her fingers on the counter, and taking perfunctory sips of the beer she'd ordered.

Watching her, Bernie couldn't help but think that Libby was correct in her assessment. Joanna had to have a compelling reason for being here. This was a woman who drank pomegranate martinis, not Bud Light out of a can, glasses being considered an unnecessary frill at Leon's. And if

Libby was correct, Joanna had a good reason for getting rid of Annabel.

Nothing like a little rivalry to get someone's homicidal juices going. Or maybe Joanna killed Annabel because Annabel had found out about Rick Crouse and was going to tell Richard, thereby cutting short Joanna's employment. Or maybe . . . as she had said to Libby, there were simply too many maybes. Until she had some facts, there was no point in jumping to conclusions. As some Shakespearian somebody had said, "That way madness lies." Or words to that effect.

And then Bernie stopped thinking about Joanna and concentrated on watching Rick Crouse walking through the door. She had to admit he had something. He'd gotten two women to meet him in places where they didn't usually go. But maybe that was part of the attraction. Maybe Annabel and Joanna had been looking for a change.

At the moment, he was chatting with the actress who played Maggie the Cat. She was looking up at him with adoring eyes. *He really is handsome,* Bernie decided. He had the cleft chin and the blue, blue eyes going for him. She wondered if his eye color was real or if it was courtesy of contact lenses. She was betting on contact lenses.

Rick was all smiles until he saw Joanna. Then the smiling stopped. One thing Bernie was sure of as she watched him: Judging from the expression of anger on his face, this was not a man who, in Marvin's words, had colluded with Joanna about anything. In fact, it looked as if he'd like to wring her neck. And take a long time doing it.

"He doesn't look happy to see her," Libby observed as they watched Rick stride over to where Joanna was seated.

"That's for sure," Marvin replied. "I wonder what they're saying?"

"Whatever it is, it isn't good," Bernie commented.

Even though Bernie couldn't hear the conversation, it

was obvious to her from their body language that Rick and Joanna were "having words," as her mom had liked to say. Rick was shaking his head from side to side and holding his hands out in the air as if he was denying everything. Meanwhile, Joanna was jabbing her finger at him accusingly, stopping just short of poking him in the chest. Bernie thought that if she did do that Rick would probably snap her finger off.

The whole interchange between them took about a minute. Bernie thought Rick told Joanna to go screw herself, but she couldn't be sure. In any case, it was enough to make Joanna practically run out the door. Bernie noted that her hands were clenched at her side.

Rick started to go after her, but the woman who played Maggie took hold of Rick's arm. He spun around with his arm raised, his hand in a fist, then realized what he was doing and dropped his arm back down to his side. He could have shaken the woman off if he had really wanted to, but he allowed himself to be pulled back. The woman started talking to Rick really fast. Bernie wondered what she was saying because his face cleared and she could see the tension flowing out of his body.

"Hey," Bernie said to Libby and Marvin. "You stay here and talk to Rick Crouse. I'm going to see what I can find out from Joanna."

"Talk to Rick Crouse how?" Libby asked.

Bernie watched as Rick went over and talked to each of the four men sitting at the bar. They all shook their heads. He turned and studied the rest of the room. She was willing to bet he was looking for them.

"Wave," she told Marvin, "so he can see you."

"I don't want to wave."

"You have to," Bernie insisted.

Marvin looked at Libby. She gave a reluctant nod. Marvin waved. Rick kept looking around.

"Wave again," Bernie told Marvin, "and make it more enthusiastic."

This time Rick caught sight of Marvin. His eyes lit up. *I'm right,* Bernie thought. *Sam told Rick about Marvin being an agent.*

"I don't think you're going to have to worry about making conversation," Bernie said as Rick started toward them. "I think he's going to do all the talking. Just remember you're with . . ."

"I know," Marvin said. "ICBM."

Bernie groaned. "No. ICBM means intercontinental ballistic missile. You're with ICM," Bernie told him. "That's International Creative Management. You're from their New York office." And with that she took off after Joanna.

Marvin and Libby watched Rick advance on their table with a determined stride. Any trace of the anger he'd shown to Joanna was erased from his face. Instead he was beaming with eagerness and goodwill.

"Hi," Rick said when he got to the table. Ignoring Libby, he leaned over, grabbed Marvin's hand, and pumped it till all the feeling in Marvin's fingers had disappeared. "I'm Rick Crouse. I understand you've been asking about me."

"My hand?" Marvin said weakly.

Rick laughed. "Sorry," he said, letting go of it.

Marvin rubbed his fingers to get the circulation going.

"My friends tell me I tend to get a little overenthusiastic about things."

"Not a problem," Marvin said.

"So what did you think?" Rick asked him.

"Think?" Marvin repeated, wondering if Rick had done permanent nerve damage.

"About my performance. What did you think about my performance?"

"Good. Very good," Marvin stammered. What else could he say?

Rick beamed. "You don't think I made Brick a little too disaffected? A little too working-class James Deany?"

"No. No. It was perfect," Marvin lied. He hoped Rick couldn't tell he was lying, because he wasn't a very good liar, a fact that had caused him a significant amount of trouble in the past one way or another.

But Marvin decided that Rick couldn't, because his smile grew even broader—if that was possible. "Super." Rick steepled his fingers together. "I wanted him to be emblematic of modern man facing this vast array of technology. I know that's not what Williams wrote, but I felt it was in the character waiting to be drawn out."

Is that what that was? Marvin wanted to say, but instead he came out with, "You did a very good job."

"Thanks," Rick said. "I like to think that if Williams were alive today he would be pleased with my interpretation. I feel that as an actor one has a responsibility to push material in new directions, ones the playwright might not have consciously been aware of when he was writing." He pointed to the open spot in the booth where Bernie had been sitting. "Do you mind if I sit down?"

"Not at all," Marvin said.

Rick nodded. He waved to the woman who had played Maggie the Cat and pantomimed getting him a beer and bringing it over to where he was sitting.

"I can't tell you how long I've waited for this opportunity," Rick confided when he was done. "I've been down in the city for four years now. My ex told me I was crazy to go—well, actually she said something less polite—but I told her that if I did the work, opportunities would follow, and they have. I mean, you're here, right?" And he gave Marvin a playful jab on the shoulder.

Marvin experienced a sharp stab of pain where Rick had punched him. "Yes, I am," he managed to get out.

"I mean, when you're bit by the acting bug, you gotta go with it, right?"

"Right," Marvin repeated as the woman who played Maggie the Cat approached their table with two beers in hand.

"No matter what the consequences are, correctomundo kemosabe?"

"Oh, absolutely," Marvin replied absentmindedly, because he was distracted by the woman approaching the table.

She looked so familiar. There was something about her mouth, the way the tip of her nose turned up, and the slight overbite. And then Marvin had it. My God. It was Priscilla Edwards, the niece of Michael Edwards, the man they'd buried two days ago. She'd gotten lost on her way to the bathroom and ended up in their storeroom.

Marvin slumped down in his seat. Maybe she wouldn't recognize him. Maybe he could plead a severe bout of a gastrointestinal illness and leave. Or maybe he could faint. Oh my God. Why hadn't he recognized the woman earlier? Why had he dozed throughout the performance? Why hadn't he read the program more carefully? If he had he might have recognized her name.

"Here he is," Rick said as Priscilla put the beers down on the table. He gave Marvin a slap on the back that sent him forward. "This is the guy Sam was telling me about. This is the agent from ICM. This is the guy who is going to make me rich and famous. Who is going to put me on the map."

Priscilla looked at Marvin and then she looked again. Her eyes narrowed. *She knows,* Marvin thought. Marvin tried to think of something to say, but he couldn't. He couldn't get his mouth to open or his limbs to move. He felt like a pinned butterfly. Libby saw Marvin's panicked expression and tried to think of something to do, but glancing at Priscilla's face she knew it was too late. Why did she listen to Bernie? That was the question.

"Really?" Priscilla said to Rick. "He's an agent? Interesting. Very interesting."

Rick looked from her to Marvin and back to her again. "What do you mean?" he asked.

She pointed an accusing finger in Marvin's direction. "He isn't an agent," she stated. "He's the son of the guy who owns the funeral home where we held my uncle's wake. He was standing by the door greeting everyone and directing traffic when we arrived. He even went and got extra chairs."

Marvin began to feel decidedly sick.

"Are you sure?" Rick asked.

"Of course I'm sure," Priscilla said. "I've got a good memory for faces."

"Fuckin' great," Rick said. "Mercury is retrograde. I should have known something like this was going to happen."

"Listen," Marvin began. "I'm really sorry. I just want you to know. . . ."

But he never got to finish his sentence because Rick stood up, drew his arm back, and punched him in the jaw before walking away.

"Nice," Marvin heard Priscilla say as she caught up with Rick.

Marvin wiggled his jaw from side to side. Nothing seemed to be broken. He ran his tongue over his teeth. They were all there. Nothing was loose. So that was good.

"Look on the bright side," Libby said.

"There's a bright side to this?" Marvin asked.

Libby thought for a moment. "Not really," she finally said.

Marvin gestured to his jaw. He could feel it starting to swell. By tomorrow it would look . . . well, actually he didn't know what it was going to look like tomorrow because something like this had never happened to him before. But one thing was for sure: it wouldn't be pretty.

"How am I going to explain this to my dad?" he asked.

"Good question," Libby said. All she knew was that it

was going to have to be an excellent story. Then she wondered how well Bernie's foundation could conceal the bruise.

By the time Bernie got outside, Joanna was already in her car.

"Wait!" she cried as Joanna started up her Miata.

Joanna turned and stared at her.

"What do you want?" she asked.

"That guy you were talking to in there?" Bernie said.

"What about him?" Joanna asked, her eyes narrowing.

"Who is he?"

"Why do you want to know?" Joanna demanded.

There was something in Joanna's face that made Bernie think she didn't wish Rick Crouse well.

"I'm here to repo his car," Bernie said.

"Funny," Joanna said. "Are you adding that to your catering as a sideline?"

"Exactly," Bernie said. "Cook by day, detective/repo woman by night."

Joanna laughed. "I'd love to see my ex's car towed away."

"You were married to him?"

"Yeah. I lent him thirty thousand dollars so he could buy into a Pita Pit franchise with it. You know what that son of a bitch did? I'll tell you what he did. He ran off to New York with it. To study *acting . . .*" Joanna practically spit the word out. "He told me he doesn't have to repay me because he considers the money an investment in himself. He calls himself the business. I may barf."

"He's not very good," Bernie observed.

"Good?" Joanna let out a hoarse laugh. "Good? He's terrible. But he's convinced he's Oscar material."

"Well, he is good-looking. That always counts for a lot."

"Hah. You should have seen him before. To be fair, he wasn't bad before, but now he's fantastic, the lowlife sleaze.

That's actually where my thirty thousand went. Or most of it. He used it to get cosmetic surgery. That cleft chin? Fake. The cheekbones? Fake. Those blue eyes? Contact lenses. The teeth? Veneers. And then Annabel, bless her heart, paid for his chest implants."

"Why would she do that?" Bernie asked, feigning ignorance.

Joanna snorted. "Why do you think? Because they were sleeping together, of course. She was such a bitch. She always had to have everything I had. So naturally she had to have Rick."

"Which is why you started sleeping with Richard?" Bernie asked. If she had expected a denial she didn't get one.

"Fair is fair. No one walks all over me." Joanna pointed to her boobs. "Rick got his chest implants and I got these. In retrospect, I should have gotten them a little smaller, but I wanted something that showed."

"Well, they certainly do that," Bernie said. "I guess Richard liked them."

"He said they were a little ostentatious—those were his exact words. I told him to go screw himself and I cut him off. 'No more sex for you,' I said. Not that he really cared."

"Why wouldn't he care?" In Bernie's experience, that was all a lot of men cared about.

"Because he was already sleeping with Melissa. I just beat him to it."

"To Melissa?"

Joanna rolled her eyes. "To kissing me off. If Richard had really cared about the sex thing I would have lost my job. But he didn't, so I'm still here."

The expression "can't keep the players straight without a scorecard" popped into Bernie's mind.

"Richard always has two women in the pipeline," Joanna continued. "Sometimes even three. Though frankly, between you and me, I think three's too many for him to handle."

"Has he always been like that?" Bernie asked.

"As far as I know. Now they're calling people like him sex addicts. I just call people like that pigs."

"Did Annabel know?"

Joanna snorted. "You bet she did. How could she not? He practically flaunted it in her face. Her friends, the women who worked for Annabel—everyone was fair game. I mean, I felt sorry for her before she started messing around with Rick. Having to put up with Richard's stuff. And she was the brains of the outfit too." She added, "I'll tell you one thing, I didn't kill Annabel, but I'm glad someone did. She had it coming. And it wouldn't surprise me at all if Rick had something to do with it."

"What makes you say that?" Bernie asked.

Joanna leaned her head out of the car. "Because he was scamming her like he was scamming everyone else, and she'd just found out. So no more money, honey."

And with that last comment, Joanna took off. As Bernie watched the receding headlights of her vehicle, she wondered how much of what Joanna had just told her was true. A second later there was a sharp screech as Joanna threw her car in reverse and started backing up. Bernie jumped out of the way as Joanna squealed to a stop in front of her.

She stuck her head out of the window again and said, "I'd talk to Annabel's best friend, Joyce, if I were you."

"The reason being?" Bernie asked.

"Because she's a best friend with a caveat."

"Why are you telling me this?" Bernie asked her.

"As they say, payback is a bitch. She's the one who introduced Rick to Annabel. She's the one who told Rick that maybe Annabel would help him with his acting career." She imitated Joyce's voice: "I was just trying to help. Trying to help." Then she said, "Ha!" as she put the car in first and zoomed off into the night.

Chapter 14

Bernie was still thinking about what Joanna had told her when Libby tapped her on the shoulder. Bernie spun around.

Libby pointed to Marvin's jaw.

Bernie put her hand over her mouth. "What happened?" she asked.

"Rick Crouse happened," Libby said. "He found out that Marvin wasn't a talent agent after all."

"He punched me in the jaw," Marvin told her. "I hope it was worth it," he added plaintively.

Poor Marvin, Bernie thought. He was always so cautious, but it didn't matter. Things just happened to him. If there was a brick nearby it would fall on his head. Not, she was sure, that Libby would see the current situation that way. Bernie lightly patted the uninjured side of Marvin's face. "You know, you look very hot this way," she said as she tried to cheer him up. "Almost irresistible in fact."

"I do?" Marvin said, throwing his shoulders back.

Bernie nodded. "Absolutely. Men with bruises always are. Right, Libby?" she asked. "Right?" she repeated when her sister remained silent.

"Right," Libby answered through gritted teeth.

But she had to admit that Marvin had perked up when Bernie had said that to him. However, that still wasn't going to prevent her from wringing her sister's neck the first chance she got.

"Where is Rick Crouse now?" Bernie asked.

"Back in the bar," Libby said. "Drinking a beer."

"The bartender didn't even call the police," Marvin complained. "He could at least have done that."

"Was there blood?" Bernie asked.

"No," Marvin said.

"Did it spill over onto anyone else?"

Marvin looked puzzled.

"Start a brawl," Bernie explained.

"No."

"Then there you go," Bernie told him. "At Leon's unless there's a fair amount of blood on the walls, a body on the floor, or five people breaking chairs over people's heads, the bartender isn't going to call the cops. And even then it might not happen."

Marvin gingerly touched his jaw, then wiggled it around a little. "You know, this is the first time in my life I've ever been punched," he admitted.

"Seriously?" Libby asked.

Marvin nodded.

"See," Bernie said, thinking of Brandon, who'd made a career for a while out of brawling. "Then this is a good thing. It adds to your cool-dude factor. Trust me. You're going to thank me later on."

Marvin looked dubious. "Thank you for this? I don't think so."

Bernie raised her hand. "I promise. You'll see."

Libby just shook her head. Where Bernie came up with this stuff she'd never know. But, on the other hand, you did have to admire her gall. She would give her that.

Bernie thought for a moment. "I'll tell you what," she

said. "You take Marvin home and get an ice pack on his jaw. I'll go back inside, talk to Rick, and see what I can find out. When I'm done I'll call and you can come pick me up."

Libby nodded. That would work, she thought, since her main concern right now was keeping the swelling on Marvin's jaw down as much as possible.

"I'll drive," she said to Marvin as she took his arm and started leading him toward the car.

"You know," he said, "I have two funerals tomorrow. How am I going to explain my jaw?"

"No problem," Libby said with more confidence than she felt. "We'll come up with a really good story."

"Well, whatever you do, don't ask Bernie for one," Bernie heard Marvin say to her sister.

"I won't," Libby replied.

When Bernie walked into Leon's, Rick Crouse and Priscilla Edwards were sitting at the bar sipping their beers and watching TV. She went to the booth where she, Marvin, and Libby had been sitting, reclaimed her jacket, got her can of Bud Light, then walked up to Rick and tapped him on the shoulder.

"Yes?" he said, keeping his eyes glued to the TV.

Bernie waved her hand in front of his face. "Hello," she said. "Don't you know it's rude to ignore people?"

He reluctantly turned to face her. "And it's rude to wave your hand in front of someone's face. What do you want?"

"I want to know why you punched my friend."

"That guy was your friend?"

"That's what I just said, didn't I?"

He gave Bernie his full attention. "Girls in stiletto heels shouldn't go causing trouble."

"I'm not causing trouble. I'm asking you a question."

Rick took a gulp of his beer and put the can back down. "Not that it's any of your business, but I clocked him one because he lied to me. That's why."

"You punch everyone who lies to you?" Bernie asked him.

"No, I don't," he replied. "Okay. I admit I lost control of myself, but this was different. He deserved it."

"Different how?"

"Because . . ."

But before Rick could finish his sentence Priscilla Edwards leaned forward and finished it for him. "Rick was really excited about meeting the agent. It was all he was talking about backstage. So when he found out that this guy Marvin was shining him on he just got a little carried away, that's all. Heaven only knows what would have happened if I hadn't been along. Poor Rick would have never known."

"That's right," Rick said. He pounded the bar. "That's exactly right."

Priscilla patted his arm in a proprietary manner. Rick favored her with a grateful smile.

"I see," Bernie said. And she did. She put her can of beer down. It was bad enough when it was cold, but it was undrinkable when it was warm. "You know, I was the one who suggested Marvin do that. I was the one who told Sam. Marvin was just doing what I told him to do."

Rick looked back at her, a puzzled expression on his face. "Why?" he finally said. "That wasn't very nice. That wasn't nice at all. In fact, it was downright mean. What did I ever do to you? That's what I want to know."

"Nothing," Bernie told him. "You've never done anything to me. I just wanted to get some information. I figured that this would be a good way of getting you talking."

"You could have just asked," Rick said. "That would have been easier."

"Agreed," Bernie said. "It certainly would have been easier on poor Marvin."

"What you did is not good for me," Rick went on as if Bernie hadn't spoken. "I have trust issues. And this whole thing has reactivated them. It's going to make it difficult for me to sleep, which is bad for my immune system. I'm going to have to call my therapist. In fact, I could call my lawyer and sue you for emotional distress."

"Do you have a lawyer?" Bernie asked him.

Rick hesitated a moment too long before saying, "Of course I do."

Bernie leaned back slightly. "That's good," she said. "Considering you might need one when the police find out about you and Annabel."

"There's nothing between me and Annabel," Rick cried.

"That's not what I heard," Bernie retorted. "But I guess I got my info wrong. I guess you weren't the go-to guy for her."

Priscilla scowled. "Why do you want to know about her?" she demanded of Bernie.

"Are you his lawyer?" Bernie demanded.

"No. I'm his friend. His good friend," Priscilla said, emphasizing the word *good*, in case Bernie didn't get it.

"Fine then," Bernie replied. "I'm asking because she was murdered and I'm investigating her death."

"She wasn't murdered," Priscilla said. "The papers said it was an accident."

"Maybe it was and maybe it wasn't," Bernie said.

"Well . . ." Priscilla began but Rick interrupted.

"Whatever it was doesn't matter," he said. "Because I didn't have anything to do with it."

Bernie raised an eyebrow. "But you were involved with her."

Rick assumed an injured expression. Bernie was surprised he wasn't holding his hands to his heart and crying, "Oh, the calumny of it all."

"She was my patron," he said. "She believed in me. She believed in my craft. So if you want to call that being involved, then yes, we were involved."

"How touching. I didn't know she had an artistic side. Tell me, does paying for your chest implants qualify as helping your acting career?" Bernie asked.

"Your what?!" Priscilla shrieked.

Everyone in the bar turned around.

"It's nothing," Rick told Priscilla as he hushed her. "Everyone does it these days."

"I don't think Laurence Olivier would have done that," Bernie observed.

Priscilla and Rick ignored her.

"Rick," Priscilla said, "you told me you got your body working out at the gym every day—that's why you needed me to pay for your training."

"Priscilla, darling," Rick told her. "My sweet. I do need the gym every day. I need my trainer and my masseuse. It's just that sometimes people need that little extra edge. That's all. It's not a big deal."

Bernie ran her finger around the edge of her beer can. "I bet Annabel thought it was. I mean, she must have liked you a lot to fork up that kind of dough. So I'll tell you what interests me. What interests me is that I hear she was cutting you off. No more money for Rick. So what did you do to piss her off? That's what I want to know. Or maybe she found someone else. Someone with a little more . . . on the ball."

Rick's face started to get red. "That's a lie."

"She gave you money?" Priscilla demanded.

"No. No. No," Rick said to Priscilla. "You don't understand."

"That's not what your ex told me," Bernie said, adding fuel to the fire. "She told me she gave you plenty."

"That bitch," Rick spat out. "I might have known. You can't believe anything she says."

"Like the fact that you owe her thirty thousand dollars."

Rick snorted. "What a crock. She gave me money for a business and I invested in one." Rick poked himself in the chest. "Me. I'm the business. I'm a gilt-edged investment. I've told her that when I get famous I'll pay her back, but she can't hear that because she's jealous that I'm going someplace, that I'm going to be rich and famous, while she's stuck in some stupid, pathetic day job. . . . "

"Hey. I have a day job," Priscilla cried.

"Not you, babykins." Rick gave her a peck on the cheek. "I wasn't talking about you. You've got . . . soul. You've got theater in your blood. Joanna is a civilian."

Priscilla pushed him away. Judging from the expression on her face she wasn't convinced. "You were taking money from Annabel?"

Rick opened his mouth to reply, but Priscilla didn't give him a chance. "You told me you were broke. You told me you were going to be out on the street if you didn't get money together to pay your rent."

"It's true," Rick said. He raised his hand. "I swear. You can talk to my landlord if you want. In fact, I insist. Here, let me write down the number for you." He patted his shirt and his pants. "Drats. I don't have a pen."

Bernie smiled. "I do."

He glared at her as she handed him the pen and a piece of paper. He scribbled something down and handed it to Priscilla, who shoved it in her bag without bothering to look at it.

"How much were you getting from Annabel?" Priscilla asked, returning to the matter under discussion.

"I wasn't getting any money," Rick replied.

The key here is the word money, Bernie decided. "Priscilla, ask him about his car," she suggested, guessing that the BMW in the parking lot belonged to Rick.

Priscilla put both hands on her hips. "Well?" she demanded.

"She insisted," Rick said in a piteous voice. Bernie could have sworn she saw the beginning of tears in his eyes. "You wouldn't want me to have hurt her feelings, would you?

She was so fragile. If I had refused she would have seen it as a rejection of her."

Bernie rolled her eyes. "Can't you come up with something better? That's so lame I'm embarrassed for you. On the other hand, I have to give you kudos for the tears. They were a nice touch. In short, I'd give your material a D- and your performance a B+."

Priscilla ignored her. "Really?" Priscilla said as she spoke to Rick and pretended Bernie wasn't there.

"Yes, really," Rick said. "The only reason I didn't tell you was that I was afraid you would misinterpret it. And you have." He clasped both of Priscilla's hands in his. "You're my muse. You know you mean everything to me. Without you I'm nothing."

Bernie could see Priscilla start to fold. In another five minutes she'd give it up. Bernie was about to say that when Libby called and told her she was on her way. It was time to go. She'd gotten as much as she was going to get anyway. Bernie put on her jacket, picked up her bag, and slung it over her shoulder. Then she picked up her Bud Light, raised the can, and poured it over Rick Crouse's head.

"This is for Marvin," she said as she started walking away.

Rick froze. This was a good thing, Bernie decided. Otherwise he might have decked her too. He was still in shock when Priscilla grabbed a bunch of napkins off the bar and started blotting at his face and neck. Then he came out of it. He grabbed the napkins out of Priscilla's hands and pushed her away.

"Leave me alone," he snarled.

Bernie kept going.

"You come back here!" he screamed at her.

Like that's going to happen, Bernie thought as she picked up her pace.

"I'm going to sue you!" Rick yelled at Bernie as she reached the door. "I'm going to sue you for millions of dollars for the pain and suffering you've caused me. That's what I'm going to do."

Bernie turned around. "Go right ahead. And I'm going to countersue you for the pain and suffering and mental anguish you've caused by inflicting on me the worst performance of Brick that I have ever seen." Which wasn't quite true, but at this moment exaggeration seemed to be the order of the day. As Bernie watched Rick ball his hands up into fists, she decided she might have gone too far. "Okay, maybe I did overstate," Bernie told him. "But you shouldn't have done what you did to Marvin either."

It didn't seem to help. Rick took a step toward her and Bernie ran out the door. Luckily Libby was pulling up alongside the door just then.

"Go!" Bernie yelled as she yanked open the van door on the passenger side and jumped in.

"What's going on?" Libby asked.

"I'll explain later," Bernie cried. "Just move."

Libby tromped on the gas. The van lurched forward and they were off—at forty miles an hour. They were clearing the parking lot when Rick came bursting through the door with Priscilla in hot pursuit.

Libby checked the rearview mirror as they made a right onto Church Street. Nobody was behind them. She sighed in relief. It would have taken all of two seconds for Rick's BMW to catch up with A Little Taste of Heaven's van.

"Don't do this again," she told Bernie as she slowed down to thirty miles an hour, the speed the van was happiest at. The van could actually do fifty if pressed, but it began to get the wobbles.

"I won't," Bernie said. And she meant it too. For the moment.

Chapter 15

It was a little after seven-thirty the next morning, and Bernie and her dad were sitting at the breakfast table talking about last night's events. The morning was cold and gray. The weather forecast had promised more snow later in the afternoon. For now, though, things were quiet.

As Bernie looked out the window, she could see the first of her customers filing in for their early morning coffee, muffins, and scones. There was Mr. Ryan, Mrs. Cortes, and the Gleason twins. The twins always came in for one cranberry muffin and one chocolate chip muffin each, plus two large coffees with double sugar and skimmed milk.

Some of the shop customers, like old Mrs. Frederiks, had been coming here since Bernie's mom had opened the place. As Bernie watched Nathan Landow come in for his walnut scone and hot chocolate after his morning run, she decided that their customers—most of them, except for a select few—made all the aggravation of running a place like this worth it.

She would miss them if—God forbid—something happened. So many small businesses were going under these days, they were lucky they were hanging on. Well, they were doing better then just hanging on. They were paying their bills and having enough left over to put some aside, which was all you could ask for, really. She even had enough to indulge her shoe addiction from time to time.

As she thought about it, she realized she would miss more than the customers. She would miss the early morning risings when everyone was asleep and the world was hers. She would miss the sweet, rich smell of butter and sugar, the feel of the bread dough between her fingers as she kneaded it out, and the satisfaction of seeing the cookies lined up on the baking sheets like so many soldiers. She was thinking about how it had happened that she'd come to embrace the shop instead of running away from it when she became aware that her father was speaking to her.

"What did you say?" she asked her dad as she took a bite of the apple crumb cake she'd decided to eat for breakfast. She'd used half whole-wheat flour and half white. It had, as she suspected, resulted in a slightly more flavorful batter and a chewier crumb.

"I was saying that I thought what you said to Rick Crouse was ill-advised," Sean replied.

Bernie raised an eyebrow.

"I'm serious. There's no point in going for a man's weak spot if you don't have to. Most of the time it just makes him madder. It's like cornering an animal. You always want to leave him a way out if you can."

Bernie took a bite, chewed, and swallowed. She'd heard this lecture before. Multiple times. "You would have said the same thing if you'd seen him onstage. In fact, you would have probably gotten up and walked out."

"Was he really that awful?"

Bernie automatically smoothed out a crease in the tablecloth before replying, "Yes, he was. And I wouldn't have said it if he hadn't punched Marvin. That went way over the line."

"Agreed." Sean grimaced. "That whole sticks-and-stones-may-break-my-bones-but-words-can-never-hurt-me thing. Whoever made up that saying got it backward."

"Well, he put on a terrific performance offstage. I will give him that. I can see how all the women love him. It's the onstage part that's the problem. Maybe I should tell him that."

"Maybe you shouldn't," Sean said as he took a forkful of home fries.

As he did he reflected that his girls always got the balance just right. The onions were slightly charred around the edges, the green pepper had a nice flavor, and the cubed potatoes were soft on the inside and crispy on the outside. Add some fresh ground pepper and he could eat these every day of his life.

Bernie poured herself a tiny bit more coffee and added a smidgen of heavy cream. She was trying to cut down on both but wasn't having much luck. "I think I'm going to have to," she said after a moment's reflection.

"Then meet him somewhere public. It'll be safer that way." Sean ate another forkful of potatoes and chewed slowly. "On a different topic," he said after he'd swallowed, "let's talk about what happened to Marvin last night."

"That was a slight miscalculation," Bernie said.

Sean raised an eyebrow. "Slight? Is that what we're calling it now?"

"That's what I'm calling it. God only knows what Libby is saying."

"Nothing very nice."

"That's what I figured," Bernie said gloomily.

"How could you?" her father asked her.

Bernie didn't give him an answer because she didn't think her father was looking for one.

Her dad continued, "Libby put enough pancake make-up . . ."

"Foundation," Bernie corrected.

Sean gave an impatient wave of his hand. "As I was saying, your sister put enough make-up on Marvin's jaw to coat an elephant. I told her not to bother. I told her it would only attract more attention, but you know your sister. Once she gets an idea in her head there's no stopping her.

"Even Marvin agreed with me. For once. He went in the bathroom and washed it off. Of course, he'll need it today. Can't have a funeral director with purple bruises. It's too distracting. No. I bet his dad was really pissed when he got a look at Marvin last night. You know Marvin's dad. It's all about the work."

Bernie swallowed another piece of the apple crumb cake. A few toasted walnuts on the top to add a nice contrasting crunch and it would be perfect. "So what's the story you guys came up with?"

Sean took another sip of his coffee and ate some more of his scrambled eggs. "Are the green flecks in the eggs chives?"

"Dad!"

"What?" Sean said in his most innocent voice.

"Tell me you didn't leave that to Marvin," Bernie pleaded. Marvin was good at many things, but coming up with alibis wasn't among his strengths.

"Well, I don't like to lie," her dad said.

Bernie snorted. "This is me you're talking to, remember?"

"It's true," Sean protested. What he did was interpretative speaking.

"Anyway," Bernie continued, "this isn't lying. This is an act of mercy. A mitzvah."

Sean gave his daughter an irritable glance. "Of course Marvin and I came up with a story. What do you think I am? We rehearsed it too, so when his dad cross-examines him he won't get flustered." Sean paused for a moment to take a sip of Libby's freshly squeezed orange juice and allow the dramatic momentum to build.

Bernie leaned forward. "Tell me, Dad."

Sean put his glass down. "Fine. Marvin rescued Libby from a mugger as she was getting into his car and got punched in the jaw for his trouble."

"That works."

"Of course it works. How could you think that I wouldn't come up with something that works?"

"I actually never doubted you would for a second." Which was true. She hadn't.

Sean looked mollified. He ate another bit of his scrambled egg. "The bigger question is: What were you thinking when you put him in that situation?"

"You already asked me that."

"I'm asking again because I didn't get an answer the first time."

"Well . . ."

"I'll tell you why you can't answer. . . ."

"Because you won't let me?"

"No. Because you can't think of anything to say. What you did was totally irresponsible."

Bernie mashed one of the crumbs on her plate with her fork. "Dad, you sound as if you're taking his side."

"I am. Poor Marvin," Sean said.

"Come on, Dad," Bernie protested. "Admit it. This was good for him. It broadens his worldview."

"Getting punched in the jaw does nothing for one's worldview. It may do something for the dentist who replaces your teeth. Like make him money. But that's about it. And I should know. I've been punched enough. Ask Brandon. He'll say the same thing I just did." Sean put his fork down and looked his daughter in the eye. "Bernie," he said, "you really have to think before you speak."

"I know," Bernie told him. "I'm working on it."

"You've been working on it since you were a little girl, and I don't see much progress in that direction." When she didn't reply, he told her, "I mean it. Words matter. They matter a lot. And you of all people should know that."

"You're right," Bernie told her father.

And he was. It was just that the moment she thought of something she tended to put it into action. Sometimes that was very good and sometimes, witness last night, it wasn't. She took another sip of her coffee.

"Marvin could have been really hurt," her dad continued.

"But he wasn't."

"But he could have been," Sean insisted. "And so could you, if we come down to it."

Bernie thought about Rick bursting through the front door of Leon's. He'd looked pretty angry. Pouring beer over Rick's head had been a satisfying but unnecessary thing to do, she had to admit.

"How did you know that Libby was going to be there at that particular moment?" Sean asked. "Exactly," Sean said when Bernie didn't say anything. "That's what I thought. I'm going to say to you what I used to say to my men: Planning is the key to everything. You have to know what you're doing before you do anything. Otherwise you're relying on luck and luck only takes you so far."

"Are you done?" Bernie asked, trying to stem the rising tide of irritation she was feeling at her dad's lecture. She hated when he kept on repeating things over and over. Like she didn't get it.

"Yes, I am," Sean said.

He ate another mouthful of home fries and scanned the front page of the local paper. Not that there was anything worth reading in it today, unless you were interested in the fact that Mrs. Gardenia had six cats living in her house, one more than the local ordinance allowed for.

A moment later, Libby came into the room. She was wearing a white terrycloth bathrobe and had a purple towel wrapped around her head.

"I don't know why you can't get white towels," she

complained to Bernie as she reached over and took a sip of coffee out of Bernie's cup.

"Hey, get your own," Bernie told her.

"I will in a minute. Why do you have to get all of these weird colors?"

"Because that's what's on sale, that's why. Have you heard from Marvin yet?"

Libby shook her head.

"So that's good news."

"I guess so," Libby said. It was true. When something bad happened, especially something with his father, Marvin always called her. "But what happens if his dad wants him to file a police report? You know what he's like."

"Marvin will tell him he doesn't want to," Bernie said.

"But if his dad insists?" Libby said.

Sean shrugged. "Then Clyde will take it and it will conveniently be buried."

The things his eldest child found to worry about continually amazed Sean. She'd been like that ever since he could remember. At five she worried about what happened to the lightbulbs when they burned out. She didn't want Rose, their mother, throwing them out because she didn't want their feelings hurt. They'd had to sneak them into the trash at night.

"Because," Libby continued, "I would feel terrible if we filed something and the police picked someone up because of it."

Sean snorted. "I wouldn't worry about that if I were you. Things that happen around Leon's don't get investigated. That's just the way it is," he said, forestalling his daughter's next question. Even though they were older he still didn't like discussing payoffs with them. He knew this was ridiculous, but there it was.

"And I certainly don't want Clyde to get in trouble," Libby continued.

"He won't," Sean assured her. "Everything will be fine. Really." He rolled his wheelchair back from the table to give himself another inch of room. "Anyway, on a different note, did you learn anything from last night?"

Libby gave Bernie a bitter look. "Besides the fact that saying the first thing that comes out of your mouth is not a good idea?"

"Yes. Besides that," Sean replied.

"We learned quite a bit," Bernie said.

Libby sat down, took a piece of raisin toast off the plate set in the center of the table, and bit into it. There was the sweetness of the raisins, the nuttiness of the whole-wheat flour, the slight hint of orange rind, and the sharpness of cinnamon. The bread was so good it didn't need butter or cream cheese. They would just mask the flavors.

Libby took a second bite of toast and poured herself a cup of coffee out of the carafe sitting on the table. "I suppose we did."

"So?" Sean prompted.

He'd gotten a general idea of what had happened last night, but between Marvin moaning, Libby running up and down the stairs to get ice packs, and she and Bernie arguing, it had been difficult to sort out the particulars.

Bernie ate the last piece of her cake. "For openers, we learned that Rick Crouse has poor impulse control."

"A lot of guys would have done what he did given the circumstances," Libby objected.

"That's true," Bernie admitted. "But an equal amount of guys would have walked away or they would have said something, but they wouldn't have punched Marvin in the jaw."

"I thought it was a bad idea from the beginning," Libby told her. "Marvin thought it was a bad idea too. We told you it was."

"Then you shouldn't have gone along with it," Bernie shot back.

"We had no choice," Libby pointed out. "You didn't

consult us. You'd already told Sam about Marvin being an agent."

"You certainly did have a choice," Bernie countered. "You didn't have to go into the bar if you didn't want to. Neither did Marvin. We could have turned around and come home. All you had to do was say something."

Sean brought his fist down on the table.

"Enough," he said as Libby opened her mouth to reply to Bernie.

"But . . ." she said.

"No buts," Sean told her. "Now are we going to try to solve this crime or am I going to have to spend the morning listening to you girls bickering?"

"Solve the crime," Bernie and Libby said in unison.

"Good," Sean said. "Let's begin again, shall we? Now, what else did you learn last night?"

Bernie cleared her throat. "We learned that Rick was sleeping with Annabel. That's number one."

Sean nodded. Bernie had told him that last night.

"She was giving him money, but according to Joanna, Annabel was cutting Rick off moneywise," Bernie said.

Sean nodded again. "Okay. Do we know whether Rick was getting any money from Annabel if she died, because if he wasn't, then he had a motive for keeping her alive, not the opposite."

"No. We don't know," Libby said.

"We should find out," Sean said.

"Yes, we should," Bernie said.

"So what else do we know?" Sean asked.

Bernie took a sip of her coffee. "We know that Rick and Joanna were married, that Annabel seduced him, and that in revenge Joanna seduced Richard."

"Wow," Sean said. "Talk about drama. And we know this how?"

"From Joanna," Bernie said. "It's one of the things she told me outside Leon's."

"Do you think she was telling the truth?" Sean asked.

Bernie thought for a moment. "Yes, I do. Why else would she have said it? I mean, she implicated herself by telling me that."

"Well," Sean said, "an alternative scenario could be that she said that because by doing so she would appear to be innocent."

"That line of thought seems a little too complicated," Libby objected. "Dad, haven't you always said that simple works best?"

"True," Bernie said. "But hurt pride in some people can be a powerful motivating force for revenge. Especially in a man. Which she is clearly not." Bernie shook her head. "Did I just say that?"

"It may be a good reason," Sean said, returning to the subject at hand. "In fact, gender aside, it is a good reason. But then the question becomes: Why now?"

"What do you mean?"

"Well, this thing with Annabel seducing Rick happened a while ago, correct?"

Libby and Bernie both nodded.

"So then why should Joanna pick now to kill her?"

"Maybe Joanna had managed to put this all behind her and something Annabel did brought it up again. Only this time it was worse than ever. This time Joanna decided to exact revenge," Bernie suggested.

"But we don't know what this hypothetical something is," Sean said.

"No, we don't," Libby said. "It's a stretch."

"Yes, it is," Sean admitted. "Anything else?" he asked.

"Joanna mentioned Joyce as well," Bernie said. "She implied that she had a reason for killing Annabel. She said that we should talk to her."

Sean drummed his fingers on the arm of his wheelchair. "And Joyce is who? Refresh my memory."

"She was Annabel's best friend," Libby told him. "She was there at the dinner."

"That's right," Sean said. "Of course, according to Annabel's last speech, everyone at the party had a motive for killing her."

"That's what makes this so tough," Libby observed.

"Correction," Sean told her. "That's what makes this so interesting."

"If Annabel didn't have a heart condition she might have survived," Bernie observed.

"How many people knew she had a heart condition?" Sean asked.

"Everyone at that party knew," Bernie said.

Sean thought over what Bernie said for a moment. He'd just come up with his to-do list when the house phone rang. Libby sprang up to answer it. She came back a couple of moments later with a puzzled expression on her face.

Chapter 16

"Who was it?" Bernie asked when Libby sat down at the table again.

"That was Richard Colbert and he wants me to meet him at his house at two o'clock this afternoon."

Bernie reached over, grabbed a piece of raisin toast, and took a bite. "You're kidding."

"Nope."

"That's interesting," Sean said.

"Isn't it, though? Richard not being one of our biggest fans," Bernie replied before turning to her sister. "Libby, he asked for you specifically?"

"Yes," Libby told her. "He did. And I said I'd be there. Maybe he wants to apologize to us."

Bernie barely managed to keep from rolling her eyes. "I wouldn't count on that if I were you." She finished her toast. "On the other hand, it does offer an opportunity. . . ." Her voice trailed off and she started to smile.

"Don't even think about it," Libby warned, catching sight of Bernie's expression. "Because it's not going to happen."

Bernie widened her eyes. "Think about what?"

"About going through the house while I talk to Richard."

"Such a thing would never enter my mind." Bernie held up her hand. "I swear."

"Do you sister swear?" Libby demanded.

"That's absurd," Bernie said, trying to summon up indignation and failing.

Libby folded her arms across her chest and leaned back. "That's what I thought."

"At least she has the good grace to blush," Sean said to Libby.

"You don't think it's a good idea?" Bernie asked him.

"On the contrary, I think it's an excellent idea as long as everyone is out of the house. This is going to be the only time, as far as I can see, that you're going to get to look around there."

"I'm pretty sure we're just talking about Joanna being there," Bernie said.

"We don't know that for sure," Libby said. "There could be lots of people working there. Maybe we should find out first."

"We don't have time to do that," Bernie said.

Libby bit her lip. "All the more reason not to do this. Besides, the house is huge."

"I'll go through as much as I can," Bernie said. "I realize it's not ideal, but I think we have to take advantage of this opportunity. What do you think, Dad?"

"If we can get Joanna out of the house, I think we should go for it," Sean said. "If Bernie meets anyone, she can always say she came in to use the bathroom and got lost."

"I still don't like it," Libby said.

"It'll be fine," Sean said. "If I thought it was dangerous, I would never put you and Bernie at risk. You know that."

"How are you going to get Joanna out of the way?" Libby asked. She hoped that would provide the metaphorical fly in the ointment. But it didn't.

"Listen and learn," Sean said. He turned to Bernie. "Brandon's pretty good at imitating voices, isn't he?" he asked.

"Yes, he is. But he's asleep."

"Then wake him up."

Richard Colbert seemed much friendlier this time around, Libby decided when he met her at the door of his McMansion. Although this place wasn't even a McMansion. It was a McMansion on steroids. She looked at the way Richard was dressed—tweed sports jacket, immaculately pressed blue and white windowpane shirt open at the neck, tan corduroy pants, chestnut brown leather loafers that gleamed; in other words, the epitome of the country squire as filtered through American designers—and wished she'd dressed in something other than her old jeans, flannel shirt, and hiking boots. But what could you do?

Okay. She could have done something. She could have worn her black slacks and black sweater, the way Bernie had suggested. But she hadn't wanted to be here in the first place—the whole thing felt wrong—so she'd decided she'd be damned if she was going to take the time to change her clothes. That would just have been adding insult to injury. She'd told her sister that and Bernie had just shaken her head and walked away. Maybe Bernie was right about dressing to fit a part, Libby decided as Richard smiled and shook her hand. But it was too late now.

"Thanks for coming," he said as he took her old ski parka and hung it in the hall closet next to an expensive-looking fur coat.

Bernie would know what kind of fur it was, Libby thought as Richard led her down the hall. But since her sister was otherwise engaged in exploring the upstairs areas of Richard Colbert's mansion, she couldn't ask her. Libby felt a stab of resentment at Bernie for making her worry this way. Then she put the emotion away and concentrated on the matter at hand.

One thing was for sure, she decided as she followed Richard down the hall: He didn't look like a man prostrate with grief. In fact, he looked pretty relaxed and happy. As if a great weight had been lifted off him. Interesting, as her dad would say. She and Richard walked past the solarium and turned to the left.

"This is the guest wing," Richard explained as they passed the exercise room, the sauna, and a room with a large loom in it. "Well, here we are," Richard said, pausing at the doorway in front of him. "I thought we'd have our little chat in the library."

"It's amazing," Libby said as she caught up with him.

"It's rather showy if you ask me," Richard said. He gestured at the floor-to-ceiling shelves of leather-bound books, the large Oriental rugs, the leather sofa and armchairs, the elaborately carved old oak desk. "Annabel bought the whole room lock, stock, and barrel from an estate on Rhode Island and had it transported here one carefully wrapped piece at a time."

"That must have been quite a job," Libby said.

"You have no idea." Richard pointed at the two stained glass windows over on the far wall. "Tiffany glass. Annabel had to have them. Had to. Was going to die if she didn't. I can't tell you how much they cost or what a pain they were to transport here. I had to get a special crew from the Metropolitan Museum down in New York City up to Rhode Island to wrap them for shipping.

"That was the only way I could get them insured. Then, of course, when they got here they didn't fit the original openings. We had to knock some of the wall down to make a space for them." Richard shook his head at the memory. "But whatever Annabel wanted that's what Annabel got."

"Well, not quite everything," Libby said, thinking of the Malathion.

Richard corrected himself. "Almost everything." He gestured for Libby to sit in one of the leather armchairs, which she did. He took the one across from her.

"So where is everyone?" she asked when she'd gotten

herself settled, no easy task in a chair deep enough for a pro wrestler to get lost in. She just wanted to make sure there were no surprises.

Richard shrugged. "Joanna had to go out on an errand and the cleaning crew comes on Tuesdays and Thursdays."

"Cleaning crew?" Libby repeated.

Good grief. That's what had been bothering her. Richard had mentioned something about a cleaning crew coming in. How could she have forgotten? She closed her eyes for a second. She could hear her dad now. The plan is only as good as the information it's based on. But, she reminded herself, she had to focus on the positive. What did Brandon always say? No harm, no foul? Fortunately, this time luck was on their side.

And Joanna was definitely down in the city, thanks to Brandon pretending that he had information about Rick's finances and asking her to meet him down in a little Italian restaurant in Staten Island—a trip that would take Joanna at least two hours to make.

"Where's Trudy?" Libby asked. She'd expected the little dog to be at Richard's feet.

Richard sat back in his chair and rested his right ankle on his left knee. A man in control of his world, Libby couldn't help thinking.

"She's in the kitchen," he replied. "Which is where she belongs. I don't want her tracking dirt over the rugs. They're quite expensive."

"Doesn't she mind?" Libby asked, thinking back to the birthday party Annabel had thrown for her. "She was the princess of the house."

"Not anymore," Richard snapped. "My wife made that dog into a child. I treat her like a dog. She stays in her crate and eats dog food. It's as simple as that."

Suddenly Libby felt very sorry for Trudy. She was thinking about how hard it had to be for her: first she lost her mother, so to speak, and then she was demoted to living in the kitchen like a scullery maid. Just like Cinderella, Libby couldn't help thinking when Richard unfolded his legs, leaned forward, and folded his hands together.

"Thanks for coming," he said in a voice dripping with sincerity. "I can't tell you how much I appreciate it. I'm sorry if I treated you and your sister rudely the other day, but I've been under a lot of stress lately. A lot of stress," he repeated in case Libby hadn't gotten it the first time.

Libby made a noncommittal sound.

He leaned forward a little bit more. "And I realize that what happened at the dinner party must have been very stressful to you and your sister as well."

"And for Annabel," Libby added. "Especially for Annabel."

"Oh, definitely. Without a doubt," Richard said hurriedly. "It must have been a little bit terrifying for you as well," Richard continued. "Not to mention confusing."

Libby wondered uncharitably how many more adjectives he'd find to apply to the situation. Maybe he'd consulted a thesaurus before she'd come.

"Yes," he said into the ensuing silence. "I can see where it would be a very confusing situation for both of you."

Confusing was not a word Libby would have chosen for what had happened.

"I don't think the sequence of events is confusing at all," Libby told him. "I thought it was extremely clear-cut. Annabel told everyone how much she hated them, she drank the wine, and she keeled over. *Punto finito.* Nothing very confusing about that."

Richard ignored Libby's clarification and went on.

"And agitating."

"You already said that," Libby told him before she remembered she was supposed to keep him talking for as long as possible so Bernie could go through the upstairs rooms. It was just that she was finding him so irritating that she just wanted him to get to the point and be done with it. Why did women find this man so attractive? It was a mystery to her.

A scowl flitted over Richard Colbert's face and then subsided. "I did?"

"Different word, same sentiment."

"I'm sorry if I'm rambling on here." Richard put his hand to his heart. "It's just that I feel guilty about all that you and your sister had to go through and I'm sure that Annabel, if she'd been in her right mind, would have felt guilty about the promise she elicited from you."

"You think so?" Libby asked, wondering where this conversation was leading.

Richard nodded emphatically. "Without a doubt. What a terrible burden to put on someone."

Actually her dad was enjoying working on the case. He loved puzzles like this. "Beats the crossword any day," he'd said. But Libby was sure this was not what Richard wanted to hear.

"It is," Libby said, seeking to draw Richard out.

She snuck a peek at her watch. She'd been here for ten minutes, but it felt like an hour.

Richard paused to regard the shine on his shoes for a moment. He strongly believed that you could tell a man's worth by the shoes on his feet and the watch on his wrist. He'd come close to losing both—after all, you can't afford custom-made shoes or a Philip Patek if you have no money—but fortunately, through no action on his part, the crisis had been averted.

He smiled and went on talking to Libby. "The police have said that what happened to poor Annabel was an accident, thereby rendering what she asked you and your sister to do null and void, to steal a legal phrase." He looked at Libby. She didn't say anything. "You do know that she was being treated for some . . . some psychological issues, don't you?"

Libby sat up straighter. "Are you suggesting that she put flea spray and Malathion in the wine herself?"

"I didn't say that," Richard replied.

"You implied it."

"No. I didn't. You did. However, since you raised that specter I will say that I wouldn't put anything past her, if doing it made her the center of attention."

"Even if she wasn't there to enjoy it?"

"She believed in the afterlife."

Libby wasn't prepared for that one. "I see," she said after a moment had gone by. "And here I thought she did it because it improved the wine's taste."

Richard's scowl came back. "Those toxins were not put in the wine. I'm telling you what I told the police. Two weeks ago, a bottle of Malathion spilled in our garage and Annabel wiped it up with paper towels. She didn't use rubber gloves—not a wise thing to do. The following week, she was at Ramona's kennel helping her treat a flea infestation. I fear the combined exposures were too much for her.

"I told Annabel to be careful with that stuff. I told her to always wear gloves when using insecticides. She was especially vulnerable given her heart condition. I told her she shouldn't even be near that stuff. But she never listened. She never listened to anything I said. And now she's dead."

"That's not what Annabel said when she tasted the wine."

"My wife was delusional."

"Well, she seemed pretty sane to me," Libby noted.

Richard took a deep breath and blew it out again before he spoke. "Not in private. She was an extremely paranoid person who always thought people were out to get her."

"You know what they say," Libby said. "Just because you're paranoid doesn't mean it's not true."

"Be that as it may," Richard said. His voice rose as he continued, "The conclusion that my wife died of accidental poisoning is not my conclusion. It is the conclusion the

authorities have come to. Annabel's death has been classi-
fied as an accident. The district attorney has declined to
prosecute. If you think otherwise, then I suggest you take
it up with them."

"How could they say anything else when you threw out
the wine bottle?" Libby demanded.

"You make it sound as if I did it on purpose."

"You did!"

"No. It was an accident."

"How could that be an accident?"

"I was cleaning up because it gave me something to do.
I wasn't thinking because I was upset. Surely you can understand that."

"You didn't look upset," Libby countered.

Richard took another deep breath and let it out. "I'm
not one of those people who wear their heart on their sleeve.
Of course I was upset. What kind of person do you take
me for?"

Richard sounded so sincere that for a second Libby believed him. Maybe he didn't have anything to do with this,
she found herself thinking. Maybe the whole thing was an
accident. Maybe Annabel was nuts.

Maybe Richard was right. Maybe she had done this to
herself in order to get back at everyone. After all, if you
were going to kill someone why do it in such a public
manner? Libby considered that idea for a moment before
discarding it. No. Annabel just didn't seem like the type.
She had impressed Libby as too straightforward for that
kind of thing. But when it came down to it, she really hadn't
known Annabel except in the most cursory kind of way.

Richard clasped his hands in front of him. "Listen," he
said to Libby. "We're getting off on the wrong foot here.
This is not the way I intended this conversation to go."

Again with the supersincere tone, Libby thought. "Okay,"
she said. "I'll bite. How did you intend the conversation to
go?"

He favored her with a boyish smile. "I intended to try to make amends for the situation. That is, if you'll drop your hostile attitude and let me."

"Really?" Libby said. Now that was interesting. She snuck a peek at her watch. Thirteen minutes. God. Bernie had asked her to keep Richard talking for half an hour at least. "Listen," she said, stalling for time. "I hate to be a bother, but could you get me a glass of water?" The moment the words were out of her mouth she wanted to take them back. After all, she'd asked the person who might have poisoned his wife to get her something to drink. How dumb could you get! But then she decided she was being nutty. Richard had no reason to kill her. People didn't kill people for no reason at all. At least, most people didn't. It was that small percentage that was worrying her.

"Not a problem." Richard sprang out of his seat and went off to the kitchen.

Libby figured that should buy her another five minutes at least. Libby got up. She'd just crossed the room to study the bookshelves when Richard came bounding back in through the door, glass of water in hand. The whole trip had taken him a minute at the most.

"That was fast," Libby said in amazement. "Did you run to the kitchen and run back?"

Richard laughed. "No. No. You didn't see it, but a little way ahead we have a guest suite with three bedrooms and a small kitchen with a refrigerator. I always keep it stocked."

"What a good idea," Libby lied as Richard handed her the glass.

"It definitely makes things easier," Richard said, sitting back down. "Actually, it was Annabel's idea. When you live in a house like this you have to be efficient."

Libby took her seat as well. Richard looked at her expectantly. Libby wondered what he was waiting for. Then she realized it was for her to take a drink.

"Thanks," she said. She raised the glass to her lips and

took a sip. It tasted okay. So far so good. She took another sip. Then she put the glass down. No sense in taking chances. "This is excellent," she said, although she never got the whole artisanal water thing.

Richard beamed at her. "It should be. I get it flown directly here from my own private glacier in Alaska."

"Very impressive," Libby murmured as she took a leaf from Bernie's book on handling the male species, instead of saying what she really wanted to say, which was, *You're kidding me, right?*

Richard's smile broadened. "I was joking."

"Good. I was worried for a second."

"I don't believe in wasting money. Tap water is good enough for me. I think people who spend two and three dollars on a bottle of water are nuts. But back to what I was saying."

Libby cocked her head and gave a masterful imitation of hanging on his every word.

"As I was saying," Richard went on. "You girls have had a terribly stressful time and I'd like to compensate both of you for all the time and trouble you've taken in this matter concerning Annabel. I really appreciate your concern. You both are such gifted cooks that I'd hate to see you distracted from your primary task by this witch hunt that Annabel has sent you on."

"So what are you proposing?" Libby asked.

"A couple of thoughts have occurred to me," Richard told her. "As you know, I'm the head of Colbert's, and I would love to have A Little Taste of Heaven cater some of our official functions down in our headquarters in the city. Naturally, you would be generously recompensed for your time. It would be a gold mine for you, a way to showcase your product to a wider audience. That's one idea."

"And the other?"

"I was thinking that you might need a sponsor."

Libby frowned. "A sponsor? Like in stock car racing?"

Richard waved his hands. "Hear me out, because I think you're going to like this. I would, in my capacity as owner of Colbert Toys, make a sizable contribution to your shop so you could remodel and possibly enlarge it—I have a connection with Hemstead Realty, the people who own . . ."

"I know who they are," Libby told him.

Richard clapped his hands together. "Of course you do. How foolish of me. In any case, in return all I would ask is that you display some items from our product line."

"Like the Puggables?" Libby asked.

"Exactly," Richard said. He smiled broadly. It was like a lighthouse beacon.

Libby stood up. Richard did as well.

"So what do you think?" he asked.

"I think you're trying to bribe us," Libby replied.

Richard's smile died. "Heavens no. What a terrible thing to say."

"Well, it certainly sounds that way to me."

Richard crossed his arms over his chest. "The reason I asked for you specifically is that I thought you were the sister with the most common sense. Evidently, I was misinformed." He took a step closer to her.

"By whom?"

Richard blinked.

"Who informed you?"

"That was a figure of speech. All I can say is that if I were you I would take my proposals back to your sister and I would think about them very carefully. Both of them are extremely generous."

"I'll ask her," Libby told him. "But I can tell you right now that she and I are going to say no."

"That would be a mistake," Richard said.

"For you?"

"No. For you."

"Is that a threat?"

"Hardly." The corners of Richard's mouth turned up

into something that resembled a sneer. "I'm simply pointing out that you'll be missing an extremely good business
opportunity if you proceed along the lines you were talking about."

"It sounds like a threat to me."

"Why would I threaten you?" Richard asked.

Libby detected a note of amusement in his voice.

"What would be the point?" he asked.

"To stop what we're doing. To stop us from poking
around."

Richard threw back his head and laughed. "Don't be
ridiculous. I'm trying to be nice to you. I realize both of
you are sincere but fundamentally misguided. If I wanted
to stop you, I would have my lawyers slap a restraining
order on you. But I don't want to do that. I want to keep this
as low-key as possible. Annabel would have loathed the
media circus that this kind of thing generates. If you want
to waste your time, go right ahead. You won't find anything. And now I think you'd better go."

Libby looked at her watch. She was ten minutes short of
the thirty that Bernie had requested.

"Could you explain what you said again?" Libby asked.
"I think I must have missed something."

"I think I was perfectly straightforward."

Then Richard looked at her. It was a calculating look,
Libby thought. As if something had just occurred to him.
Something having to do with her. She might have overstayed her welcome. No. She had definitely overstayed her
welcome. She should never have asked him for an explanation of what he'd just said. She should have left. Bernie
would do fine. She always did.

"I'll let you know what my sister says," Libby told
Richard as she hurriedly gathered up her belongings and
headed for the door. But before she could get there, Richard
stepped in front of her, blocking her way.

"You keep looking at your watch. The whole time we

were talking you were looking at your watch. Why is that?" he demanded.

"I have an appointment after this," Libby said, putting as much conviction into the lie as possible.

"Is that a fact?"

Libby looked up at him. "Yes. It is. Or perhaps I just found our conversation boring."

"Maybe yes and maybe no."

"That I found our conversation boring?"

"That you have an appointment."

"What's that supposed to mean?"

"It's obvious, isn't it?" And Richard reached over and grabbed Libby by her shoulder.

"Not to me," she told him as she tried to twist away and failed.

"Let's go see if your sister is upstairs. Shall we?"

"What a ridiculous thing to say," Libby spluttered. "Let me go."

Richard laughed.

"If you don't I'll call the police," Libby threatened.

"Be my guest." And Richard dug his cell out of his pocket with his free hand and handed it to her. "Well," he said when she hesitated to take it. "That's what I thought."

"I just don't want to embarrass you," Libby told him, remembering her father's words of wisdom: In situations like this, never explain. Take the offensive. Of course, Libby reflected, if it wasn't for her father she wouldn't be in this situation. Maybe she should have followed her mother's words of wisdom: if it feels wrong, don't do it.

Richard raised an eyebrow. "Really," he said. "And here I am thinking that you don't want to see your sister arrested."

"Arrested for what?"

"Breaking and entering."

Now it was Libby's turn to laugh. "Hardly. If she were

here, and I'm not saying she is, the most that would happen to her would be a trespassing charge."

"Well, we can discuss that when the police arrive."

"They're not going to arrive, because she's not here."

"Then you'll have my apologies if I'm wrong and you'll be facing court action if I'm not."

"How about at least letting me go? You're hurting my shoulder."

Which was true. But only up to a point. Actually Libby was mildly uncomfortable. But that didn't have the same ring to it.

"You'll survive," Richard told her.

"Thanks," Libby replied. "I have to say I don't think your wife was the delusional one in this partnership."

"Let's go before I lose my temper," Richard said.

"Is that what happened to Annabel? Did she get you angry?" Libby asked.

"I refuse to have my privacy invaded by the likes of you," Richard said as he dug his fingers more deeply into Libby's shoulder and dragged her toward the stairs.

Chapter 17

Bernie heard Richard and Libby coming. The carpet muffled their footsteps, but Libby was doing a pretty good job of talking as loudly as possible. Fortunately, Bernie thought, this was a new house and sound traveled. So maybe there was something good about using wallboard after all.

She'd been through four rooms of the right wing and had at least six more to go that she was aware of, and there were even more rooms than that, because she didn't know what was in the left wing of the house. This had been a mistake, Bernie decided, as she tried to figure out a way to get out of the house.

A big mistake. And she had no one to blame but herself. Libby had been correct—not that Bernie would ever tell her that. And to top everything off, you'd think that a place this size would have more than one staircase. Talk about chintzy. But it didn't, so she was pretty much boxed in.

Actually, this had been more than a mistake. It had been a blunder. She hadn't counted on the fact that there were simply too many rooms and too little time. Most importantly, she didn't have a clue what she was looking for. Therefore, she couldn't narrow the field down to drawers or closets. And—surprise—so far she hadn't found anything that said, "Here. I'm the person who put the poison in the wine bottle. Arrest me." And she probably wouldn't either. That was usually the way these things went.

What she had found were more bedrooms than a Mormon polygamist would need. Why had the Colberts built a house this large? Because they could. With the exception of two, most of the bedrooms she'd been in looked uninhabited. One was obviously Richard Colbert's room, while the second one, which was three doors down from the first, was the sleeping quarters of the late, apparently unlamented Annabel Colbert. Both rooms were surprising in their lack of personal touches. Bernie had the feeling that everything in them, from the bedding to the pictures hanging on the walls, had been chosen by a decorator with an eye to proclaiming the wealth and taste of the inhabitants.

There were no dirty clothes hung over the back of a chair. No shoes on the floor. No pictures of little Annabel or baby Richard on the walls. There were no family photos. No pet photos. No hokey snaps of Richard and Annabel either together or separately in a gondola on a canal in Venice, lying on a tropical beach sipping a rum and Coke, or waving from a cruise ship. The bedrooms were like stage sets, which made Bernie wonder where Richard and Annabel conducted their real lives. If they had real lives. Maybe everything was just for show.

Besides the color schemes and the products in the attached bathrooms, the only real difference between Richard's and Annabel's bedrooms lay in the fact that Richard's room had three Puggables in his closet, while Annabel had two bags of mini Snickers in hers. Must have been her secret vice, Bernie thought as she contemplated taking one but rejected the thought. In fact, it struck Bernie that for a couple who ran a toy company Richard and Annabel's house was surprisingly devoid of anything that could remotely be construed as fun.

Bernie was in Annabel's room looking at the handbags

in Annabel's closet. She was thinking that Annabel's taste was somewhat pedestrian when she heard Libby proclaiming in an indignant voice that she saw no need to go through the bedrooms and that her sister was definitely not in the house. Drats, Bernie thought as she glanced at her watch. Ten more minutes and she would have been out of here. Oh well. No point in thinking about that now.

Now she had to think about what she was going to do. Of course, she could always stay. That was one option. All Richard would do was call the police. But that could be a problem. Especially if they decided to take them into custody. They might be sitting in a jail cell until tomorrow. And that would not be good, because then there would be no one to make the pot roast, the kreplach, the chicken soup, and the rugelach for Mrs. Stein's dinner party. So that left her with option number two: escape.

Since there was only one stairway and Richard was on it, that precluded that path. And she definitely didn't want to do something like hide in the attic, or in a closet, or under a bed, because Bernie was 100 percent sure that Richard would go through every nook and cranny in the house looking for her. Richard liked to win and to him this was one big game. Which meant she didn't have lots of choices. In fact, there was only one good one that she could think of.

Jumping out the window. Wonderful. Thank heavens she was wearing her house-breaking-into outfit—a black, long-sleeved James Perse cotton and spandex T-shirt, black parachute pants, a black quilted vest, and the only sensible shoes she owned, a pair of Gortex hiking boots that she'd gotten because Brandon had made her—instead of something like a pencil skirt, leggings, and stiletto boots. Then she'd really be in trouble.

Bernie went over, pulled the silk drapes back—talk about expensive, the material alone for these had probably cost several hundred dollars—and peered down at the ground.

Nothing to it. Piece of cake. Ha. Ha. Luckily there were no foundation plantings, because landing on a cedar branch would be exceedingly uncomfortable. At best. And there *was* about two inches of snow on the ground, which would help cushion the fall—slightly.

She cranked the window open and leaned out. The windowsill was narrow. There was no ledge. Basically she'd have to climb out, hang down, and push off with her feet so she wouldn't hit the wall. For a brief moment she thought about reconsidering, but then she thought about Mrs. Stein's pot roast. She'd be very disappointed if she didn't get it. At ninety-four she couldn't cook anymore, and her children and grandchildren were coming. How could there not be food on the table? Bernie decided jumping was the only way to go.

She concentrated on Libby's and Richard's voices. They sounded closer now. They'd cleared the steps. It was only a matter of time before they'd look in this room and Bernie wanted to be well away before Richard came in here. The last thing she wanted was for him to look outside and see her running away. Well, she wouldn't run. That would be a mistake. She'd walk. If he yelled at her to stop, she would. And then she'd tell him that she was just taking a stroll around the grounds while Libby went in and talked to him. Let him prove different.

Yes. That would work. No need to panic. Bernie took a deep breath. Richard and Libby were getting closer. She had to stop dithering around and decide what she was going to do. And anyway, how high was twenty feet, really? She was five feet six inches. If she was hanging by her arms, that would add another foot, so now you were talking almost seven feet. If you subtracted that from twenty feet, she was only dropping thirteen feet at the most. That wasn't bad. Not really. Although, to be honest, she wasn't that fond of heights. But at least she wasn't as bad as Libby in that regard. Sometimes, Libby got queasy going over bridges.

Bernie checked her pockets to make sure her wallet, cell phone, and keys were where they should be. She rechecked the buttons on her pockets to make sure they were closed.

"You go, girl," she whispered as she cranked open the window and began climbing out.

The getting out part proved to be a little trickier than she imagined. The whole turning around business didn't work very well, mostly because she couldn't decide what she should do first. But she finally got it figured out. Except for that moment or two where she thought she was going to fall. She managed to keep her grasp, though. Then she hung down and pushed off from the wall with her feet.

The impact on landing was bone rattling. She could feel the shock reverberating up her body as her feet hit the earth. Then she collapsed in the snow. A moment later, she regained her breath. Another moment after that, she managed to sit up. Her left ankle was throbbing slightly.

Probably just a sprain, she thought. She became aware that her behind was cold. That's what came of sitting in the snow. She got up, brushed her rear end off, and headed toward the van at what she judged to be as good a pace as she could manage with her ankle.

Richard Colbert entered the fourth bedroom with Libby in tow.

"See," she was saying for the hundredth time. "No one is here. I told you."

He ignored her as his eyes swept the room. Everything seemed in place. He checked the closet. It was empty. He gave the bathroom a quick once-over. Nothing. He pulled the shower stall panel back. The bathtub was empty. He felt Libby wiggling away from him. This time he let her go, confident that she would stay there to protect her sister, whom he had yet to find. But he would. He promised himself that.

And he would enjoy having Bernie arrested. She was

making trouble for him—this whole thing with Annabel could be a potential PR nightmare. He could just see the headlines now: TOY EXEC OFFS WIFE. NO CUDDLES FOR PAPA PUGGABLES. Nope. He paid his people big bucks for damage control. So far they'd done an excellent job. He was damned if their efforts would be undone because of two girl detectives. Girl detectives. His mouth curled up in a sneer. They had obviously read too many Nancy Drews when they were younger.

He got down and checked under the bed—not that he expected Bernie to be there—but he was a methodical man, which is how he'd gotten where he was. In fact, he expected Bernie to be in the crawl space in the attic. There was just enough space there to get into, but there was nowhere to go once you were inside. The space went in about a foot and stopped.

Anyone in there was stuck. For a moment, Richard played with the idea of moving a trunk against the space and trapping her in there. Libby wouldn't know she was in there and Bernie wouldn't say anything. And even if Bernie had her cell phone she couldn't call out. There was no signal up there. Then he'd go on vacation for a couple of weeks. If she was alive when he got back, all well and good. If she wasn't . . . oh well. The thought was attractive, delicious really, but it was a fantasy, nothing more, and he had enough to deal with as it was. Opening the door and seeing her in there would be pleasure enough.

"Can we stop this nonsense?" Libby said as Richard got up off his knees.

"When we're done. And not before," he told her. "Go if you want to," he added, testing his hypothesis.

As he suspected, Libby didn't move. He was right again, he noted with satisfaction. Actually, not that he liked to brag, but he was rarely if ever wrong. He turned to leave and then turned back. There was something here. Something that was bothering him. He stood there for a moment trying to figure out what it was. Everything looked the way it should. And yet . . . He rubbed his hands together. It was drafty in here. Yes. That was it. He strode over and swept the draperies back. The window was open. The conclusion was obvious.

"She jumped," he told Libby.

"Don't be ridiculous," Libby scoffed. She was pretty sure Richard was right, though. What a relief! "She was never here, so how could she jump?"

"Then why is the window open?"

Libby shrugged. "How would I know? Maybe one of your people forgot to close it."

"My people don't forget things."

"Then yours are the only ones," Libby retorted.

Richard pointed to the snow. "And what are those?"

Libby looked. "What 'those'? I don't see anything," she lied.

"Look harder!" Richard yelled. "Can't you see those tracks?"

"There's no need to shout," Libby told him. She squished up her eyes, pretending she was having trouble seeing. "Footprints?" Libby asked after a moment.

"Exactly," Richard said. A triumphant smile played around the corners of his mouth. "They're your sister's footprints."

"Don't be ridiculous," Libby scoffed. "She'd never wear shoes that made prints like that."

"We'll see," Richard muttered as he ran out of the room. "Yes indeed. We certainly will."

"Where are you going?" Libby cried.

Richard flung the words "To get your sister" over his shoulder as he hit the landing. Libby went after him.

Richard had it all figured out. He'd follow the footprints. Bernie Simmons thought she was smart, but he was way smarter. Leaving a trail like that. Really. He had to admit he was a little disappointed. He'd been looking forward to cornering her in the attic, but he'd settle for intercepting her in the snow.

Bernie was sitting in the driver's seat of A Little Taste of Heaven's van sipping a cup of French roast from her thermos, eating half of a crunchy peanut butter and radish sandwich on country bread, and listening to NPR on the radio when Richard Colbert yanked the door open. Libby was right behind him.

"That's rather rude," Bernie told him.

"Show me your shoes," he gasped, because he was winded from running.

"Are you out of your mind?" Bernie answered.

He put his hands on his knees and took a couple of breaths before straightening up. "No. I want to see them."

"I have lots of shoes. Is there any particular kind you'd like to see? Boots? Sandals? Ballet flats?" Bernie broke off a quarter of her sandwich and carefully rewrapped it in Saran Wrap. "For later," she explained as she stowed it in her bag. "Although I can't see why you're interested in my shoe collection. Unless, of course, you're one of those men who are into cross-dressing. Because if that's the case, I don't think my shoes will fit you. However, there are sites on the Web you can visit. If you'd like I can tell—"

"I'm talking about the shoes on your feet," Richard growled. Then he whirled around. "What are you laughing at?" he demanded of Libby.

"Nothing," Libby said. "I'm not laughing."

"She's not laughing," Bernie said. "She's giggling."

Richard turned back to Bernie.

"Don't tell me you have a foot fetish," she said. She put her hand to her mouth. "Oh dear. You do, don't you?"

Richard's face was now crimson. How had the situation gotten so out of hand so fast? This was a nightmare. This woman was just babbling on and on. He had to get control back.

"I'm not kidding," he growled. "I want to see the shoes you're wearing and I want to see them now."

"Well," Bernie replied in a reasonable tone of voice. "Why didn't you say that in the first place, although you still haven't told me why." And she stuck out her foot and showed him her Manolo Blahniks. "Nice, aren't they? I got them at the end-of-the-season sale. Fifty percent discount. What about the purple bow? Do you like it or do you find it distracting? Brandon likes it, but I'm not sure."

"See," Libby said to Richard now that she'd finally managed to suppress her giggles. "I told you you were wrong. Someone else made those tracks. Maybe you have a prowler on the grounds. You should check and make sure."

Richard ignored her. "You had on different shoes," he said to Bernie.

Bernie took a sip of her coffee. "I already told you I have lots of different pairs of shoes—not as many as Imelda, but I do try to do my fair share to keep the American economy moving. And I try to wear a different pair of them each day so I don't wear them out. If you'd like to come to my house I'd be happy to show you my footwear collection. No?" Bernie said. "Fine. There's no need to glare at me like that. I was just being polite. Now, I'm going to ask you once again, do you want to tell me what this is about?"

Richard took a deep breath and tried to relax. He was sure his blood pressure was in the red zone. *I will not yell*, he told himself. *I will not give this woman the pleasure of losing control.* Instead he took another deep breath and focused on what he was going to say.

"It's about you searching my house, while your sister was talking to me and keeping me occupied," he said through gritted teeth.

Bernie took another bite of her sandwich and chewed it

thoroughly before speaking. "Allow me to point out that you invited my sister to come here and talk to you. She did not initiate the meeting."

Richard shook his finger in her face. "Which you took as an opportunity to do a little ad hoc exploring."

"And why would I want to do that?"

"To find evidence that I murdered my wife."

Bernie ate the last eighth of her sandwich and wiped her hands on her napkin. "And did you?" she asked.

"Of course not," Richard cried as he wondered once again how he'd been so thoroughly bested. "It was an accident."

"Then why do you keep bringing the subject up?"

"I don't. You do."

"No. You do. You know," she said to Richard, "I'm so appalled by those accusations that I'm not even going to dignify them with a response. Come on, Libby, let's go. We have work to do."

Richard's jaw dropped. By now he was so upset all he could do was splutter. Libby edged around him and climbed into the van. Bernie started up the vehicle.

"So what happened to your shoes?" Libby asked once they'd cleared the gate.

"I changed them of course," Bernie said. "Lucky I always keep a spare set of stilettos in the van for emergencies."

"Doesn't everyone?" Libby replied. And she started to laugh.

A moment later Bernie joined in. "It was pretty funny," she said.

"I don't think Richard Colbert thought so," Libby observed.

"Not at all," Bernie replied.

Libby extracted a Lindt truffle from her pocket, unwrapped it, and popped it into her mouth. The chocolate melted on her tongue. That's what made good chocolate so special. Its melting point was near body temperature. Libby had tried making chocolate truffles at the shop, but they never came out this well. She reflected that she'd take a chocolate truffle over a real one any day of the week.

"Richard Colbert is not a good person to make an enemy out of," Libby observed once she'd finished enjoying every last ounce of flavor the truffle had to offer.

"No, he isn't," Bernie agreed.

"You probably shouldn't have said what you did."

"Probably not," Bernie allowed. "He'll probably get his lawyer to sue us on some grounds or other. But you have to admit it was funny. When I asked Richard whether he was a cross-dresser, I thought he was going to explode."

Libby started to giggle at the memory. A moment later Bernie joined in. They were still giggling when they pulled up in front of Joyce Atkins's house ten minutes later.

Chapter 18

The van let out an unpleasant squeak as the vehicle came to a stop in front of Joyce's house at 106 Passerville Drive. Not good, Bernie thought. They were definitely going to need a new vehicle soon. She looked at her watch.

"We still have time," she said to her sister.

"Not that much," Libby protested.

"Enough. You always overestimate how long things will take."

"And you always underestimate," Libby retorted. "Which is why you're always late."

"I'm not late," Bernie protested. "I'm just not prompt."

"How can you say that stuff with a straight face?" Libby asked.

"Practice. Lots of practice. Now, do you want to go see Joyce now or do you want to do this tomorrow?"

"Definitely not tomorrow," Libby said.

Tomorrow would be even worse, she thought. They had two dinners they were catering, plus a large order from their supplier coming in that would have to be put away, plus one of them would have to go to Sam's Club, always a time-consuming process, plus, for some reason Libby could never figure out, Monday was always a busy day for lunch.

"This probably won't take long," Bernie said, more to convince herself than her sister.

"You might be right," Libby said. "If this visit follows the way we've been going, Joyce will probably throw us out of the house as soon as we say hello."

"Probably," Bernie agreed. She was feeling much cheerier since her little encounter with Richard. Even if it turned into a Pyrrhic victory. What could she say? She liked winning. "But it's worth trying," she pointed out. "Joyce could tell us a lot, being Annabel's best friend and all."

"True," Libby said as she studied the house Joyce Atkins lived in. "But she would have to want to do that."

"There is that," Bernie agreed. "But we know she was pissed at Annabel over the dog biscuits Annabel was about to start selling. That was pretty clear. Maybe she'd like a sympathetic ear."

"Maybe," Libby said.

Actually, she was sorry Joyce's car was in the driveway. It was true she'd told Bernie she'd come to Joyce's after they'd gone to Richard's—no one had twisted her arm—but on further reflection she realized she hadn't thought the whole scheduling thing out very well.

"Still worrying about the time?" Bernie asked.

"I didn't say that."

"But you were thinking it," Bernie said. "You know," she continued, "we have some meat raviolis in the freezer."

"So?" Libby said.

"Well, if we're crunched for time we can use those instead of the kreplach."

Libby gave her The Look.

"It's not so bad," Bernie said. She was stung by Libby's unvoiced criticism.

"Bad? It's terrible. How could you even suggest that?" Libby cried. The thought outraged her.

Bernie gave a sheepish shrug. "I just wanted to save a

little time. And raviolis and kreplach are pretty similar. Essentially, they're both dumplings with a meat filling."

Libby pounded on the dashboard of the van. "They're not similar," she said. "Not at all. That's like saying roast beef and roast pork are similar because they're both meat." Bernie opened her mouth to say something, but Libby steamrolled over her. "And aside from everything else, there is—as you know—a big difference between fresh-made and frozen anything."

"I don't think most people can actually tell the difference," Bernie said gently. "Especially with something like pasta."

Libby pointed at herself. "*I* can. And I would consider doing that a breach of everything our shop stands for. We don't substitute ingredients and we don't serve frozen food— even if it's our own frozen food—when we tell someone we're making it fresh. Especially for something like this. And you know what else? I bet Mrs. Stein can tell the difference between fresh and frozen. I bet she'd know in an instant."

"You're right. You're right," Bernie said. "I don't know what I was thinking."

"Neither do I," Libby replied. And she crossed her arms over her chest and went back to studying the house.

The house at 106 Passerville Drive was a cute little cottage. The houses on the block had all been built in the thirties and forties. They mostly consisted of well-maintained capes and ranches with a few colonials thrown in. The street was lined with old maples and oaks, and in the summer it was positively Norman Rockwellian.

"Quite a change from the Colbert place," Libby observed as she took in the white stucco, the green tile roof, and the mint-green door of Joyce's house.

"And how," Bernie said. "That place was like a barn."

"I wouldn't mind living in someplace like this," Libby said. She nodded toward the house.

"It's very quaint," Bernie observed.

Libby knew that *quaint* was a code word for *kitschy* in her sister's vocabulary. But she didn't care. She liked the place anyway. She liked the way the cobblestone path curved as it went from the sidewalk to the front door. She liked the snowman banner hanging from the porch pillar and the pinecone wreath on the door, things that Libby knew her sister considered beyond the pale design wise. She liked the way the foundation plantings were neatly clipped. Somehow she knew that in the summer and the spring irises and daffodils would be growing out front. To Libby's mind, the cottage projected an air of calm self-sufficiency, of being comfortable without being sloppy.

Libby pointed at the Hyundai parked in the driveway. "Nice car," she commented.

"Inexpensive car," Bernie noted.

Unlike Annabel's. She had driven around in a Beemer.

"So what do we know about her anyway?" Libby asked Bernie as her sister took the key out of the ignition. "Aside from the fact that she was pissed about the dog biscuit business, that is."

"You want the gospel according to Clyde?"

"If you please."

"Okeydokey. For openers, Joyce has no priors. Never even got a ticket, if you can imagine that." Bernie certainly couldn't.

"Besides that," Libby said.

"Well, we know that Joyce has been on her own for a while. We know that her husband took off with a twenty-two-year-old hottie to New Mexico. We know that her daughter is a dog walker in New York City. We also know that Joyce used to work as a receptionist for a big insurance company in the city until they got bought up and downsized. Now she temps and sells Avon."

"She's never bought much from us," Libby said.

"I don't think she has much money. Her husband left

her in pretty rocky shape financially when he took off. Although she was wearing that Chanel jacket," Bernie said as she thought of what Joyce had on the day of the party. It was ratty but it was still Chanel, which told Bernie that Joyce had had money at one time in her life. Sometimes that made losing it even harder.

"That's it?" Libby said.

"That's all she wrote," Bernie answered. "Ready?" she asked her sister.

"Very," Libby replied, with visions of Mrs. Stein's kreplach dancing in her head. The sooner they got in, the sooner they would get out.

"Then let's go get her," Bernie said, and she opened her door and stepped outside. Libby followed.

It had gotten colder since they'd left Richard's place. The wind had picked up. *Maybe it's going to snow again,* Libby thought as they walked up the path and rang the bell. The weatherman had said it would be clear and sunny, but these days with the weather being so weird—one day it was hot, the next day it was cold—you never really knew. She was still thinking about that when Joyce answered the door.

"I expected you sooner," Joyce said as she beckoned them in. Joyce's pug, Conklin, sniffed at their feet as they stepped inside the hallway.

The comment struck Bernie as puzzling. *Did Richard call Joyce and tell her we were coming?* Bernie wondered as she handed her jacket to Joyce, who hung it up on one of the big metal hooks around the hall mirror. Libby followed suit.

Bernie and Libby looked around. The small hallway they were standing in led directly into the living room, which in turn led into the dining room. The walls had been painted a light yellow and gone over with a varnish finish, the end result reminding Bernie of an old Italian villa.

"Nice," Bernie said as she gestured at the paint job.

"It's easy," Joyce said. "I got a book out of the library

and that was that." She pointed to the oak baseboards. "I also stripped those—they had about forty-nine coats of white paint on them—and put up that tin ceiling. It had those horrible acoustical tiles. I also stripped that molding and the seat in front of the window, re-covered the cushion, and made the pillows."

"I'm impressed," Bernie said. And she was. Her mother had been an avid knitter, crocheter, seamstress, and all-around do-it-yourselfer. On the other hand, Bernie was an avid shopper. It seemed as if the only gene she'd inherited from her mother was her cooking gene.

Joyce shrugged. "I enjoy doing it. And anyway, when you don't have lots of money it pays to be handy. Fortunately, I discovered I had a knack for it when my husband took off." At which point she led them to the living room and indicated they should sit down on the oversized tweed-covered sofa.

"I should just tell you," Joyce said as she sat down in the matching armchair and picked up the knitting sitting in the basket on the side table, "I've already talked to my lawyer."

"About what?" Bernie asked.

"About my talking to you about Annabel, of course," Joyce said as she started knitting. "It's a sweater for Conklin," she informed them without being asked. "I'm using a cashmere and mohair blend. The poor dear really can't tolerate the cold."

"And what did your lawyer say?" Bernie asked.

"He obviously said it was all right," Joyce said. "Otherwise we wouldn't be having this conversation."

"Obviously," Bernie repeated. "And how did you know we'd want to talk to you?"

"Because you promised Annabel that you would investigate her death, and since you think she was murdered, and I was in the room, and she said what she did, it makes sense that you'd want to talk to me."

Libby leaned forward slightly. She could feel the sofa material through her pants. "And you don't think she was murdered?" she asked.

Joyce shrugged her shoulders. "No. I don't."

"Then what do you think happened?" Bernie asked.

Joyce frowned. Then she crossed and uncrossed her ankles. "Frankly I think she set the whole thing up. It would be just like her."

"That's what Richard said," Libby told her.

"Well, he's correct," Joyce replied.

"That's quite a statement," Bernie observed.

Joyce silently counted stitches before answering. "Not if you know her, it's not. And I told that to the police, as well."

Bernie raised an eyebrow. "So, in essence, you told them you thought she committed suicide."

"That is correct."

"And that she accused everyone for no reason at all," Bernie said.

"Yes. Exactly."

"That's a pretty serious charge," Libby commented.

Joyce shrugged. "It's the truth."

"Why would she want to do that?" Libby asked.

"Because she was mean, and spiteful, and it would amuse her."

"I'm having trouble believing that," Bernie told Joyce. "Setting something like this up is a fairly odd way to amuse yourself. I mean, it's not as if she was going to be around to enjoy the results."

"Well," Joyce said, "she was one of those people who would cut off her nose to spite her face. That's just the way she was. And she probably thought she didn't have long to live, with her arrhythmias getting worse. Her health problems just made her meaner. Some people rise to the occasion when they get a serious problem. Others don't. Annabel didn't. It's as simple as that."

"Okay," Bernie said. "Assuming she was that vindictive,

you're telling me that no one gave her any cause to be that way?"

"That has nothing to do with the situation."

"I don't agree," Bernie said.

Joyce put her knitting down. "She had no one to blame but herself for some of the things that happened."

"How so?" Libby asked. "She seemed nice enough to me." Which wasn't true, but she wanted to hear what Joyce would say.

"That was the thing," Joyce answered. "How nice she seemed. But she wasn't. She wasn't nice at all. She felt entitled to do anything she wanted."

"For example?" Bernie asked.

"For example, Rick. She just had to have him. Had to. That's all she talked about. I told her not to, but she wouldn't listen. Then, of course, she made sure that Joanna found out—because what's the fun of doing something like that if your victim doesn't know? Which, of course, was why Joanna came on to Richard. Annabel didn't even like Rick all that much. Annabel just liked the idea of being able to do it. She was like a cat flexing its claws."

Joyce's description of Annabel reminded Bernie of some of the girls who'd called themselves her friends when she was in high school. "So given how you described her, why did you stay friends with her?" Bernie asked.

"She was different in high school. Or maybe she was like that all along only I didn't see it. I don't know."

"So what made her change?" Libby asked.

"I'll show you." And Joyce got up, went to the breakfront standing next to the wall near the dining room, opened a drawer, and pulled out a class yearbook.

Bernie and Libby watched as she leafed through the pages. When she found the ones she wanted, she crossed over and handed the book to Libby and Bernie.

"Here," Joyce said.

Libby and Bernie both looked. Across the top of the two

facing pages was a banner proclaiming, SPANISH CLUB TRIP TO NEW YORK. Down below was a montage of photos arranged in a fan.

The one on the far left consisted of three teenagers standing in front of Rockefeller Center. One was clearly Joyce, the second one was a skinny dark-haired girl wearing jeans and a parka, while the third one was Annabel. All three of the girls looked cold and unhappy.

"Annabel was a lot heavier then," Bernie commented. *Probably over two hundred pounds,* she thought.

"She lost a lot of weight after her dad left them. To be honest, I don't think she ever recovered from his departure. After that, everything had to be about her. I don't know. I should have just walked away, but I didn't. I felt sorry for her. I guess when it comes down to it I'm not very bright. Sometimes you see what you want to see, not what's really there."

"So did she sleep with your husband too?" Bernie asked.

Joyce laughed. "No. She was too old for him. He likes them young. Once they get over twenty-five they're past their sell-by date. She would have been welcome to him, believe me. No. I wasn't that lucky."

"You guys were still friends when she died," Libby said.

"I thought we were," Joyce replied. "But evidently I was wrong."

"What happened?"

Joyce took a deep breath and let it out. "You're going to find out anyway so I'm going to tell you. She stole my ideas."

"Your ideas?" Libby echoed.

"Exactly. The Puggables were my idea. In fact, I even sewed up a few of the original models. But Annabel never gave me any credit. More importantly, she never gave me any money. She used my ideas to make herself rich. If it wasn't for me, Annabel and Richard Colbert would still be living in their little ranch on Buttermilk Drive."

"You could have sued her," Libby pointed out.

"It wasn't that simple. First of all, I didn't have any proof. Secondly, you have to have money to hire a lawyer. Thirdly, she made me doubt myself."

Now it was Bernie's turn to lean forward. "What do you mean, doubt yourself?"

"I mean this," Joyce said. "I just sat down one night at my sewing machine and created this family of pugs out of some leftover fabric that I had. I made them for Annabel's birthday, because I thought it would be this nice thing to do. I stuffed them, put bows around their necks, and gave them to Annabel. She loved them. In fact, she loved them more than she loved Trudy. I know for a fact she didn't like the dog. In fact, Richard was talking about getting rid of her.

"But they must have seen the commercial possibilities because the next thing I knew, I saw ads in the paper for the Puggables. Then they had to keep Trudy." Joyce picked up her knitting again. "And while it's true I didn't name them, they looked exactly like the ones I'd made for Annabel."

"Didn't you go tell her that?" Bernie asked.

"Of course I did, but she told me I was wrong. That the ones I'd made were different. This all happened right around the time I was having trouble with my husband and mentally I wasn't in a state to question anyone. I believed her— probably because I couldn't bear to think she was screwing me over as well.

"Later when I asked to see the ones I'd made for her, she told me she didn't have them. That Trudy had ripped them to shreds." Joyce spread her hands apart. "I suppose I was an idiot, but she was my friend and I wanted to believe her."

"Of course you did," Libby said.

"And then everything settled down. And she gave me stuff—like the Chanel jacket that I wore to Trudy's birthday. Sometimes she'd take me with her when she went to Florida. Then last year I had this idea for the dog biscuits that we were going to call Trudy's Treats. The recipe was totally unique. And we were going to make them into different vegetable shapes. Each vegetable would be a different flavor. And Annabel loved it. She said we'd sign a contract. We'd go into business together. I kept asking when that was going to happen, but she kept putting me off."

"So when did you find out that wasn't the case?" Bernie asked.

"At the party."

Libby cocked her head. "Not before?"

"No. Not before."

"You're sure of that," Libby said.

"Ask Ramona if you don't believe me," Joyce said. "Ramona," she repeated. "Trudy's trainer. In fact, if you want someone who had a motive to kill Annabel, talk to her. Yes. Definitely talk to her."

"And why should we do that?" Bernie asked.

"Because two days before the party, Annabel told Ramona she was going to hire someone else to mount Trudy's campaign for Westminster."

"So?" Libby said.

"What do you mean, so? This was Ramona's chance. Losing that was a real slap in the face. Everyone in the dog world would know. They'd figure something had to be wrong. Otherwise why would Annabel let her go? She'd probably never get another chance like that again. Plus, she'd lose the house she's living in. The new trainer would move in. Not that Trudy had a chance of winning. This was just another one of Annabel's vanity things—like the house that she built."

"And may I ask why you're telling us this?" Bernie inquired.

"Let's just say that Ramona is not one of my favorite people and leave it like that." And Joyce rose, indicating that it was time for Bernie and Libby to go.

"So what did you think?" Libby asked Bernie once they were outside. "Do you believe Joyce?"

"About Ramona? About the story she told us?"

"Both."

Bernie thought for a moment. "Well, I certainly believe what she said about Annabel and Richard not liking Trudy. That squares with everything we know. And I believe what she said about Annabel being a bitch. I don't think there's any argument on that score."

"Well," Libby said, "she was certainly anxious to steer us in Ramona's direction."

"Those two must have quite a history," Bernie observed as she reached into her bag to get her keys.

"I would say," Libby agreed.

Bernie put the key in the ignition. The van started with a loud grinding noise that seemed to be coming from the rear. She tried it again. Definitely the rear. Then the noise stopped.

"Joyce seems really nice," Libby observed.

"One never can tell," Bernie said as she pulled out onto the road. "Just because someone knits doesn't make her a good person."

"Have you ever heard of anyone knitting who was a bad person?"

Bernie smiled. "Madame Defarge in *A Tale of Two Cities*. I believe she was knitting the names of the people about to be beheaded into the scarf she was making."

Libby sighed. She'd never been able to get into Dickens.

The van was three-quarters of the way down the block when Libby happened to glance around.

"Now that's interesting," she said.

"What?" Bernie asked.

"I think I just saw Joyce getting into Richard's car and both of them driving away. She must have called him right after we left."

"Or, more likely, before she answered the door," Bernie said, doing the math in her head. "Are you sure it was Richard's car?"

"It was the same one parked out front when we went to Annabel's house the first time."

"Well, he certainly didn't waste any time getting here," Bernie observed.

"I wonder what they have to talk about," Libby mused.

"Somehow," Bernie said, "I don't think they're reminiscing about dear old departed Annabel."

Chapter 19

Sean hung up the phone and thought about what Clyde had told him. It was highly speculative, but still worth pursuing. In cases like this, one had to follow every tiny lead wherever it took one because you never knew. Things that seemed ridiculous to him were things that could drive other people to a homicidal rage. And had. He should know. He'd seen someone get stabbed over a penny debt once.

He'd tell Bernie and Libby what Clyde had told him when they got home and see what they wanted to do with it. It would probably amount to nothing, but there it was. Of course, in the old days he would have jumped in his car and gone off to find out. But this wasn't the old days. This wasn't even close. Not even remotely. Who would have thought he would end up like this?

Sean sighed. Okay. He was being negative and he hated people who were like that. Things could always be worse. But still. There was no denying that he wasn't happy. For valid reasons. He was not happy because it was the middle of February. He was not happy because it was another cloudy, dreary day.

He was not happy because the shop had run out of lemon bars, so he couldn't have one for dessert with his lunch.

He'd had to settle for a piece of Linzer torte, which he also liked, but it just wasn't what he wanted at that moment. He was not happy because his daughters seemed to be spending most of their time these days bickering and he was tired of hearing it. What they found to argue about never failed to amaze him. Really.

But he was most especially not happy because Ines had planned to come over to play Scrabble with him at one o'clock, but she'd had to cancel due to an emergency at the Longely Historical Society, although what could go wrong there, besides a fire or a flood—which there wasn't—was a mystery to him. Not that he was wasting much time wondering. He was pretty sure he'd find out when she called later.

Then he'd wanted to work on his crossword puzzle and finish reading his book. But he couldn't find either of those. Bernie had cleaned the house and put them heaven knew where. Given Bernie's penchant for relocating things to odd places, he'd probably find them in the laundry basket three weeks from now. And then he'd just about decided to break down, call Marvin, and see if he could drive him to the mall—this not being able to drive was a terrible thing—when his day had gotten even worse.

A girl with pink and purple hair had burst in on him. She was carrying a dog in her arms and demanding to speak to his daughters. And when he told her they weren't here, she'd put the dog down and burst into tears, which he couldn't deal with at all. Well, it wasn't that he couldn't deal with it—between being married and being a law enforcement officer, he'd dealt with plenty of crying females in his life one way or another—it was that he didn't want to deal with it. All that emotion just tuckered him out.

He'd had to calm her down, which he had done by feeding Samantha but-you-can-call-me-Sam the last of his chocolate-covered almonds, the expensive French ones that Ines had gotten for him when she'd been in Paris. And now, some-how or another, he had a snorting, wheezing pug sitting on his lap.

Actually, the pug had run straight over to him, stood up on her hind legs, and clawed at his pants. Samantha had picked up the pug and put it on his lap, saying, "Isn't that cute. She really likes you," before he'd had a chance to do anything. Like give the thing a little swat on the behind with the flat of his hand.

He didn't think it was cute at all. He was not a big fan of dogs. Actually, he was not a big fan of animals of any kind. It's not that he disliked them. In fact, he liked them. To a degree. But he'd grown up in the country and firmly believed that animals belonged outside, not sitting on him and trying to filch the last piece of his Linzer torte off the table.

"I assume this is Trudy," Sean said to Samantha as the dog looked up at him with big bug eyes. Her tongue curled out of her mouth. She looked like an alien. What were these things used for? Nothing. They had no earthly use at all as far as Sean could see. Why would you breed something like this?

Samantha nodded. Her eyes began to mist up again. "I've done a terrible thing," she wailed.

"I'm sure it can't be that bad," Sean said hastily. Actually, he couldn't imagine the girl in front of him doing anything worse than jaywalking. If that. When you got beyond the hair color and the weird clothes, she looked like a skinny, frightened little girl.

"It is. I'm going to be put in jail. That's why I came to see your daughters. I needed their advice, but they're not here." And Samantha started to sob again.

"Okay," Sean said hastily. "Tell me instead."

"Thanks for the offer, but you can't help me. No one can. When my father hears what I've done, he's going to throw me out of the house. Then I'll have nowhere to go. I'll have to live on the street and they'll find me frozen to death."

Sean interrupted her rant. "Let's not get overly dramatic. I used to be the police chief here, so I think I'm certainly qualified to advise you on any situation you've gotten yourself embroiled in."

Samantha wiped her nose on her sleeve. "You don't know what I've done," she said as the tears streamed down her cheeks.

"You killed someone."

Samantha stopped crying. Her eyes widened in indignation. "What? Are you kidding me?" She put her hands on her hips. "Of course I didn't kill anyone. Don't be stupid."

"Then you sold coke to an undercover agent and you're looking at serious jail time," Sean said as he pushed the dog away from the food.

"Don't be ridiculous. What a thing to say!"

"Okay. You took Trudy."

"How did you know I took Trudy?" Samantha asked.

"Because you're here and Trudy's here, so great detective that I am, I put two and two together."

"How do you know she's Trudy?"

Sean shrugged. "Who else can she be?" Sean was not someone who believed in random events.

"Cool," Samantha said as she got up off the floor and went into the bathroom to wash her face, leaving Sean alone with the dog.

Trudy leaned against Sean's chest and licked his hand.

"You want to get down?" Sean asked.

Trudy snorted. He tried to push her off, but she proved to be amazingly hard to move for something of that size.

"You just want to get closer to the food, don't you?" Sean asked her.

She wagged her tail and gave Sean's hand another quick

lick. Well, she might not have it in the looks department, Sean thought, but she was smart. He'd give her that.

"All right," he said. "I guess everyone deserves dessert now and then." And he broke off a piece of the Linzer torte and held it out to Trudy, who very carefully took it out of Sean's hand and ate it. "You have manners too." Also not a bad thing.

Trudy snorted and worked her way deeper into Sean's lap. She lifted her head up and gazed into his eyes. Actually, Sean reflected, she was kind of cute in an ugly sort of way. And really, if he thought about it, dogs like this did do valuable work. In a sense. They couldn't herd sheep or protect a house against prowlers, but he could see that they would be good companions. And that was important too. Especially for shut-ins and people who couldn't get around easily.

Of course, there was always the flea problem. He hated fleas. You got them in your house and you never got them out. They were scary little things. They could hibernate for up to two years. Then when the conditions were right, they'd spring out and bite you.

"Okay," Sean said when Samantha came out of the bathroom. "Why don't you tell me why you stole Trudy?"

"I didn't steal her," Samantha replied indignantly. "I rescued her."

"Just tell me," Sean said.

He wasn't in the mood to get into a semantic discussion right now. As he listened to Samantha's story—and it *was* a story and not a very good one at that—he began to formulate a plan. This situation might not be so bad after all.

"Do you have a car?" Sean asked Samantha when she was done talking.

Samantha looked at him as if he was crazy. "Of course I have a car. How do you think I got here?"

"Good," he said. "Because we're going to drive over to Ramona's place."

Samantha twisted a lock of pink hair around her finger. "Why would we do that?"

"Well, you just told me you found Trudy wandering outside."

"I did?" Samantha asked.

"Yes, you did," Sean said. "I distinctly heard you say that. You didn't say you walked into Richard Colbert's place and took her, because that would be stealing, correct?"

Samantha nodded. "If you say so."

"I do. I'm just making sure we're on the same page," Sean told her.

"We are."

"Good. Because we're going to knock on Ramona's door and ask her if Trudy is missing."

"But she wasn't wandering near Ramona's place."

Be nice, Sean told himself. "True," he said to Samantha, "but Ramona doesn't know that."

"Oh," Samantha said after a moment. "I get it. We're going to play detective."

"I don't 'play' detective," Sean said, stung to the core. "I *am* a detective."

"Oops. *Sor*-ry." Samantha bounced up and down on the sofa. "If you're a detective, then I'm your trusty sidekick, right?"

"Right," Sean said.

After all, Ramona was on the list of people who needed to be talked to and his daughters hadn't gotten around to her yet, so why not take advantage of the opportunity that had been offered to him?

This way he'd get to see firsthand Ramona's reactions to the questions that needed to be asked of her. That definitely beat listening to Bernie and/or Libby tell him what had happened. He'd always believed that in cases such as these direct experience was best. He'd believed it when he was the Longely chief of police and he believed it now.

Anyway, talking to her certainly beat sitting around here doing nothing.

"This is so cool." Samantha sprang up off the sofa. "Let's go." She was almost to the door when something else occurred to her. "Trudy is staying here, right?"

"Well . . ." Sean said.

"You can't take her back there. You can't."

"I . . ." Sean hedged because he'd been planning on doing exactly that.

"Trudy's a good girl. She'll be fine." Samantha ran over, got down on her knees, and grabbed Sean's hands. "*Please*," she begged.

"Get up," Sean said.

"Not until you say yes." Samantha gestured at Trudy, who was gazing at him with adoring eyes. "How could you consign her to a fate worse than death?"

"That is a little excessive. Now get up."

"You promise?"

"All right," Sean said. After all. Really. What could it hurt? How much harm could the dog do in the flat? All the furniture was old anyway and the carpet did need to be replaced. "But when we get back we have to figure out what to do with her, because she can't stay here."

Samantha jumped up and kissed the top of his head. "You are definitely the best."

Sean felt himself beginning to blush.

Chapter 20

The moment that Sean and Samantha got down the stairs he regretted his prior suggestion to Samantha. He should have waited for the girls. So, he'd been a little bit bored. So, he'd been feeling a little bit sorry for himself. So what. It would have passed. But he hadn't waited. He'd been in such an all-fired hurry to get out of the house. And now he had to contend with the matter of Samantha's car. A Mini Cooper.

"Isn't she too cute?" Samantha had squealed when he saw it. "Her name is Esmeralda. Don't you think that's a good name? You know, green? Emeralds? Get the connection?"

"Of course," Sean muttered.

He didn't think the vehicle was cute at all. It reminded him of a fancy tin can that had been painted green with checkerboard trim along the sides. Even the bumper cars in the amusement parks that he used to go to when he was a kid were better made than this thing.

Personally, he liked solid metal between him and every other vehicle on the road. He didn't even want to think about what would happen if one of these things collided with an SUV or a pickup truck. That's why he hadn't let

Bernie buy one when she'd wanted to. He'd told her the vehicles were too dangerous and now he was going to be riding in one. Terrific. *Karma, baby,* as Bernie would say. She would find it funny. He, however, did not.

He looked at the Mini Cooper again. Of course, he was going to have to get into the thing first before he went for a ride. And that was going to be difficult. It was fine for a twenty-something like Samantha, who popped up and down like a jack-in-the-box. It wasn't fine for someone like him, someone large and stiff in the knees. Even when he was younger it would have been a tight fit. In order to get in he was going to have to fold himself into an accordion shape. Frankly, he was too old to be pleated.

The only good thing was that Trudy wasn't along. If she were she'd be sitting on his lap. Since there wasn't room to move, his legs would probably go numb from her weight. Now that would be a disaster. They might go numb anyway if the ride was long enough, which he didn't think it would be. And he didn't even want to think about having to get out of the blasted car. That was a whole separate issue.

It would be worse than getting in. He could see it now. He'd get stuck and Samantha would have to grab his wrists and pull. He'd finally pop out and fall on his face like one of those clowns in the circus. Or maybe the fire department would have to come. That would be unspeakably degrading. No, he wasn't going to think about that.

He swore that he would never complain about riding in Marvin's hearse again. Ever. Well, at least not for a month. Unless Marvin was using it to pick up a client, as he so euphemistically put it. But really that had happened only twice. And it couldn't be helped. It wasn't that Sean had anything against dead people. He'd seen plenty of them in his time. It just seemed kind of ... well, tacky ... to be combining errands, as it were.

And speaking of Marvin, Sean would never complain

about his driving again. Samantha's was even worse, Sean decided once he was in the car. Mario Andretti she was not. She'd peeled away from the curb in front of the shop without looking and had come within two inches of tearing off the sideview mirror on Mrs. Gupta's Infinity. Then they'd torn through the streets without regard to pedestrians, or traffic, or lights, with Samantha shifting with gay abandon.

"You are all right, aren't you?" Samantha asked as they sped through a yellow light at Ashcroft, Ashcroft being one of those tricky intersections where five lanes of traffic merge. It was just sheer luck that the SUV that Samantha had cut off had been able to brake in time.

Sean came out of his state of shock for a moment. "Are you talking to me?"

"Who else would I be talking to?" Samantha demanded.

"The traffic police," Sean couldn't help saying.

"Ha. Ha. Very funny."

"It's not funny. It's true."

"I'm not driving too fast for you, am I?" Samantha asked as she took the corner at Ash and Oak at fifty miles an hour. They actually went up on two wheels. "I mean, I know old folks like to go slow, so if you want I can gear down."

Sean considered that option for all of two seconds. He wanted to say, *Yes, please slow down, I don't want to die yet*, but his pride wouldn't let him. Sometimes it sucked being a guy.

"No. It's fine," Sean heard himself telling Samantha. "In fact, you can go even faster if you like." What had his mom said about pride being a terrible thing? Well, it looked as if she was correct.

"Good," Samantha said as she revved the car back up. "You know, you really are pretty cool."

"Despite being practically an antique?"

"Yeah. Despite that," Samantha said as they whipped

around Longworth and headed toward Route 63. A few minutes later they were on it.

"I still don't see why you can't keep Trudy," Samantha said to Sean as they bounced down the road toward Ramona's house.

"Because I would be receiving stolen property," Sean explained for the hundredth time. Somehow he managed to keep off the topic of Samantha's driving.

"Trudy isn't property," Samantha protested. "She's a living, breathing thing. And I didn't steal her; I acquired her."

"Oh. Excuse me. Acquired. I like that. Listen, I'm not arguing with you. I'm just telling you that in the eyes of the New York State Agricultural Code, a dog is considered property."

"That's terrible."

"It may be terrible, but there it is. The law is the law."

"It needs to be changed."

"Then call up your congressman and complain. Get a petition going."

"I know what I could do," Samantha said. "I could call up Animal Control and complain that Trudy is being treated meanly. Then they'd take her away and I could adopt her."

"You could," Sean agreed, who doubted that Animal Control would ever set foot in Richard Colbert's house no matter what the cause. "But somehow I don't think that being kept in the kitchen and being fed dog food would be considered cruelty to animals. That's what a lot of people do. And I'm sure your father wouldn't be too pleased if you brought Trudy home."

"First of all, Trudy is locked in a crate," Samantha protested. "And if that isn't cruel, I don't know what is. How would you like to be in a cage all day?"

"I'm not a dog," Sean replied. "So I wouldn't know. And remember, you told me you found her wandering outside, which means she wasn't in her crate."

"Oh, yeah," Samantha replied. "I forgot."

"Don't forget," Sean said.

"It's true. She was lost," Samantha continued. "The poor thing didn't even have her coat on. And no one noticed. I was there two days after Annabel died and Trudy was whimpering. It was heartbreaking. When I tried to take her for a walk, Richard yelled at me."

"Why did he do that?"

"He said he didn't want Trudy tracking dirt through the house. But my therapist said that Richard was treating Trudy badly because she was Annabel's dog. Or something like that."

Sean thought that might be true.

Samantha continued, "My therapist calls it displaced anger. But Trudy is lonely. She needs to be with people. And anyway, she used to be treated like a princess when Annabel was alive. I mean, even if Annabel didn't love her she got good food and walks and doggie treats."

"You're telling me she was a trophy dog?"

Samantha stared at him.

"Like a trophy wife," Sean explained.

"Oh. I get it," Samantha said. "Yeah. That's what she was and now she's like Cinderella BPC."

"BPC?" Sean repeated.

"Before Prince Charming, of course."

"Of course," Sean agreed. Who didn't know that? Of course, he'd just recently learned what OMG and LOL stood for. He could still hear Bernie saying, "Dad, I can't believe you don't know what that means." Well, believe it.

Sean gazed out the window at the snow piled up on either side of the road. He hadn't driven Route 63 since he'd chased the Lipton boys down for stealing the high school principal's Lincoln Continental and spray painting it purple. The road wasn't in any better shape now than it was back then. But why should it be? There were no big developments on it; hence, no tax dollars were spent on maintaining it.

The road had no traffic signs and very few vehicles, which meant that Samantha could go as fast as she wanted on it. And she was. Never mind the ruts in the road. Actually, he was amazed Samantha could get as much speed out of the Mini Cooper as she was getting.

"She handles pretty well," Sean heard himself observing.

"She does, doesn't she?" Samantha responded. "I was pretty surprised. But it makes sense considering who manufactures them."

"You didn't buy this car?"

"With what? No. My dad gave it to me, so he wouldn't have to deal with me. He figures that way I can go off on my own and I don't have to bother him."

"That's too bad," Sean said, thinking of all the time he'd spent driving his daughters. Some of their best conversations had occurred when he'd picked them up from school. "He doesn't know what he's missing."

Samantha shrugged. "I don't care. I'd rather have the car anyway."

Then she stopped talking. Sean could see she was blinking the tears out of her eyes. They finished out the ride in silence. Five minutes later, they pulled up in front of Ramona's house. Sean looked at his watch. It would have taken any normal person half an hour to drive there. It had taken Samantha ten minutes. Maybe even eight. On the plus side, at least his legs hadn't had time to numb up.

Samantha parked. Then she reached into her pocket and pulled out a pack of cigarettes.

"Do you mind if I smoke one of these before we get out?" she asked.

"Only if you give me one," Sean replied.

This was the first good thing that had happened today, Sean thought as Samantha held out the pack for him.

"Just don't tell my daughters," Sean cautioned Samantha.

"They don't know?"

Sean shook his head. "No. They don't know that I started again."

"That's okay," Samantha said as she blew a smoke ring and watched it drift across the front window. "Neither does my dad."

"You shouldn't be smoking," Sean admonished.

"Neither should you," Samantha shot back.

"Yeah, but you're young. I'm old, so it doesn't matter."

"I'm not that young," Samantha said. "In two months, I'll be twenty-one."

"That's very old," Sean told her with a straight face. "I didn't realize you were an antique."

Samantha giggled. "I suppose it's not that old from where you sit."

"Not exactly," Sean said wryly.

Samantha rolled down her window, cupped her hand, tapped the ash from her cigarette into it, and dumped it out the window. "Not to change the subject or anything, but what if Ramona's not here?"

"Then we'll come back another time," Sean said, doing the same thing with his cigarette that Samantha had done.

"I don't see her car."

"It's probably in the garage."

"We should have called first."

Sean shook his head. "No, we shouldn't have. Then we'd give up the element of surprise."

Samantha just grunted and took another drag.

Sean took a moment to study the structure in front of him. It was one of those ramshackle buildings that seem to have grown themselves. The place was tucked away on the back end of the Colbert estate. It was separated from the main building by the swimming pool, the tennis courts, and the flower beds on one side, and bounded on the other side by Route 63 and Freemont Woods. You had to know it was there to find it.

Sean decided that the structure must have been built—or maybe cobbled together would be a better description—with the intention of housing the hired help. If the house that Richard Colbert lived in was built for show, this place was built for function. The bungalow-style cottage had once been painted red, but although patches of the original color remained close to the ground, the wind and the weather had combined to scour the color off the rest of the walls. An empty dog run and a small garage stood a short distance away.

Samantha pointed. "That's probably where Ramona keeps Trudy when she stays here."

Sean didn't doubt it. "Some people keep their dogs in places like that," Sean said. His dad had always kept his hunting dogs in an outside run. *Otherwise they'll get spoiled,* his dad used to say.

"Maybe," Samantha answered. "But Trudy isn't that kind of dog. Trudy has outfits. And shoes. My, there are a lot of cats here," Samantha noted, changing the subject.

"Yes, there are," Sean agreed.

He couldn't believe that he hadn't seen them at first, but maybe they'd been scared off by the sound of Samantha's Mini Cooper when it roared to a stop. He knew he would be. And then after a few minutes of quiet, they'd crept back out. He counted ten at least. Maybe twelve. Most of which were hanging out near the garage. Then he spotted another couple near the blue spruce over to the left.

"I bet she feeds them all," Sean said as he opened the car door.

Otherwise they wouldn't be hanging around. Cats were opportunistic in that way. No food and they found somewhere else to go. He remembered when his grandma had started feeding the barn cats. In the end, much to his dad's disgust, they'd had twenty of them lounging about. *It's a waste of food,* he remembered his dad saying. Gram hadn't cared. But at least they hadn't had any mice, Sean thought. Not too many birds either, come to think of it. Then his mind turned to the problem of removing himself from the Mini Cooper. In situations like these, planning was key.

He'd just managed to extract himself after a five-minute struggle that Samantha had the good grace to look away from when Ramona Birdwell came barreling around the corner. She was wearing a black wool watch cap, a bright yellow parka, matching snow pants, Gortex boots, and thick brown leather work gloves. Sean couldn't help thinking that she reminded him of a walking fireplug.

"Who are you and what do you want?" she barked as she drew closer to where Sean and Samantha were standing.

Sean introduced himself and Samantha.

Ramona gestured toward Sean with her chin. "So are you related to the Simmons sisters, the ones who catered Annabel's party?" Ramona asked.

"I'm their father," Sean explained.

The expression on Ramona's face made it plain that this did not improve his standing in her eyes. "That turned into quite a fiasco, didn't it?" she said. Her tone exhibited a certain amount of smug satisfaction that Sean found particularly distasteful. It was almost as if she was glad that the whole affair had turned out the way it did, that she thought Annabel had it coming.

"Well, under the circumstances," Sean replied, "I don't see how it could have been anything else *but* a fiasco."

Ramona snorted. "I told Annabel the whole idea was ridiculous. Trudy is a dog, not some fancied-up child. But Annabel wouldn't listen. Never would. Had to have the party even though I was trying to get Trudy's weight down by half a pound. She always had to have things her way. Money just makes some people stupid."

"And others envious," Sean observed.

"Not me, if that's what you're implying," Ramona answered as she pointed to Samantha. "And you," Ramona snapped. "What's your excuse for being here?"

Samantha looked around nervously.

"She's the one who found Trudy," Sean said before Samantha could answer.

A furrow appeared just above the bridge of Ramona's nose. "What do you mean, found Trudy?"

"Near your place. She found Trudy near your place. So we came to see if you were missing a dog."

"My place?" Ramona repeated.

"Yes. She was outside by the road," Sean lied.

"The road?" Ramona's voice quivered with outrage. "That's absurd. You're making it up."

"At least we think it's Trudy," Sean continued. "Maybe it's not. I have to confess that to me one pug looks just like another."

"Not to me," Ramona snapped.

"Obviously," Sean observed.

"Was she hurt?" Ramona asked.

"Not at all," Sean replied.

"I'd like to see her," Ramona said.

"The pug?"

"Who else would I be talking about?" Ramona growled.

Sean shrugged. "Sorry. The pug's fine. She got into some stuff, so one of my daughters took her to get cleaned up. Of course, we'll need proper documentation before returning her to Richard. She could be someone else's dog." Then before Ramona could say anything else, Sean gestured toward the cats. "Are these all yours?"

Ramona's voice softened. Her body relaxed. "Those are my outdoor kitties. I have more inside."

Sean rubbed his hands together. "Speaking of inside, do you think I can make use of the facilities?"

Sean could tell from the frown on Ramona's face that

she was anxious to let him in her house. "Please," he said. "Just for a moment."

"Do you like cats?" Ramona asked.

"As well as the next man. Why?"

"You'll see," Ramona said. And then she added, "But I want you to just do your business and go. I don't want you poking around in there."

Sean drew himself up. "I hadn't intended to."

"Good," Ramona replied. "Because my babies aren't used to people and I don't want them to get spooked."

"Neither do I," Sean said.

And he meant it. One or two cats were fine. But he suspected he'd find multiple cats in Ramona's house, and that was a different story. So, it was with some trepidation that Sean followed Ramona inside. The first thing Sean and Samantha noticed when they stepped inside was the cats. They were everywhere. Lounging on the window seat, sitting on chairs, draped over the back of the sofa, lying on the rugs. Sean lost count after fifteen. And he was willing to bet there were more in the other rooms of the house. Many more. The second thing Samantha and Sean noticed was the lack of smell. He realized he'd been unconsciously girding himself for the reek of kitty litter, but it wasn't there.

"Training dogs is my business, but cats are my weakness," Ramona said.

"I can see that," Sean said as he carefully picked his way to the bathroom.

When he came back, despite what Ramona had just said to him about doing what he had to do and leaving, she and Samantha had seated themselves on the sofa in the living room. Samantha was stroking a three-legged ginger-colored tabby who was sprawled across her lap, while Ramona was brushing the back of a large black and white tomcat. Two gray cats and a tortoise shell looked on.

"I told Richard not to do that," Sean heard Ramona saying to Samantha. "But he didn't listen. He never does."

"You must be relieved to be reinstated," Sean said, interrupting the two women's conversation. He was standing against the wall because all the other possible seats were being taken up by felines. And anyway, if he sat down he'd just have to get up again, and transitions like that were hard for him.

Ramona shot him a sharp look. "What do you mean, reinstated?"

"Well, I'd heard that Annabel was hiring someone else to mount Trudy's campaign for Westminster," Sean said, repeating what Clyde had told him earlier that afternoon.

"That's ridiculous," Ramona spluttered. "She would never think of doing such a thing. I've been with Trudy since the beginning."

"I'm glad to hear that. You know what gossip is like in a small town like Longely."

"Yes, I do," Ramona said. "People here are like a bunch of piranhas. They have way too much time on their hands if you ask me."

Sean was just about to say that piranhas had fins, not hands, but he managed to restrain his inner Bernie. Instead he said, "I also heard that you were going to have to move out of here because the house comes with your job."

Ramona's eyes narrowed. "What a lot of drivel. Where did you hear that from?"

Sean shrugged. "You know how people talk."

"I bet it was Joyce or Melissa, wasn't it? They would say something like that. They've always hated me. Especially Joyce. She couldn't bear to think that I was important to Annabel. She has a nasty mean streak in her. My cats can't stand her. Or Melissa, for that matter. And they are very good judges of character."

"No. It wasn't them," Sean assured her.

"Are you sure?"

"Positive."

"Then it was Joanna."

"It wasn't her either. Really," Sean said. He could tell Ramona didn't believe him. "But I'm glad to hear that's not the case. It certainly would be hard to find a place given the cats. They must cost a lot of money to take care of," he observed.

Ramona didn't say anything, but Sean could see from the way she'd stiffened up that he'd hit a home run with his comments. Score one for Clyde.

The question, though, was: Was that enough of a motivation for murder?

If Ramona was about to lose everything—her job, a place to live, her beloved animals—then Sean thought the answer to that question could be yes.

As he and Samantha left the house, Sean was glad he'd come out here. He'd learned a lot. It had definitely been worth the ride, and given the circumstance that was saying quite a lot. On the way back to the car, he walked over to the garage, scattering cats as he went, and peered in the window.

Through the dirt and the cobwebs, Sean saw bags and bags of cat litter, cat food, flea spray, as well as three brown quart bottles that he was positive were going to turn out to be Malathion. He was about to try the garage door when Ramona came out and started screaming at them. At that point, he figured it was time to go. He and Samantha beat a hasty retreat, or as hasty as he could manage, got into the Mini Cooper, and zoomed off to pick up Trudy.

Chapter 21

Samantha looked at Ines. Ines looked at Sean. Sean looked at Trudy. Trudy didn't look at anyone. She was happily exploring the carpeting in the back room of the Longley Historical Society.

"You want me to do what?" Ines asked Sean.

Sean explained again. "It'll just be for a few days," he assured her. "Till we get everything straightened out."

Ines put her hands on her hips. Sean thought she looked particularly good in the black turtleneck sweater and suede straight skirt she was wearing,

"What is 'everything' exactly?" she demanded.

"Really, you'd be better off not knowing," Sean told her. Which was true.

"Because it's illegal?" Ines asked.

Sean waved his hands in the air. "No. No. It's nothing like that," he lied. "Absolutely not."

Of course the sheriff might not see it that way. Scratch that. Considering the sheriff was Lucy, there was no "might" about it. He'd arrest Sean without a second's pause. What was Trudy worth? Fifty thousand dollars? Twenty? Ten? He really had no idea. But even if it was two thousand, it was still felony land. And Lucy would be happy to put him there. Sean couldn't believe he was doing this. It went against everything he'd been trained to do. He should take the dog back to Richard. It was a dog, for heaven's sake. Just a dog. All this trouble over an animal. He had to be nuts. And yet . . . and yet something in his gut wouldn't let him.

"Why don't I believe you?" Ines said.

"It's just an awkward situation."

"How awkward?"

"Awkward enough."

"I'd like to be the judge of that."

"I'll tell you the whole story later. I swear."

"Is that a fact?"

"Really. Boy Scout's word of honor. And I have to say you're looking very nice today. Did you just get your hair done?"

Ines laughed. "Nice try."

"It's true," Sean protested. "You're looking particularly lovely today."

"Absolutely," Samantha put in. "Love your cardigan. Is it vintage?"

"Yes, it is. Just like me," Ines answered. Biting her lip, she looked down at Trudy, who was snuffling around one of the legs of the oak table in the center of the room.

"Come on," Sean wheedled. "Look at her. She's adorable."

"I admit she's cute in a spectacularly ugly kind of way," Ines conceded.

"Exactly," Sean said. "She needs some love. And a nice home for a little while."

"Lots of love," Samantha put in.

Ines looked at her. "Why can't you take the dog?" she asked Samantha.

"Because . . . because," Samantha stuttered.

"Because her father's violently allergic to animals," Sean said.

"Exactly," Samantha reprised.

Ines looked skeptical. "And she can't answer for herself?" she asked Sean.

"Sometimes I forget things," Samantha explained. "It's the hair dye."

"Really," Ines said. The corners of her mouth twitched as she tried not to laugh. "How curious. I've always heard that pink was toxic to brain cells. I just never knew it was true."

"Personally, I think it's the purple," Samantha said.

Ines couldn't contain herself any longer. She burst out laughing.

Sean hastily changed the subject, as Ines wiped the tears from her eyes. "You don't have any pets right now," he pointed out.

"There's a reason for that," Ines told him. "I like being able to come and go when I want."

Sean put on his most engaging smile. "Please. This is just for a couple of days. Maybe a week at the most."

"Okay," Ines said. "I heard why Samantha couldn't do this. Now, why can't you? Are your daughters allergic too?"

"Yes, they are," Sean replied. "Fine," he said under Ines's unfaltering gaze. "The truth . . ."

"For a change . . ."

"The truth is that the dog just can't be at my place," Sean told Ines. "You have to trust me on this. It's complicated."

"Everything with you is complicated," Ines said dryly.

Sean drew himself up. "I wouldn't go that far."

"I would."

"She needs a good home," Sean said, getting back to the matter at hand. This wasn't the time to discuss his personal stuff. No time was, but that was a different matter. "And it's only for a couple of days."

"You said it could be for a week."

"At the outside."

"I'd have to go out and get dog food and treats. . . ."

"Oh, we have them in the car," Samantha said. "I'll go get them." They'd stopped at Pets Are Us on the way and Samantha had run in.

"You swear it's for a week at the most?" Ines asked.

"Oh, absolutely," Sean said. "And remember, if anyone asks about the dog tell them you got Mathilda . . ."

"Mathilda?" Ines's eyebrows went up. "What kind of name is that for a dog?"

"I think it's a nice one," Sean said. What was wrong with Mathilda? Mathilda was a perfectly reasonable name as far as he could see. It certainly wasn't any worse than Trudy. In fact, he figured it was a whole lot better.

"All I can think of is that calypso song 'Matilda.' " And Ines started humming it under her breath.

Now it was Sean's turn to smile.

"What's calypso?" Samantha asked.

"Something that happened before your time," Sean and Ines said in unison.

Sean continued. "Be that as it may, the important thing to remember is that you got her from your cousin in Scranton. . . ."

"I don't have a cousin in Scranton," Ines informed Sean.

"Well, you do now," Sean told her. "A distant cousin. One you just reconnected with by the name of Elsiver Crandall."

Ines's eyebrows went even higher this time. "Elsiver Crandall? You've got to be kidding me. Where do you get your names from?" she asked in wonderment.

Sean pointed to his head. "They're just there," he said. "Pretty terrific, huh?"

Ines groaned.

"Or," Sean said to Ines, "you can say you found the dog wandering around outside and took her in until you could find the owner."

"I like that better," Ines said. She looked down at the little pug, who was now sitting on her feet. "I think I'm going to call you Edna," she said.

Sean blinked. "How is Edna better than Mathilda?" he asked.

"It just is." And Ines bent over and scooped the little dog up in her arms.

As Sean watched Ines and Trudy interact, the churning in his stomach quieted down. For the first time since Samantha had invaded his home, he felt certain he'd done the right thing.

By the time Sean left fifteen minutes later, Ines had replaced Trudy's collar with the one Samantha had bought at the pet store and was busy feeding her a piece of leftover Swiss cheese from her lunch. She didn't even look up when Samantha and Sean said good-bye, just gave them an absentminded wave.

Which was a good thing, Sean thought as he reinserted himself in the Mini Cooper. He was incredibly grateful that Ines was distracted by the dog. Otherwise, she would have insisted on walking him out and he didn't know what he would have done. He'd be beyond mortified if she saw him getting into this dratted green tin can. She'd want to help and that was simply not happening. In fact, as far as he was concerned, after today he'd never set foot in this vehicle again.

"Can I ask you why you said what you did in there?" Samantha asked after Sean managed to fit himself back in the Mini Cooper.

"Certainly you can ask," Sean told her as he reached over and fastened his seat belt.

"Seriously."

"I am serious."

"So, you're not going to tell me," Samantha said.

"I am," Sean said as he struggled to get his legs into some sort of reasonable position. "It's called the doctrine of plausible deniability."

Samantha just looked at him.

"Okay," Sean said. "Now, if we leave Trudy in my house and the police come looking for her, I can say I found her wandering around outside and I thought she was just your average stray. They won't believe me, because Bernie and Libby are involved in the case. The facts aren't plausible. But if they come to Ines's house and she says that to them, they'll believe her. Why shouldn't they? Up to this point she hasn't been involved with Trudy in any way, shape, or form."

"Do you think the police will really come looking for her?"

Sean shrugged. "Let's put it this way. Probably not, but I wouldn't be surprised if they did. Even they can sometimes put two and two together. It really depends on how much pressure they get to find her."

"You're not a big fan of our police department, are you?" Samantha asked.

"That would be putting it mildly."

"My dad said you got what you deserved, but considering my dad, I think that means you got a bad rap."

"Thank you," Sean said.

But as it turned out it wasn't the police who turned up at the Simmons's flat. It was Richard Colbert.

Chapter 22

Bernie and Libby had gone straight to the shop after their visit with Joyce and gotten to work on Mrs. Stein's order. When they were finished, they went upstairs expecting to tell their dad about their visit with Joyce. There was only one problem. He wasn't there.

"Try his cell," Libby suggested.

Bernie punched in their dad's number. It went straight to voice mail.

"Great," Libby said when Bernie told her.

"He's probably fine," Bernie said.

"Probably," Libby agreed.

But she felt this uneasy tugging in her gut and she could tell from Bernie's expression that she felt it too. Their dad was always there—unless he was out with Marvin or Clyde.

"He's probably out with Clyde," Bernie suggested as she dialed Clyde's number. Only he wasn't.

"And Marvin's working," Libby said.

Both girls looked at each other and headed out the door. The first thing they did was ask Amber and Googie if they'd seen their dad, but both of them had been busy and hadn't noticed him. And anyway, as Bernie pointed out, there wasn't a view of the entrance to their flat from the shop. If their dad had gone to the left, they wouldn't have seen him.

For the next fifteen minutes, they searched the neighborhood. No Sean. And given the pace at which Sean moved, neither Libby nor Bernie could see his getting much farther. Especially since he had to be extra careful because of the ice on the streets.

Bernie pushed her hands down in her jacket's pockets to warm them. "We're making too big a deal of this," she said.

Libby nodded. Her breath was visible in the air. "It's good that he can get around on his own again."

"Absolutely," Bernie agreed. Then she said, "I hope he's not dead, because I want to kill him when I find him."

"And I'll join you," Libby told her as she wound her scarf more tightly around her neck. She looked at the sky. Black clouds were hovering in the west. "I think it's going to snow," she observed.

"Terrific," Bernie said. "That's just what we need. More white stuff."

"I'm sure there's a reasonable explanation for where Dad is," Libby said as they did one last turn around the neighborhood.

"I'm sure there is," Bernie said. The problem was that she couldn't think of one. "He should have called."

"We should go home and check the house phone," Libby suggested. "Maybe someone called on that."

Bernie grunted. Even though Libby hadn't said the words, Bernie knew she was talking about the hospital or the police.

"Yes. We should do that," she said quietly as she turned toward their house.

They'd just gone back upstairs and hung their coats in the closet when their dad walked through the door. The girls ran over to him.

"Thank God," Libby said.

"What do you mean, thank God?" Sean asked, even though he knew exactly what she meant.

"Where were you?" Libby demanded of him. "We were worried."

"Well, you shouldn't have been," Sean shot back. He was hungry and tired, and he was stressed from the Mini Cooper. He needed a cup of tea. He didn't need to be attacked. Okay. Maybe his daughters had a point, but they could be more tactful about it. "I'm not two," Sean told them. "I'm perfectly capable of taking care of myself, thank you very much."

"Why didn't you answer your phone?" asked Bernie. She decided it would be better to skirt the topic her dad had raised.

Sean took out his phone and looked at it. "Guess I forgot to turn it on."

"You're always forgetting to turn it on. What's the point of having it if you don't use it?" Libby said.

"He uses it," Bernie told her. "He just uses it when he wants to."

"Are you saying I turned it off?" Sean said as he struggled to take off his jacket. He was damned if he was going to ask either of his daughters for help.

Bernie nodded. "That's exactly what I'm saying."

"I'm entitled to some privacy now and then," Sean responded.

"We never said you weren't," Libby said.

Her dad glowered at her. "These cell phones are the curse of the modern age. We'd all be better off without them."

Bernie rolled her eyes. "Let's not go on that rant, shall we?"

"I'm not sure you do value my privacy," Sean told her as he wiggled his left arm out of his sleeve. The right sleeve was easy. "I'm not sure you do at all."

Bernie lifted her hands in the air and let them drop back

down. "The point of having the phone is so we can call you too."

"Thank you for the technological update," Sean snapped. The last thing he needed was to be chastised by his children. He wasn't some old fart they had to keep track of twenty-four/seven and he'd kill himself before he'd let that happen. No nursing home for him, that was for sure.

"We were worried," Libby said. "Because you're usually . . ."

Sean gestured to the wheelchair. "Sitting there."

"Yes," Bernie said. "I'm glad that you're feeling stronger, but we were getting concerned."

"You don't have to be."

"The least you could have done was leave a note," Libby said.

That made Sean even madder, mostly because he knew it was true. "In case you've forgotten, I'm your father," he informed them.

"We know," Bernie said. She paused while she thought of the right thing to say. When he got this bullheaded, it was difficult to know how to proceed. "Have you ever considered the fact that we may need to call you for advice?" she finally said.

Sean softened slightly. At least his daughters cared for him—even if they were inclined to smother him, a trait they'd gotten from their mother. But still. They did love him. Which was more than a lot of other people could say about their children. So, in that sense he was lucky.

"I talked with Ramona," Sean said, changing the subject.

Libby frowned. She didn't understand. "Ramona? Did she come here?"

"No. I went there."

"How did you get out there?" Bernie asked. She'd figured her dad had gone off on a walk someplace. "She's out on Route Sixty-three."

"I know where she is. Samantha drove me."

Libby's eyes widened. "Samantha? As in Samantha with the ever-changing hair color? That Samantha?"

"That's right. That Samantha." Sean heard a roar from outside as she took off.

"You went in her Mini Cooper?" Bernie asked.

Sean drew himself up. "Why are you so surprised?"

"It's just that you're too . . ."

"Old?"

"No," Libby said. "That wasn't what I meant."

"Infirm? Hidebound?"

"We're just surprised that you'd ride in one," Bernie said. "Considering your opinion of them and all."

"People change," Sean said as he made his way to the straight-backed armchair next to the sofa.

The chair had just the right amount of padding and depth. If he used the arms on either side for support, he could get in and out of it by himself. And even though his wheelchair was actually more comfortable, he'd sit in the armchair for as long as he could possibly manage it. In fact, he was going to ask Bernie to fold the wheelchair up and put it away. He didn't even want to see the dratted thing. He was just going to assume that his remission would last forever.

"So does this mean I can get one?" Bernie asked.

"Ha. Ha. Very funny."

"I'm serious."

"So am I. My answer is no. Under no circumstances. Those vehicles shouldn't be on the road," Sean opined as he slowly lowered himself into his chair. Boy was he glad to be back. This afternoon had tired him out more than he thought.

"How did you and Samantha get together?" Libby asked.

Sean was just about to tell Libby that if she'd get him some tea and a couple of chocolate chip cookies he'd tell her when he heard the bottom outside door slam.

"Are you expecting anyone?" Sean asked.

Both Bernie and Libby shook their heads.

Then they heard footsteps on the stairs. They were coming up hard and heavy. Before anyone had a chance to do anything Richard Colbert burst into the room.

"Where is she?" he demanded.

"What are you talking about?" Sean asked.

"You know what I'm talking about," Richard shot back. His face was red with anger. "I'm talking about the dog."

"Are you nuts?" Bernie demanded for the second time that day. "You can't come barging in here like this."

"I certainly can," Richard said. "I have."

"Obviously," Bernie said.

Richard pointed to Sean before Bernie could go on. "Ask your dad."

Bernie took a step forward. "Ask him about what?"

"About the dog," Richard cried. "I just told you. What are you, some kind of moron?"

"I'm going to pretend I didn't hear that," Bernie told Richard.

Richard ignored her and moved closer to Sean. "Ramona called just after you left. She told me that you and Samantha had been out to her house to ask if she was missing a dog."

Sean steepled his fingers together. This was going to be interesting. "We didn't know it was your dog," Sean explained in a reasonable tone of voice, a tone that seemed to piss Richard off even more. "For that matter, we still don't know."

"Who else could it be?" Richard snarled. "Lassie?"

"I thought Lassie was a collie," Sean said. Then he went on before Richard could say anything else. "Samantha found the dog wandering out by the road. There was no collar on her."

"How could it be out on the road?" Richard demanded. "The thing was in its crate in the kitchen."

"Then obviously it's not your dog," Sean replied.

"Of course it is!" Richard yelled.

"Maybe someone let it out," Sean said.

"I bet Samantha did," Richard said promptly. "It would be just like her to do something like this. She's always going on about the rights of animals and stupid stuff like that. Wait till I tell her dad. She's going to be out on the street in two seconds flat. All the things I've done for her and this is how she repays me, by stealing my dog?"

"You should calm down and think about what you're saying," Sean said.

"Calm down!?" Richard yelled. "Calm down?!"

Bernie started to reach for her cell but Sean gestured for her to stop. He didn't want the police up here—for several reasons. But mostly what he wanted was to study Richard Colbert's reactions. At the moment, Richard seemed to Sean to be a man who had a low frustration tolerance.

He waited for another second and then he said, "First of all, as I said, we don't know this dog is Trudy."

"Don't be ridiculous. Of course she is."

"Is she microchipped?" Sean asked.

Richard shook his head. "Annabel never wanted to do it."

"Any special markings?"

Richard shook his head again. "Just call her. She'll answer to her name."

"That doesn't prove anything. She could be Trudy, but not your Trudy." Sean put up his hand to forestall Richard's comments. "But even if the dog that Samantha found is Trudy, why would she steal her and then tell Ramona she had her? Think about it. What you're suggesting makes no sense. Why would she tell me, for that matter?"

"I don't know," Richard said. "Maybe because she knew your daughters were investigating the ridiculous allegations my late and not too lamented wife made, and she thought Trudy could tell them something."

"Can you hear yourself?" Bernie said to him. "Trudy telling us something? Come on. I mean, I know Trudy is famous, but I didn't know talking was one of her talents."

A spurt of anger crossed Richard's face before he managed to erase it. He made a fist with his right hand and slammed it down into the open palm of his left hand. "Then you tell me what happened. I'm waiting to hear."

Sean shrugged. "The obvious answer is that someone let the dog out. The question is, who? Maybe it was Joanna."

Richard shook his head. "She'd never do something like that."

"Maybe it was an accident," Sean said.

"Joanna doesn't do accidents."

"Then someone else," Sean replied.

Richard's face contorted while he thought. "Melissa," he muttered. "The little bitch. I've had about all I can take of her."

That's interesting, Sean thought, as he waited for Richard to say more about Melissa. But he didn't. Instead he said, "I'll sort everything out later. Right now I need the dog. Where is she?"

Sean tried to put on an expression of sincere regret. "I would have told you if you'd given me the chance."

"Told me what?"

"Unfortunately, Trudy ran away immediately after Bernie got her washed. Bernie was putting her in the van when she just took off after a squirrel. Bernie looked forever, but she couldn't find her. Isn't that right, Bernie?"

"Oh, yes," Bernie said, taking up her father's lead. "It was terrible. Poor thing. But now that I know it's Trudy, I feel even worse."

"Is that a fact?" Richard said.

"It most certainly is," Bernie told him.

"All I can say is that that dog had better be around someplace."

"I'm sure someone will find her. In fact, we'll go out looking," Bernie said, which Sean thought was going a tad too far. "If we see her, you'll be the first to know," she chirped.

Richard rounded on her. "That tone doesn't fool me. I know you have something to do with this. I just don't know what. Yet."

Bernie put her hands on her hips and drew herself up on her stilettos. "Is that a fact? Well, maybe you're the one who helped her disappear. Maybe you did to her what you did to your wife. You had a motive."

Richard's eyebrows shot up. "Are you saying I killed her?"

"The dog? Your wife?" Bernie asked. "Which?"

"Both."

"No. *You* are saying that, not me," Bernie pointed out.

"You really are crazy," Richard said. He turned to Sean. "Your daughter is nuts. Do you know that?"

Sean didn't bother to suppress a smile. "She does elicit that reaction from some people."

"I think it's interesting that Annabel and Trudy are both female," Bernie said.

"I don't have to listen to this," Richard cried. But he stayed put.

Bernie continued, "From what I've heard, you have lots of problems with the female sex, but then I guess that's what happens when you get greedy. What did Annabel think of your running around? She can't have been happy about you screwing Joanna, then moving on to Melissa. And I'm not even going to talk about Joyce," Bernie said, taking a random shot. "No wonder her husband wanted a divorce."

"Is that what Joyce said?" Richard asked, his voice tight with suppressed emotion.

"Yes," Bernie lied. "It is."

"Really?"

"Really," Bernie repeated, feeling a small stab of guilt at what she was saying. The operative word here was *small*.

"You go ask her about her business," Richard said.

"You mean selling Avon?" Libby asked.

"Her other business. The one she was trying to develop."

"You mean the dog treats. We already know about those," Bernie said.

"I think it was too much for her, Annabel using another one of her ideas. I think it flipped her out."

"So Annabel stole the idea for the Puggables?" Libby asked.

"I wouldn't say *steal*," Richard said. "I'd say she was inspired by the dogs Joyce made."

"Inspired?" Bernie asked. "That's not the word Joyce used."

"I have no doubt of that. Annabel and I tried to work out something with her. We tried to come to some sort of understanding. But she wanted an immense sum of money—which we didn't have at the time. The agreement we were trying to work out fell apart. Annabel felt guilty. She tried to make it up to her, but I don't think Joyce ever forgave her. Not really. She's someone who can hold a grudge for a long time."

"Does she hold a grudge against you?" Libby asked.

"Yes, she does," Richard said. "We hardly speak. That's why I find her allegations about me so absurd."

"Interesting," Bernie said. "Then why were you over there?"

Richard blinked. "What do you mean?" he asked.

"Exactly what she said," Libby replied.

Richard's face froze. "I don't understand."

"We saw you, you know," Bernie informed him. "We were three-quarters of the way down the street when you pulled up to Joyce's house. Boy you made good time getting there. Was Joyce in this with you? Is that why you hightailed it over there? Or did she need some consolation? I'm told that grief and fear do that to some people—you know, awakens their sex drives. Tell me. I'm curious. Inquiring minds want to know."

"You'd better be careful what you say," Richard hissed.

"Or you'll what?" Bernie countered. "Kill me too?"

"Something much worse," Richard said.

"Oooh," Bernie said. "I'm scared."

"You should be," Richard said, and he turned and stomped down the stairs. "My lawyer will be in touch."

"Nothing like pissing people off, I always say," Sean commented as soon as he heard the door slam.

"What do you think he'll do?" Libby asked her dad.

"Get in touch with his lawyer."

"What could he sue us for?" Bernie demanded.

Sean shrugged. "Who knows? Lawyers can always find something."

Libby turned to her sister. "Really, Bernie, you didn't have to be so harsh."

"Harsh? Richard Colbert comes barging in here screaming and yelling about his dog and I was harsh?" Bernie cried, stung by her sister's criticism. "We're talking about someone who might have poisoned his wife in cold blood." Fixing her gaze on her dad, Bernie continued, "And as long as we're apportioning blame, Richard wouldn't have come up here if it wasn't for Trudy going missing."

"That's true," Libby acknowledged.

"Dad, where is the dog?" Bernie demanded.

"Yes. What is going on here?" Libby asked. "Please explain."

"I don't know where Trudy is," Sean told his daughters. It was the principle of the thing. He didn't like being interrogated by anyone, but especially not by his daughters.

Bernie raised an eyebrow. "What a big fat lie you just told."

"I don't lie," Sean blustered. What had happened to the

whole respect-your-father deal? He would never have talked to his dad this way. Ever. He wouldn't have been able to sit down for a week if he had.

"That's true," Bernie said. "You don't lie. You evade, omit, and confabulate." She continued, "Now I know you had the dog. I'm guessing that's why Samantha came up here, right? She took the dog and she wanted to speak to one of us. Only you were here instead."

"Why would she take the dog?" Sean asked.

"I guess we'll have to ask her," Libby said to Bernie. "Maybe we should call her up."

Sean crossed his arms over his chest. "Be my guest. Question your father's integrity."

"Spare me," Bernie said.

"Go ahead. Dial."

Bernie sighed. "What's the point? She'll just say what you told her to."

Sean certainly hoped that was the case. "You have no patience."

"Patience?" Bernie echoed. "What does patience have to do with anything? Next you're going to tell me that all will be revealed in time."

"Well, it will."

"When?" Libby demanded. "Can you give us a time frame here?"

Jeez, Sean thought. *She sounds just like me.* "I can't tell you," Sean answered. "Honestly. I would if I could, but I can't."

"Can't, or won't?" Bernie challenged.

"Both," Sean admitted. "It's for your own good."

Bernie snorted. "Ha. I don't believe that for one minute. If you're going to make up an excuse, at least make up a good one."

But what Sean had told them was true. The less they knew the better.

For a few seconds he debated about explaining that to

them but decided that would bring up a whole host of other questions he didn't want to answer. Sean almost wished he were back in the Mini Cooper with Samantha. That was actually easier than this. He watched Libby chew on the inside of her lip while she thought. Never a good thing.

"She can't be at Clyde's," she mused. "For one thing, Mrs. Clyde is allergic to dogs, and for another, I don't think Clyde would do something illegal."

"Never," Sean managed to get out without dissolving in a fit of laughter.

Libby turned to her father in alarm as another idea occurred to her. "Tell me you didn't get Marvin involved in this."

"I'm telling you I didn't get Marvin involved in this."

"I'm serious, Dad."

"So am I. I wouldn't do something like that." Aside from everything else, Marvin would probably lose the dratted dog when he took Trudy out for a walk. Sean raised his hand. "I swear. There. Is that good enough for you?"

Bernie tapped her nails on her thighs. "Well, she's got to be somewhere. Is she with Amber or Googie?"

Sean remained silent.

Bernie answered her own question. "No. That wouldn't work. Neither of them could have left the store and both of them live in places that don't allow pets. So that leaves only one person."

Sean put his poker face on as he waited for Bernie's conclusion.

"The dog's in Ines's house, isn't she?" Bernie asked.

"No," Sean lied. "She's not."

Bernie inspected his face. She was pretty sure her dad was lying, but when he got like this she could never be absolutely certain. "This was a bad idea, Dad," Bernie said. "A very bad idea." When she got hold of Samantha she was going to wring her neck. She had enough drama in her life without this.

Sean leaned forward slightly. Never defend. Always attack. That was his motto. It had served him well over the years and he wasn't about to change it now.

"I'll tell you what's a bad idea, Bernie. Saying what you said to Richard. Now that's a bad idea. You obviously haven't learned anything from your encounter with Rick."

Bernie looked unrepentant. "I was just trying to shake him up."

"And you certainly did that," Sean agreed.

"So what's the problem?" Bernie asked. "You always said that was a good thing to do, to get things moving."

Sean took in a deep breath and let it out. He knew he had said that in the past. And it *was* a good thing to do. But it was one thing having his men doing it and another thing having his daughters do it. Not that he was going to say that. Even he knew better than that.

"Next time, just leave that kind of thing to me," he told her instead. He judged that to be a fairly neutral comment.

Evidently Bernie didn't think so, given the look on her face. She put her hands on her hips. Her mouth fairly quivered with indignation. "After everything that's happened? After all the criminal cases we've been involved in, you don't think I can take care of myself?" she cried. "How can you say something like that?"

"Of course I think you can take care of yourself," Sean told his daughter. "I raised you, didn't I? I taught you the three deadliest judo moves, didn't I?" Much to his wife's dismay, he could have added. "You and your sister have done a great job solving the cases we've taken on. Better than some of my men. I guess I get a little overprotective from time to time. You know, your mom would come back from the other side and kill me if anything happened to either of you. And I'd deserve it."

Bernie felt all her annoyance and anger flow out of her. She went over, bent down, and gave her dad a hug. Libby did the same.

"Nothing is going to happen to any of us," Bernie said. "I promise."

Libby nodded. "And I second that promise. Let's stop arguing."

Sean grinned. "Works for me."

Suddenly he felt better. The truth was, he hated being the bad guy to his girls, and had ever since they were little. He'd left that role to his wife, much to her chagrin. He was the one who'd given them candy before meals and let them drive his car around the parking lot when they were twelve.

His wife, Rose, had called him a pushover when it came to them. And he was. And always would be. Not that any of his men or the civilians he dealt with over the years would have believed that about him, but fighting with his daughters just upset him. It was as simple as that. He leaned back as his daughters settled themselves on either side of the sofa across from him.

When they'd both gotten comfortable, Libby putting her feet up on the coffee table and Bernie folding her legs into a lotus position, he said, "I think it's time that someone talked to Melissa."

"Richard's probably talking to her already," Libby observed.

"I'm counting on it," Sean said.

Bernie gave him a quizzical look.

Sean explained, "Now that you've stirred up the pot, so to speak, we might as well take advantage of it." He looked out the window. It had begun to snow. Big fat flakes. They reminded him of Ivory Snow, the detergent his mom had used. "How about some tea?" he said to Libby. After this afternoon, he could certainly use something warm and soothing. "And a piece of your coconut cake wouldn't be so bad either."

Libby cocked her head. "You never eat coconut cake, Dad. You always eat white cake with chocolate icing."

Sean folded his hands in his lap. "Well, I've decided that today is a day for trying new things. Having a piece of coconut cake is one of those new things."

"Maybe we should see Joyce on the way over to Melissa's," Bernie suggested.

Sean nodded his assent. "Sounds like a plan to me."

Then he turned and watched the snow. It had gotten heavier in the past minute. It looked as if they were in for another storm. That would be two in the past week. He could be in Buffalo given the snow they were getting. Hopefully, this would be the last of it.

He'd liked snow when he was younger, liked the way it made the town quiet and clean, liked riding around in his squad car helping people out of the ditches they'd slid into, but that was when he could walk without thinking about it. Now, he wasn't so fond of the stuff. Even though it looked pretty, it was just another obstacle for him to have to overcome if he wanted to get from place to place. He shook his head to clear the negative thoughts away. No point in entertaining them. They didn't help anything anyway. But lately they'd been swarming around him like a bunch of no-see-ums in the spring.

A few minutes later, when Bernie and Libby had gone downstairs to get the tea and cake and check on things in the shop, Sean took his cell out of his pocket and called Ines. He wanted to see how she and Trudy were getting on. And, if truth be told, he liked hearing her voice. She had a knack for making him laugh.

Chapter 23

The snow kept up all Wednesday afternoon and well into the evening, drawing a veil over Longely. It piled up on the roads and snarled commuter traffic coming in from the city. Except for a few walk-ins, A Little Taste of Heaven was dead. At six-thirty Libby decided to send Amber and Googie home.

She and Bernie kept the shop open for another half hour and then closed when it was obvious that everyone this evening was going straight home. They spent the rest of the evening drinking hot chocolate, watching the news, and playing Scrabble with their dad. By the time the storm had moved over to Pennsylvania, it had dumped ten inches on Longely, an amount the town was ill-equipped to deal with.

Bernie and Libby got up early the next morning to shovel the sidewalk in front of their store.

"I can't believe we're doing this again," Libby groaned as she picked up the red plastic shovel she'd used yesterday and the day before that.

"Believe it," Bernie replied. She remembered that she had to go to Sam's Club to get the stuff she'd forgot to get yesterday, which meant digging out the van—again. Well, at least she didn't have to go to the gym. Shoveling definitely counted as her cardio workout for the day. "I bet we're going to get slammed today, just like we did after the last storm," she concluded, thinking of all the work that lay ahead of them.

"Well," Libby said, pausing at the curb, "at least the storm is good for our bottom line."

Bernie grunted. "If this kind of thing keeps up, we should hire someone to clear our sidewalk."

"Definitely," Libby said, unbuttoning her jacket. She'd just begun shoveling and she was getting warm already. "It'll be money well spent, in my opinion."

"What I want to know is, whatever happened to global warming? I thought we were going to turn into the tropics, have beachfront property, and be rich," Bernie complained as her cell started ringing.

It was Amber telling her she'd be an hour late. At least. Five minutes later, Googie did the same thing.

Bernie slipped her cell back in her pocket. She'd been expecting the calls, but that didn't mean she was happy about them. "I have a feeling we're going to be stuck in the shop all day today."

"I have a feeling you're right," Libby said. "If we'd been smart we would have baked extra last night."

But they hadn't been, so they spent the day making muffins, scones, brownies, and fruit pies, not to mention ginger chicken, Swedish meatballs, potato and leek soup, and apple and butternut squash bisque to feed the ravening hordes, although their dad pointed out that Mrs. Stein and Mr. Patella could hardly be considered ravening, much less part of a horde. It wasn't until Friday that they made it out to Melissa Geist's house.

She lived ten miles outside of Longely, on a back road to which the county plow had given what their dad would have called a lick and a promise. Basically, the road was fine for SUVs, but it wasn't so fine for top-heavy vans with rear-wheel drive.

"We should have waited another day," Libby said as Bernie fought to keep their vehicle on the road.

Bernie didn't say anything, because she was too busy concentrating on her driving.

Libby popped a piece of apricot bread in her mouth, glad that she wasn't the one behind the wheel. Bernie's nerves were steadier than hers in situations like this.

"I wonder where Joyce is?" Bernie mused.

As per their plan, they'd stopped at Joyce's house on their way to Melissa's. However, her car hadn't been there and no one had answered the doorbell.

"Maybe she's out selling Avon," Libby suggested.

"Or taking a vacation," Bernie replied.

"Now that would be an interesting thought," Libby said. She hadn't taken a vacation in ten years or more. "I think I've forgotten what that's like."

Bernie slowed down to a crawl over a treacherous piece of road. "Ah, the joys of being a small-business owner."

"Do I denote a bit of sarcasm?" Libby asked.

"Just a trace," Bernie replied.

Libby looked at her sister. She wasn't wearing any make-up this morning except for some black eyeliner, and she'd twisted her hair up on top of her head with a clip, but she still looked stunning in her black turtleneck sweater and black puffy vest. Now, if Libby was wearing that outfit she'd look like a schlep, but somehow Bernie made it work.

"Do you ever regret giving up your magazine job and coming back from California?" Libby asked. It was something she wondered about from time to time.

Bernie considered for a moment before answering. "You know, I really don't. I even like the snow—just not as much as we've been having. Don't get me wrong, it was fun out there, but I'm glad I came back. I like being home with you guys. And there was the boyfriend issue. That was huge."

"Yes, it was." And it hadn't been a good issue either, Libby recalled only too well. Bernie had arrived at the shop with just the clothes on her back. Figuratively speaking, of course. "Good," she said. "I'm glad you're back too."

"And I'm glad that you're glad," Bernie replied.

Libby laughed and went back to talking about Joyce. "We really should speak to her," she said, remembering what Richard had told them when he'd been up at their place. "Maybe she's gone to St. Croix and we could interview her there."

Bernie smiled. "Works for me. I could definitely use a little beach action."

Libby took another bite of her slice of apricot bread. "You sure you don't want some?" she asked Bernie, who shook her head.

"It's good," Libby told her.

"I'm certain that it is," Bernie answered.

Libby had added a touch of chopped candied ginger and some macadamia nuts to the batter and the combination had turned out better than expected. She ate the rest of the slice, even though she'd told herself she'd save some for later—talk about delusional behavior—dusted the crumbs off her puffy coat, and went back to looking out the window. The snow was like a white goose-down comforter blanketing everything. With the sun glinting off it, she had to scrunch up her eyes to see. As she was looking out she remembered something. She turned toward Bernie.

"You know that article that was in the paper about Annabel Colbert buying up the land to make that children's camp?"

"What about it?" Bernie asked.

Libby gestured to the land outside the window. "Well, this is the land she wanted to buy."

"Are you sure?"

"I'm positive. And look," she said as she pointed to the brown house coming up on their right. The cap of snow on the roof made it look like a mushroom. "There's Melissa's house. Right smack in the tract that Annabel was going to buy."

"Well, that's certainly interesting," Bernie said as she slowed down to make the turn into the driveway. "Can we say hello eminent domain, good-bye house?"

"Would the county do something like that?" Libby asked.

"In a heartbeat," Bernie told her. She gestured to the surrounding land. "A place like that would bring in people and businesses. It would give them tax dollars. There's nothing here now, at least nothing of any value."

"You think Melissa knew about Annabel's plan?" Libby asked.

"Yes, I do. How could she not? Especially given Annabel's personality. I don't think she could resist telling her, or at least hinting enough so that Melissa would find out."

Libby nodded as she studied Melissa's house. It was a small colonial, set back from the road by a couple hundred feet. A scrim of evergreens rising up like a phalanx flanked the house on either side. It wasn't fancy. But it was still Melissa's. Libby imagined how she'd feel if the town of Longely decided it had to widen the road and told her she'd have to move A Little Taste of Heaven. It wouldn't matter if the price the town offered her family was market value or not. She'd still be furious. And if it was a "friend" who was doing it, that would just make it worse.

Libby pointed to the small sign off to one side that read, PRECIOUS PUG. "Shouldn't that read Precious Pugs?" Libby asked as they drove past it and up toward the house. Now that they were closer, they could hear the sounds of dogs barking.

"Yes, it should," Bernie said as she maneuvered the van over three small piles of snow in the driveway. Evidently the snowblower had broken down or the person using it had given up, Bernie decided.

She parked on the right side of the driveway next to a

green Ford pickup truck and a large black Explorer. The Explorer had the words *Grooming by Appointment* lettered on the side, while the pickup truck had the logo *Precious Pug*. She turned the van's engine off. Now the sound of the dogs was louder, but not as loud as she'd expected.

It didn't sound to Bernie as if there were that many dogs in residence. Most of the noise seemed to be coming from the small building behind the house, to which outdoor runs were attached. When she thought about it, she realized that this seemed like an amateur operation, what a magazine she'd read had called "a backyard breeder." This had not been intended as a compliment. She'd expected Precious Pug to be bigger. More professional.

"It looks as if Melissa has company," Bernie noted.

"And there she goes," Libby said as a thin, black-haired woman walked out of the house a moment later.

She was dressed in jeans, serious snow boots, and a blue parka with the hood up. As Libby and Bernie watched, she marched over to her truck, got in, and took off. A plume of smoke marked the truck's progress until it hung a right onto Strafford three miles away and vanished from view.

"Let's do it," Bernie said. She swung her door open.

A blast of cold air rushed in. Somehow it felt even colder here than it had in town. She and Libby were almost to Melissa's house when the front door opened. The sound of barking followed Melissa as she stepped outside into the cold. Today, she was dressed in jeans, a flannel shirt, a down vest, and work boots, which contrasted with her bleached blond hair, crimson lipstick, and bright blue eye shadow. Two spots of bright pink on her cheeks completed the botched make-up job. Looking at her made Bernie want to send Melissa off for a month of enforced stay at remedial make-up school.

Bernie decided that she was one of those women who'd been pretty when they were younger and were still clinging to their youth. Never mind that the realities of the situation had changed.

Obviously when Melissa looked at herself in the mirror, she didn't see that the downward lines around her mouth and the furrows in her forehead gave her a look of perpetual discontentment. She didn't see that they offered nooks and crannies for her make-up to cake up in. She was definitely not aging well. Bernie wondered how she herself looked to other people. She wondered if she was deluding herself the way Melissa was.

"I take it you want to talk about Annabel," Melissa said to them when she got to the bottom step.

"Maybe we want to buy a pug," Bernie said. She wondered as she spoke what it was that Richard saw in her. Maybe it was that she was female and available? Because it certainly wasn't her looks or her charm.

"Sorry," Melissa said. "I don't have any available right now."

"How disappointing," Libby told her. "Can we see the dogs that you have?"

"No. You may not. They're all spoken for. Have you tried the Longely shelter?"

"No. We haven't," Bernie replied. "But thank you for the suggestion."

Melissa nodded.

"We probably should look there," Bernie said. "After all, come to think of it, we really don't need a dog with dental problems."

Melissa stiffened. "That New Hartford thing was absurd."

"That's not what Ramona said," Libby put in.

"Ramona doesn't know anything about dogs and neither did the judge. He was used to judging spaniels, and she knows as much about pugs as I do about Croatia. But you didn't come out here to discuss the disqualification,

did you? Just like you didn't come out here to buy a dog."
When neither Bernie nor Libby replied, she answered herself, "No. I didn't think you did. It looks as if I was right
the first time. You want to talk about Annabel. It makes
sense. I've been expecting you."

Everyone was expecting them, Bernie thought. Obviously, they were becoming too predictable.

"According to Richard, you've talked to everyone else
who was there when Annabel died. I'm the last one left.
Probably because I'm the most inconvenient to get to, is
that correct?"

Libby allowed how she was correct.

"You should have called first. It would have saved you
the trouble of coming out here. I have nothing to say to
you. Absolutely nothing. In fact, Richard gave me the name
of his lawyer in case you showed up. You can talk to him."

Bernie stamped her feet. She should have worn her Uggs,
because even though she had socks on, the cold was seep-
ing up through her motorcycle boots.

"Now I find that very interesting, because Richard's the
reason we're here, isn't that right, Libby?"

"Indeed it is," Libby replied, wondering where Bernie
was going with this.

"He's the one who said we should come and talk to you
about Annabel—and he didn't mean it in a nice way, if you
get my meaning—so I'm having a little trouble believing
he gave you his lawyer's phone number. I call that a case of
wishful thinking," Bernie said.

The lines around Melissa's mouth turned down a little
more. "What do you mean?"

"What do you think I mean?" Bernie replied.

"I don't have a clue."

Now it was Bernie's turn to look at Melissa as if she was
the idiot. "Think about it. He implied—no, he did more then
imply—he stated that you had information about Annabel's
death."

Melissa remained silent.

"He implicated you in her death," Libby told her.

"I don't believe you. Richard wouldn't say anything like that," Melissa declared. But Bernie could see by the way she was biting her lip that her confidence was slipping away.

"Indeed he did," Bernie replied.

"You're making that up."

Bernie buried her hands in her armpits to warm them up. Why she hadn't worn her gloves she didn't know. "Do I look as if I am? What did you think? That sleeping with Richard would give you special treatment? That he would protect you? The only person he really cares about is himself. He's a classic, textbook narcissist."

Melissa blinked.

"And yes, to answer your unasked question, he told me that you two were sleeping together," Bernie lied. "Not that he had to. Everyone knows." Changing strategy, she said, "He doesn't seem as if he's a very nice man. Trying to lay the blame for his wife's death off on you is pretty tacky."

Melissa shook herself. Bernie decided she looked as if she'd been slapped.

"I didn't have anything to do with that," Melissa said.

Bernie didn't say anything. Neither did Libby.

"Why would I?" Melissa cried.

Libby wound her scarf more tightly around her neck. If she didn't get back in the car soon, she was going to turn into a Popsicle. "Oldest reason in the world," she replied. "Because you were jealous and you wanted Richard all to yourself."

"Oh puh-leez," Melissa said. "Then why didn't I kill Joanna?"

Bernie smiled. "Because she's not sleeping with him anymore."

Melissa pointed her finger at Bernie. "Hey, I had everything to gain by keeping Annabel alive."

"Do tell."

"No. It's true. If Trudy went to Westminster and won, it would make my reputation as a breeder. My dogs would be worth thousands and thousands of dollars. Why would I do anything to jeopardize that?"

Bernie smiled. "Why would you indeed? Did you think you were doing Annabel a favor sleeping with her husband? Did you think she didn't care?"

"She didn't know."

"Are you so sure?" Bernie said.

"And even if she did know, she didn't care."

"If she didn't care, why did she say what she did at Trudy's dinner party? I don't remember you being excluded."

Melissa opened her mouth and closed it again.

"Exactly," Bernie said. "Maybe that's why Annabel was buying this land and having it plowed under and turned into a camp for disabled children. Maybe that was because of you and Richard."

"So what?" Melissa said, confirming Bernie's opinion that she'd already known about the deal. "That doesn't have anything to do with me. I own this house."

"I know you do," Bernie said. "But you and I both know that the county would seize it under the eminent domain statute in a heartbeat if the sale went through. They wouldn't let someone's house stand in the way of something like this. If I remember correctly, and I think I do, your house happens to be in the middle of where the park is supposed to be.

"Then you wouldn't have a kennel. I would think it would be difficult to find a new spot. Well, not difficult. Irritating. I know I'd be furious if it was happening to me. It would make me want to kill the person who was doing it. At least that's what I thought when I read about it in the local paper. But then maybe you're a calmer person than I am.

"Of course, luckily for you, now that Annabel is dead,

she can't buy the land for the Annabel Colbert Park for Children, or whatever she was going to call it. Sounds like a motive to me," Bernie said. "What do you think, Libby?"

"You know what Dad says," Libby replied. "If it sounds like a duck and looks like a duck . . ."

Bernie finished the sentence for her. "It is a duck."

"It really was a brilliant strategy, if you think about it," Libby said. "With one stroke, Annabel becomes a benefactress and punishes her husband and his latest squeeze—meaning you—at the same time."

"What's your take on it?" Bernie asked Melissa.

"My take," Melissa spit out, "is that I don't have to talk to you. I'm not going to talk to you anymore. I've wasted enough time listening to your nonsense, and I think you should go to hell. Now get off my land."

"Tsk-tsk," Bernie said. "So rude. Didn't your mother ever tell you you attract more bees with honey than vinegar?"

"You'll be sorry if you don't." And with that Melissa turned, stomped up the stairs, opened the door to her house, went in, and slammed the door shut. The noise sounded like a shot and set the dogs barking again.

"I have to say she doesn't have a very good disposition," Libby said as she and Bernie made their way to their van.

"Libby, what do you think about taking a quick peek at the kennel before we go?" Bernie asked. She jerked her head in the direction of the garagelike structure at the back of the house.

"I think it's time to go back to the shop, that's what I think."

"It'll just take us a minute."

"Maybe so, but Melissa is watching us from the front window, and given what she just said, I think she might actually come out with a shotgun if we don't get out of here pretty soon."

"Don't be ridiculous," Bernie replied. "She was just talking."

"Maybe. But it's a well-known fact that everyone in the country has some sort of firearm," Libby said.

"Please. You've been watching too many grade B movies. We're talking about Westchester here. Westchester is not the country."

Libby indicated the surrounding land. "Well, if this isn't country, what is it? The city?"

"I meant country country. Like up near the Tug Hill Plateau."

"Wherever that is."

"It's in New York State, for heaven's sake."

"Fine," Libby said, conceding the point. "But realistically what are we going to see peering through the window anyway, except a lot of pugs?"

"True," Bernie allowed.

"Plus, I'm freezing. This wind is killing me. I need to be somewhere warm."

Now that, Bernie wasn't going to argue about. She was freezing too.

"And we can always come back if we need to," Libby pointed out.

"True, for the third time," Bernie said, and she smiled and waved at Melissa. "Bye-bye," she called out.

The window shade went down. Libby and Bernie both got in the van. Bernie started up the engine and turned on the heater, which supplied an anemic blast of warm air. Still, she reflected, it was better than nothing.

"The question is," Bernie said as she began to back out of the driveway, "is the whole land thing enough of a motive for Melissa to kill Annabel?"

"Losing your house, losing your business," Libby replied. "I gotta say it would be for me."

"Me too," Bernie agreed. "I hope Richard was worth

it," she said as they got onto the back road again. "But somehow I doubt it."

"I know what Annabel would say, if you could ask her that question," Libby said. She moved the heat lever up another notch. Not that that was going to help much. The heater had been having issues since the van hit 125,000 miles.

"So do I," Bernie replied, clicking the radio on.

The sisters spent the rest of the way back talking about a dinner they were about to submit a menu for and about the feasibility of doing Rock Cornish game hens on individual potato pancakes as a main course.

Chapter 24

It was seven o'clock at night and R.J.'s was empty. The pre-dinner crowd had departed, while the post-dinner crowd hadn't arrived yet. This was the time Bernie liked the place the best. And it wasn't only because she could hang out with Brandon now.

It was because the place had a reassuring, old-fashioned quality to it that was apparent when no one was there. Bernie wasn't sure if it was the peanuts you had to shell, the popcorn machine, the dartboard on the far wall, the faded posters of movie stars hanging on the walls, the comfortably worn seats, or just the fact that she'd been coming to this place for as long as she could legally drink. But whatever it was, it worked for her. She felt calmer here, less agitated.

She and Libby had come home from Melissa's, checked on the shop, and fed their dad corn chowder and a grilled Black Mountain ham and imported Swiss cheese sandwich on freshly baked olive and rosemary French bread, along with a small salad composed of rocket, endive, and finely chopped walnuts. Then they'd closed the shop and gone over to R.J.'s to meet Marvin and Brandon for a drink. It had been a long and not terribly productive day, and both Bernie and Libby felt in need of one.

"Why don't you have a drink with us too?" Bernie asked Brandon as he poured a Guinness into her glass. "No one is here."

Brandon shook his head. He made it a point never to drink on the job. He'd seen too many bartenders take that route and nothing good ever came of it. Drinking could also get him fired. His boss had strict rules about that.

Bernie popped a peanut in her mouth. "I don't like drinking alone."

"You're not drinking alone," Brandon pointed out. "You're drinking with Marvin and Libby."

Bernie batted her eyelashes. "But I want to drink with you."

Brandon snorted. "You're just telling me to drink because you're in a bad mood and you want to cause trouble."

"Me, do something like that?" Bernie asked. She used her best little-girl voice.

"Yes, you."

Bernie didn't say anything, because what Brandon said was true. She was in a bad mood and she did want to cause trouble. It wasn't nice, but there it was.

"You want to talk about it?" Brandon asked.

"Why I'm in a bad mood?"

"Yes."

"Not really," Bernie said.

"Sure you do."

Bernie took a sip of her Guinness. The beer was good but filling. What had the company advertised it as? A sandwich in a glass? Something like that.

"No, I don't want to talk about it," she answered Brandon after she'd swallowed.

"You'd rather brood and be miserable," Brandon said.

"Exactly," Bernie said. "I like wallowing in my misery."

"Well, we don't allow that at R.J.'s."

"The wallowing or the misery?"

"Both. So, how are things coming?"

"The phrase is, 'How are things going?' "

"Fine. How are things going?"

"They're going nowhere fast," Bernie replied.

"I take it you're talking about the Annabel Colbert case?"

"What else would I be talking about?"

"Global warming. Dogs. Business."

"No. It's Annabel Colbert. She was a pain in the butt when she was alive and she's a pain in the butt now that she's dead."

"Bernie!" Libby cried.

"Well, it's true," Bernie retorted.

Brandon took a sip of hot chocolate and put his cup back by the register. "It's that bad?"

"It's depressing," Libby said.

"Very," Bernie said. "We've talked to everybody and we're making no progress whatsoever. We're totally bogged down. Maybe everyone is right. Maybe we should give this up. We have tried. It's not as if we're going to have Annabel's ghost following us around if we call it a day."

"You never know," Libby said. "She was pretty demanding when she was alive. Maybe she's the same way dead."

Bernie groaned. "An eternity with Annabel Colbert. What an unattractive thought."

"And you did promise," Brandon said.

"We swore," Libby said. "That's even worse."

Marvin took a sip of his IPA. "This is not like either of you."

"It's probably the weather," Bernie said.

"I wish," Libby said. "Basically we're no further along now than we were when we started this thing."

"Not at all?" Marvin asked.

"Not really," Libby said. "We've found out a lot of stuff, but nothing leads any place. It turns out that everyone seems to have had an equally good motive for killing Annabel."

Brandon laughed. "Oh, to be rich and hated."

"It's not funny," Bernie protested.

"Sure it is," Brandon retorted.

"She was not a well-liked person," Libby observed.

Bernie snorted. "You think?"

Marvin built a man out of peanuts. "Well, it seems that knowing the motives is a kind of progress," Marvin said when he was done.

"It is and it isn't," Libby replied. "If everybody has a motive, it's like nobody has a motive—if you get me."

"Not really," Marvin admitted.

"I don't get it either," Brandon said. "After all, some people's motives have to be better than other people's motives. It's just a matter of ranking them."

"I don't think it's that simple," Bernie said as she swept the pile of empty peanut shells she'd managed to accumulate onto the floor with the side of her hand.

"Try us and see," Marvin suggested.

"Yeah," Brandon said. "It's not as if we have anything else to do right now."

Libby put her hand out to Bernie. "You start," she said.

"Okey dokey." Bernie ate two more peanuts. Then she began. "Let's start with the husband, Richard Colbert."

"It's always blame the guy," Brandon interjected.

Bernie shot him a look.

Brandon held up his hand. "Sorry," he said. "Go on."

"Thank you. He probably has the biggest reason," Bernie continued. "According to Clyde, Annabel was going to leave him. Unfortunately for Richard, she had all the assets in her name. All the liabilities were in his."

"My aunt and uncle did something like that for tax purposes," Brandon said.

"As did the Colberts," Bernie said.

"So, you're saying that Annabel owned everything," Marvin said.

"Exactly," Libby replied.

"But why not get a divorce?" he asked. "He would still be entitled to a large part of the property. Wouldn't that be simpler?"

"Evidently not to him. He must have thought this was a more straightforward way of solving his problem," Bernie answered. "Divorces can be long and messy and very, very expensive. And then there was his string of infidelities. That wouldn't go over well in court. But poisoning someone . . . Hey. Problem solved."

"Not if you get caught," Marvin pointed out.

"Well, there is that minor inconvenience," Libby replied. "But so far no one has been. Annabel's death hasn't even been declared a homicide. And even if it was, the body was cremated. Basically, there's no way this is going to come back and bite Richard in the ass."

"Next," Bernie went on, "we have Joyce, the best friend, who isn't really a best friend to Annabel at all. She seems to be consumed with rage and jealousy toward Annabel, because she thinks that Annabel stole her idea for the Puggables and got rich off it."

"Did she?" Brandon asked.

"I'm not sure. From the way Joyce tells it, yes. Absolutely. I'm sure Annabel would have a different take on the matter, but, unfortunately, I can't ask her. However, whether Annabel did or didn't steal Joyce's idea isn't really relevant. What is relevant is that Joyce believes that's the case. She claims that she made the actual models the Puggables are based on as a present to Annabel.

"And now, according to Joyce, Annabel was about to do the same thing to her all over again with the idea for the dog treats that Joyce had come up with. Joyce claims that Annabel promised to sign a contract with her, but never did. Joyce isn't that well off. And of course Annabel is—*was*—filthy rich, thanks to Joyce's ideas."

"What do they say?" Marvin asked. "Fool me once, shame on you. Fool me twice, shame on me."

"My mom used to tell us that all the time," Libby noted. "In any case, you can see where Joyce would be a little bit annoyed at Annabel one way or another."

"Just a tad," Brandon said.

"Next," Libby continued, "we have Ramona, the dog trainer. She was about to lose her shot at mounting Trudy's campaign for Westminster. Annabel, for reasons we're still not clear on, had decided to replace her with someone else. Now this is a very big deal for Ramona. Mounting a campaign is serious stuff. If Trudy even got into the show, that would be a big step up for Ramona careerwise. Kind of like riding a horse in the Kentucky Derby. Plus, there's her house."

"What about it?" Marvin asked.

"The house comes with the job. If she loses her job, she'll lose the place she's living."

"That's not such a big deal," Brandon interjected. "She'll find a new place. People do it all the time."

"Ah, yes," Libby said. "There's only one problem. The cats."

"The cats?" Marvin echoed.

"Evidently, she's a cat person."

"And?" Marvin said. "So what?"

"Dad said she had twenty—"

"He said more like fifty, maybe more," Bernie corrected.

"Cats that she cares for inside her house. There are more outside. I'm guessing that leaving them—which she'd have to do if she moved—would be a wrenching experience," Libby said. "She told my dad that cats were her passion. Given what he saw, that certainly seems to be the case."

"So she's one of those scary cat rescue ladies," Brandon said.

Bernie nodded. "Exactly. And she was about to lose her base of operations, a base that would be difficult to replicate. Next, we have Melissa, Trudy's breeder. Annabel was about to take her house away, possibly because she was sleeping with Richard. Well, she wasn't going to take her house away directly, but she was going to buy Forrester's Way and set up a camp for disabled children called Puggables' Paradise."

Brandon made a retching sound.

"Unfortunately for Melissa," Bernie said, ignoring Brandon's antics, "her house and kennel are in the middle of the land that Annabel was buying. She'd have to move."

"So we have four people who are going to either lose their livelihoods, or be severely inconvenienced thanks to Annabel," Brandon summarized.

Libby nodded. "And then we have Joanna, now Richard's assistant, who once was Annabel's assistant. It turns out she had a grudge against Annabel because Annabel seduced her husband, Rick Crouse, for the pure fun of it. And lastly, we come to the aforementioned husband, Rick Crouse, the wannabe actor, who was getting money from Annabel for his 'art.' "

Brandon turned to Bernie. "How come you're not giving me money for my 'art'?"

Bernie rolled her eyes. "You don't really want me to answer that, do you?"

"Not really," Brandon said after a moment's thought.

"Good," Bernie told him.

"What happened with Rick Crouse?" Marvin asked.

"Annabel cut him off," Libby said, taking up where she'd left off. "So even though he didn't gain directly from her death, his ego—and it's pretty large—might not have been able to take the rejection."

"Hurt pride?" Brandon said. "That's a pretty good reason right there."

"Yes. The male ego is a fragile thing," Bernie said.

Brandon reached over and got his hot chocolate. "You wound Marvin and me to the quick."

Bernie laughed. "You both look it. And speaking of male pride, have we mentioned that Richard was sleeping with Melissa, and heaven knows who else while he was married to Annabel?"

"Yes, you have," Marvin said.

"What happened to Ramona?" Brandon asked. "Did you forget to mention her?"

"I think she may not worship at that altar, if you get my meaning," Bernie said.

Everyone was quiet for a moment.

"I see what you mean," Marvin said after he'd drunk some more of his beer.

"Okay on the motive," Brandon said. "Let's move on to the means."

"The means are simple," Libby said. "Someone put a cocktail of insecticides in a bottle of Annabel's wine and then sealed it back up. Under ordinary circumstances it might not have proved fatal, but since Annabel had a heart condition it was enough to kick her over to the other side."

"And everyone knew about her heart thing?" Brandon asked.

Bernie ate another peanut. "Everyone who was at that dinner knew," she said.

"And Richard poured the wine?" Marvin asked.

Libby nodded. "That would be correct. He was also the one who opened the bottle."

"Then that seems pretty clear-cut," Brandon opined.

Libby stifled a yawn. It had been a long day and she was beginning to crash. "Not really. The wine was opened at the table in front of everyone," she said. "Someone had to have put the insecticides in earlier."

"How did they know which bottle to put it in?" Marvin asked. "Maybe the poison was meant for someone else?"

Bernie shook her head. "This was the only kind of wine Annabel drank."

"Who knew that?" Marvin asked.

"Probably just about everyone who was there. I think Annabel told me she'd been drinking it for a year. The bottle was very distinctive. And she didn't share."

"Where did the wine come from?" Brandon asked.

"Spain," Libby answered.

"No. I meant where was it bought?"

"At The Grape," Libby told him.

"Ah, yes," Brandon said. "The fancy schmancy liquor store that charges a thousand percent markup."

"Yes. That one," Bernie said.

"When was the wine delivered?" Marvin asked.

"Good question," Libby said. That would give them a timeline. "Unfortunately, we don't know the answer."

Bernie whipped out her cell phone. "This is true, but I know someone who might," she replied.

"And who might that be?" Marvin asked.

"Our man on the inside," Bernie quipped as she punched in Samantha's number.

"Sam," Brandon said.

"Does she come in here?" Libby asked.

"Everyone comes in here," Marvin said.

"Samantha," Bernie said. "Samantha, I can't hear you. The connection's bad."

Marvin, Libby, and Brandon stopped talking.

"That's better," Bernie said. Then she asked her question. "Sam says they didn't get any wine deliveries when she was there," Bernie repeated, for the benefit of everyone else. Then she added, "Since she says she got to the house a little after nine and The Grape doesn't open until eleven, it's a fair bet that nothing was sent over."

"Ask her about the day before," Libby said.

Bernie did. "She wasn't there the day before," Bernie told them after she'd said good-bye to Samantha.

"I have an idea," Brandon said as he picked up R.J.'s house phone and dialed.

Now it was Marvin, Libby, and Bernie's turn to wait. There were a fair number of *yups* and *I sees* from Brandon as Peter Mahir checked the invoices after Brandon asked him about deliveries to the Colbert house.

Peter Mahir was the owner of The Grape. A chatty kind of guy, he'd inherited the shop from his dad. It had been the kind of place that specialized in two-dollar wines and three-dollar bottles of the hard stuff. With the help of his wife and assiduous attendance at all the charity functions and balls, Peter had worked the store up to someplace that now catered to the rich and the superrich. Bernie figured it had to generate a million or so a year easy. Not that she was jealous or anything like that. Well, maybe just a tiny bit.

"The Grape has not delivered to the Colbert house in the past three weeks," Brandon announced after he'd hung up.

"Richard could have ordered from someplace else," Libby observed.

"Possibly, but unlikely," Brandon said. "Richard has an account with The Grape and the other places around here don't carry Annabel's wine."

Everyone was quiet for a moment as they digested the latest piece of information.

"It doesn't matter anyway," Libby finally said after eating two handfuls of peanuts. "The salient point here is how did someone reseal the bottles? I saw them in the pantry and they all looked perfectly fine."

"Would you have noticed if anything had been amiss?" Marvin asked.

"Yes, I would," Libby declared. "I had to move the bottles to make room for some of the appetizers. And everyone was in the room when Richard opened that bottle of wine."

"How many bottles of wine were there?" Marvin asked.

"Four altogether," Libby replied. "And they were all sealed. We're not talking about cartons' worth here."

"So how did they get the insecticides in the bottle?" Marvin asked.

"That's the easy part," Brandon said.

Everyone looked at him.

"Truly," Brandon said.

"I could see how you could get the cork out and put it back in," Bernie said. "It would be a pain, but with a pump you could do it. What I don't see is how you could seal the bottle back up so it's not noticeable."

"Allow the Great Brandolini . . ."

Bernie raised her eyebrows. "Brandolini?"

"Do not mock The Great One."

"The Great One?" she echoed.

"Yes. The Great One," Brandon said firmly as he rummaged behind the counter and came up with two bottles of wine. The first one's cork was covered in foil, while the second bottle's cork was covered in plastic.

As Bernie, Libby, and Marvin watched, Brandon tried to take the foil covering off. It was a no-go. Next he took the bottle with the plastic bottle cover, positioned his hands on either side of the bottle, and gently lifted it off. Then he very carefully put it back on.

"Voila," he said, holding out his hand. "Presto chango. The Great Brandolini has once again demonstrated his magnificence."

"Let me try," Bernie said, leaning over and moving the

bottle toward her. "This is easy," she said after she lifted the cover off and carefully put it back on again.

Brandon nodded. "It works with some bottles but not with others."

"I think we should see if they have a bottle of Annabel's wine at The Grape and find out," Marvin suggested.

Libby nodded. "But even if it's true, I don't see how it helps us that much."

"Spoilsport," Brandon said.

"Seriously. I'm guessing that everyone who was at the birthday party had access to that bottle of wine at one time or another. They all either lived in the house or visited fairly frequently. Except for Rick."

Bernie took another sip of her beer. "I wouldn't count him out if I were you. He could have been up there with Annabel when everyone else was gone."

Libby nodded. "I suppose."

"The bigger question is," Bernie continued, "how many people know about what Brandon just showed us?"

"Anyone who works in the bar business knows," Brandon said.

Libby and Bernie looked at each other. "Rick," they said simultaneously.

"Why Rick?" Marvin asked. "I thought he was an actor."

"He is," Bernie said. "But lots of actors either tend bar or wait tables to make ends meet while they're waiting for their big break. I think it's time for another chat with Rick Crouse."

"I think I should come with you," Brandon said.

Bernie thought for a moment. Considering the way she and Rick had parted company that might not be such a bad idea.

"Here's my question," Marvin said before Bernie could answer Brandon.

Everyone waited.

"Why did whoever poisoned Annabel do it then?" Marvin asked.

"I don't get what you mean," Libby said.

"Okay. Why did whoever killed Annabel choose to do it then, with all those witnesses? Annabel always drank that wine, right?"

"According to Peter Mahir, she'd been drinking it ever since she and Richard came back from Spain about a year ago," Brandon said.

Marvin stifled a cough. "So why not try to poison her when no one was around? Then she would have gone into a coma and died and everyone would have thought she died of her heart problems."

"Maybe whoever killed her had just discovered whatever it was that Annabel had done to piss them off," Bernie suggested.

"But even then, why not just put it in the bottle and wait? Why make her death a public event?"

"Because someone wanted it witnessed?" Libby said.

Marvin nodded. "That's the logical conclusion."

"But why?" Bernie asked.

Marvin shook his head. "I don't know, but I have a feeling if you find out the answer to that, you'll discover who your murderer is."

"I think you're making this thing way too complicated," Brandon objected. "I think whoever put the poison in Annabel's wine did it then because they wanted the pleasure of seeing Annabel die. It's as simple as that."

"You may be right," Bernie said after a moment.

"I always am," Brandon said smugly.

Bernie laughed and punched him in the arm.

Chapter 25

Samantha dropped her cell back on her lap. "That was your daughter asking me about wine deliveries at the Colbert house the day Annabel was killed," she informed Sean.

"I know," he said.

"How did you know?" Samantha asked as she made a one-handed turn onto Applegate.

Sean wished she'd use two hands on the steering wheel, but he decided not to say anything on that topic. He'd noticed that any criticism of her driving seemed to incite Samantha to new heights of recklessness. And, he told himself, things could be worse. She could be driving with her knees and texting at the same time. Thank heavens for small favors.

"You haven't answered me," Samantha said as they tore down the block, scattering slush as they went.

"That's simple—I know because I'm a great detective."

"Seriously," Samantha said.

Sean readjusted his legs to get slightly more comfortable before replying. "Seriously," he said. "I know because you used the name Bernie at least twice in the conversation."

"I could know other Bernies."

"You could, but it's not a very common name, at least not these days."

Actually, it was a rather old-fashioned name, which was one of the reasons he liked it—not that the name had influenced his younger daughter's behavior in the least. Sean was on the verge of saying that to Samantha, but when she swerved around an oncoming pickup truck, he lost his train of thought in the ensuing flash of terror he felt.

His next thought when he recovered was that he couldn't believe he was riding in Samantha's Mini Cooper again, an idea he'd been trying to repress for the last five minutes or so. And he was riding with her at night, no less.

After all, you could hardly see the thing when it was light out, let alone when it was dark. And Sean didn't even want to think about what would happen if it snowed. Then the dratted thing would probably be invisible. For the first time, he was happy Esmeralda was painted lime green. The only good thing was that most people were home now eating dinner and watching TV, which meant less traffic on the road.

Not that he had anyone else to blame for his predicament this time but himself. He'd wanted to see how Ines and Trudy were doing together. Okay. He felt slightly guilty about what he'd done and he wanted to make sure everything was okay. He knew if he called, Ines would tell him everything was fine even if it wasn't. The only way to make sure everything was all right was to go there.

As his dad used to say to his mom whenever he was about to do something she disapproved of, sometimes a man's got to do what a man's got to do, which in this case had entailed calling up Samantha and asking her for a lift over to Ines's house. Given the circumstances, she was the only person he could turn to.

And this time, to be on the safe side, he'd left a note for his daughters telling them he'd gone out. That way they wouldn't start looking for him, like they had the last time—

or even worse, perish the thought, call the police. How embarrassing would that be? He didn't even want to think about it. If that happened, he'd hear about it from Clyde every day for the rest of his life. He repressed a shudder and considered the conversation he'd just heard.

"Were there any deliveries at all that day?" Sean asked, picking up on the line of questioning Bernie had initiated with Samantha.

Samantha chewed on her bottom lip while she thought. "No," she finally said. "No one."

"How about the florist?"

Samantha shook her head. "Annabel wasn't having flowers. She thought the Puggables were enough in the decoration department."

"Cleaning crew?"

Samantha shook her head. "They were there two days before."

"Could they have had access to where the wine was kept?"

Samantha shook her head again. "Richard keeps the wine in this wine-safe thing under lock and key. I think it makes him feel important."

Scratch that line of inquiry, Sean thought. "Any food deliveries?"

"Except for your daughters, no." Samantha frowned as an idea occurred to her.

"What?" Sean asked.

"I'm just thinking that maybe I should have told Bernie that you're with me," Samantha mused, changing the subject. "It didn't occur to me. But maybe I should have. It feels kind of weird not saying anything. I don't know why, but it does. Maybe I should call her back."

"No," Sean answered quickly. "You don't have to call her. It's not necessary. It's not necessary at all."

"Why?"

"Why what?"

"Why isn't it necessary?"

"Because it's just not," Sean snapped.

He felt foolish explaining to Samantha that he didn't want his daughters to know where he was going. In truth, there was no reason they shouldn't know. In fact, he knew that Bernie and Libby would be perfectly happy to hear he was at Ines's. Actually, to be honest, they'd probably be overjoyed.

They'd been trying to bring them together for years. They liked Ines and she liked them. Maybe he just couldn't bear admitting that they'd been right. Maybe it was the Trudy issue, which he didn't want them to have any official knowledge of. Or maybe it was that he just liked to have a space of his own where his children couldn't intrude. He knew he was being ridiculous and pigheaded and all those other words his wife used to call him. But there it was. And there it would stay.

"Are you always this grumpy?" Samantha asked.

"Always," Sean retorted. "I make it a point of honor."

Samantha laughed, and after a few seconds Sean laughed with her.

"You know," she said, "the police came to my house and asked me about Trudy, just like you told me they would."

"And what did you tell them?"

"What you told me to say."

"And what happened?" Sean asked.

"Nothing happened. They took my statement and left. I don't think my father believed me when I told him I didn't know anything about Trudy, but tough beans on him. He doesn't believe anything I say anyway. Neither does my Nazi stepmother and her spoiled-rotten little spawn."

"Spawn?" Sean repeated. "How many children does your stepmother have?"

"Two spoiled brats. Why?"

"Because spawn implies lots." God, he thought as that

sentence left his lips. He'd been infected by the Bernie virus.

Samantha shrugged. Sean noted that she seemed unimpressed with his linguistic differentiation.

"Whatever," she said as she zoomed into a parking space in front of The Right Paws.

The Right Paws was a high-end pet shop that specialized in things like real pearl collars and cashmere sweaters for "companion animals," also known as pets in a less PC time.

"Why are we stopping here?" Sean asked once they came to a full halt.

Looking in the window, which featured a rhinestone collar, a mohair doggie bed, and an all-leather cat carrier, Sean couldn't help thinking that some people in this town definitely had way, way too much money in their bank accounts.

Samantha's eyes widened in astonishment. "To get Trudy a little something, of course. You wouldn't want to go there empty-handed, would you?"

Sean snorted. "Perish the idea. Trudy is a dog. Trudy won't care."

"Of course she will. Even dogs have feelings."

"Up to a point," Sean said "Only up to a point."

"What point? They get scared, they miss people, they get excited, they get depressed."

"Fine," said Sean, conceding the issue.

"They have birthday parties," Samantha continued.

"Not most of them."

"My mom always used to buy our bassett hound Victor two Big Macs and a large order of French fries on his birthday. And he liked to watch reruns of *Sea Hunt*."

Sean threw up his hands. "I get it. I get it. But then, what's wrong with Petco or Sam's Club?" he asked. "Why can't we get something there instead?"

Samantha shot him a disapproving look. "Most of the

stuff in those places is made in China. Do you want Trudy to get sick?"

"No. But surely not all—"

"Do you want to take that chance?" Samantha said, cutting Sean off.

He decided it wasn't worth the trouble finishing his sentence. He wasn't having much luck in that department with Samantha. Actually, she was worse than Bernie in that way. Or maybe he didn't want to pursue the topic because he was having trouble thinking.

Every time he looked at Samantha's orange hair, bright pink T-shirt, red leather jacket, and pink-and-purple-striped mittens, he got a mild case of vertigo. That was another thing he liked about Ines. He could count on her clothes being . . . well . . . just regular clothes. They made her look nice without calling attention to themselves.

"Anyway," Samantha continued, "my friend in there will give us a discount."

"Super," Sean muttered as he began to extract himself from the Mini Cooper.

Now a box of dog biscuits would probably cost him only fifteen dollars instead of seventeen. When he was a kid, his mom had gone to the butcher and gotten the scraps. That's what their dogs had eaten. They didn't have any dog food. They didn't have any treats. They ate what everyone else ate and got along just fine. Now they had ninety-seven varieties of dog food on the market. It was ridiculous.

"You're doing better getting out of Esmeralda," Samantha said as Sean exited the car.

Sean grunted. He didn't say anything, but secretly he was delighted that that was the case. Either he was getting better physically or he was learning the technique of exiting a car built for a midget. Both were acceptable to him. His feeling of satisfaction, however, vanished when he got in the store and saw a poster tacked up on the bulletin board near the cash register. There was a picture of Trudy front and center. Underneath, in twenty-point type, were the words *Lost Dog. Reward: $1,000 for information leading to her return.* And then it gave a phone number to call.

Sean was about to ask who had put up the poster when Samantha started talking.

"Wow," she said to Sean. "A thousand bucks. That's a lot of money. Maybe we should start looking for that dog. Whaddaya think?"

Sean reflected that she did everything but nudge him in the ribs and wink at him. "Sure," he said as he gritted his teeth. "Why not?"

Samantha tugged at a lock of her hair. "I sure could use the money."

"Me too," the girl behind the counter said.

She has to be the friend Samantha was talking about, Sean decided. He knew this because the girl's hair was green, her nose was pierced, and she was wearing overalls and a black T-shirt. This is what made him a great detective. He noticed the details.

"Megan, this is Mr. Simmons. Mr. Simmons, this is Megan," Samantha said as she introduced them to each other. "Mr. Simmons used to be the police chief here."

"Cool," Megan said. "Did you arrest any bad guys?"

"Lots," Sean said.

"Do you carry a gun?"

"Not anymore," Sean said.

"Pooh," Megan said, making a face.

"Megan is my best friend," Samantha announced.

"Her only friend," Megan corrected.

"That is so not true."

"I meant here in Longely."

"There's Jenn," Samantha protested.

"Not since she's been going out with J.T."

"True," Samantha said. "She's gone over to the dark side."

She plopped her bag on the counter, knocking over a bunch of business cards sitting next to the register.

"Drats," Samantha said as they tumbled onto the floor.

She bent down and began picking them up and handing them to Sean, who glanced at them before handing them to Megan, who restacked them neatly.

There was a whole cottage industry here he wasn't aware of, Sean reflected as he watched Megan rearranging the cards. There were dog walkers and dog groomers and doggie dental hygienists. There were dog sitters and dog breeders, dog behaviorists, doggie psychics, and doggie daycares, as well as nutritional consultants and people who offered to cook meals for dogs and deliver them directly to your house.

"I think my daughters are in the wrong business," he commented as he handed Megan several cards.

"A lot of these people are deeply weird," Megan said. "They don't relate to people at all."

"Do they make a good living doing this?" Sean asked, thinking of Melissa, Trudy's dog breeder, and her trainer, Ramona.

Megan thought for a moment. "Some do, but not most," she said.

Samantha straightened up and began looking in her bag for some bubble gum. "The weird thing is most of them don't like dogs. Or maybe they do—maybe that's why they go into it—but they become kinda hardened. . . ."

"Like doctors with their patients," Megan said.

Samantha nodded. "It's like their career and they don't think about what's best for the dog. Like Ramona with Trudy. Got it," she said, holding up her gum. "Want some?" Samantha asked Sean as she took out a piece of bubble gum, unwrapped it, and popped it into her mouth.

Sean was about to refuse the offer and then changed his mind. Why not? He was tired of saying no to things. He'd had a piece of coconut cake the other day, and he was riding in a Mini Cooper. He decided to experiment with saying yes more often.

As he tasted the gum's sweetness he realized he couldn't remember when the last time he'd chewed a piece of bubble gum was. He tried making a bubble. And succeeded. Evidently this was a skill one didn't forget. The bubble was small, but in this case small was good enough. Next time he'd blow a larger one. And the time after that it would be even bigger. For some reason, he felt absurdly proud of himself.

"Megan's going to live with me in Fort Green," Samantha announced after she'd blown her own bubble and popped it.

Megan beamed. "It won't be long now." She gestured at the poster. "I hope they don't find her," she said. "I'd never turn her in."

"Not even for the reward money?" Sean asked.

"Not even for the reward money," Megan said.

"Even if you needed it?"

"I do need it and I'm not doing it," Megan stated.

She looked him square in the eye, which got Sean to thinking that thanks to Samantha, Megan knew exactly where Trudy was.

"Why is that?" Sean asked Megan.

"Because no one in that place really liked her, not even Annabel, and no one, animal or human, deserves to live like that. It's too awful."

"See," Samantha said to Sean. "I told you so." She turned to Megan. "He didn't believe me."

"How do you know?" Sean asked. "After all, she gave Trudy this big birthday party. That has to mean she liked her."

"No," Megan said heatedly. "That means she wanted to throw a big party and Trudy was just the excuse. It's the whole *Mommie Dearest* thing. And believe me, I know whereof I speak. Annabel used to come in the store and buy stuff all the time. You could tell she was only doing it because she thought that Trudy had to have the best. She was like an accessory or something to her. And here's the weird part. She wasn't comfortable with her. I don't think she knew how to handle her. It's like she wasn't used to dogs or something."

"I don't understand," Sean said.

"That's because she probably wasn't," Samantha said. "When I was there working I was always the one who walked her. Or Ramona did. Or the groomer. Aside from an occasional pat on the head, Annabel never had much to do with her."

Sean frowned. "She brought her to the store when she talked to my daughters."

Samantha gave him a how-dumb-can-you-be look. "Duh. That's because that was in public. She was always very nice to Trudy in public. It's in private that I'm talking about. It's like Trudy was another one of her obnoxious stuffed animals. In fact, I think Annabel preferred those."

"Even in here," Megan said. "She never let Trudy pick out what she wanted."

Sean was about to observe that Trudy was a dog and that dogs don't pick out things, but he decided that would just get the conversation off on a different tangent. Instead he said, "Do most people let their dogs pick out their own toys?"

Megan gave an emphatic nod. "It's so cute. We just had a German shepherd and his human in and the dog picked out this sheepskin lamp. He carried it out to the car. And as for him—"

"Him?"

"The husband. Richard. He doesn't even like animals. Not one single bit."

"How do you know that?"

"Because the woman who grooms Trudy, she used to go to school with Annabel and Richard, and she said—"

Sean held up his hand. "Wait a minute. I didn't know

Annabel and Richard went to the same high school," he said. Not that there was any reason he should know, but somehow he felt remiss that this bit of information had escaped him.

"And the same community college too," Megan told him. "My mom knew them both. He was a couple of grades ahead of her. My mom said he was a real turkey. Came from the wrong side of the tracks, so he had to prove to everyone how great he was. Now he's this big deal around here with this gigundo house. But he's just mean. The only thing he cares about is moolah." Megan made a rubbing motion with her thumb and forefinger. "And sex. According to my mom, he screwed—if you'll pardon the expression—anything that moved. One girl tried to commit suicide when he broke up with her. I don't know why anyone would do that. Guys are so not worth it.

"Anyway," Megan continued, "my mom used to live across the street from him. And my mom and my uncle had this dog named Sparky, and sometimes Sparky would go sit on the Colberts' lawn. He didn't do anything. He just liked to sit under this big old red maple tree they had. And it was okay with Richard's parents. But not Richard. In fact, my mom said she saw him kick Sparky really hard one day when he thought no one was looking. They had to take Sparky to the vet because Richard broke something.

"He swore he didn't and everyone believed him, but my mom knows what she saw. And he was mean to cats. My mom saw him throwing rocks at this stray cat that used to come on his property and pee in the bushes. No one believed her about that either." Megan paused for a breath. "They got into this big fight and she never spoke to him again after that."

"Well, that was a long time ago," Sean said. "People change."

"Nope," Megan said. "Not with that kind of stuff. Either you're an animal lover or you're not."

"You could be indifferent," Sean suggested.

Megan thought that over for a moment. "I suppose," she conceded. "But all I know is that Richard came in here one day yelling about all the money that Annabel was spending on Trudy."

That was something Sean actually couldn't fault him on.

"He was really, really angry. I just thought it was weird, given all the money they had, that he would care about his wife spending two hundred dollars on a cashmere sweater for a dog."

"I would care," Sean said.

"Yeah, but two hundred dollars is a lot to you," Samantha pointed out. "To him, it was probably like ten bucks."

"You know," Megan said, "I bet Annabel was just buying those things to piss Richard off. Jessica's mom used to do that to Jessica's dad a lot before they got divorced."

Sean pointed to Trudy's poster. "He's offering a thousand dollars' reward. That has to mean something."

"He's doing it for show," Megan said. "It's part of his shtik. Like this whole going-to-Westminster thing. That's a crock. She's never going to win. Not with those teeth."

"Then why is everyone so anxious for her to go?" Sean asked.

"Because it makes everyone look good. It gives Richard status. And it's a way for Ramona to make money. She knows Trudy doesn't have a chance in hell. She just kept telling Annabel that so she'd have a job. None of those people know one end of a dog from another. Nor do they care. Westminster is disgusting. It's worse than human beauty pageants. It should be disbanded."

"Wow," Sean said.

Megan ducked her head. "Sorry," she said. "I tend to get carried away."

As Sean watched, Samantha went over to one of the

shelves and picked out a box of dog biscuits. "Here," she said, bringing it over to the counter.

Sean took a look. The box had a picture of a dog and a rabbit on it. The type read: *Rabbit stew in a biscuit form. Hand cooked and hand rolled. Everything from our farm to your table with love. Human grade. No pesticides or antibiotics. If you want to indulge with your pet go ahead.* The price on the box read twenty-five dollars.

"Twenty-five dollars!" Sean yelped. "Don't you think that's a bit steep?"

"Don't worry," Megan said. "I'll give it to you for cost. That'll be ten." She looked at the clock on the wall. "If you hurry you can get to the florist before he closes."

"And why would I want to do that?" Sean asked.

"Duh," Megan said. "So you can get something for In—" And she clapped her hand over her mouth.

"Megan!" Samantha shrieked. "You promised."

"Well, I'm sorry," Megan said.

"Who else did you tell about Trudy?" Sean asked.

"No one." Samantha raised her hand. "I swear."

Sean sighed. This is what he got for getting involved with this kind of stuff.

"And I won't either," Megan told him. "They can pull my fingernails out and I wouldn't tell."

Sean thought an hour in the Longely jail would be enough.

"I just want you to know that I really admire what you're doing," Megan said. "I think it's a really good thing. If more people followed their hearts, the world would be a better place." And she came around the counter and gave him a kiss on the cheek.

"I know," Samantha said once they were back in her vehicle. "And I'm sorry. It's just that she's my best friend."

"When you keep a secret, you don't tell it to anyone. That is the definition of a secret."

Samantha hung her head. "I had to have someone to talk to."

Sean rubbed his forehead. He could feel a headache developing. What had he expected given the fact that he was dealing with a teenage girl? "Well, I hope your friend can keep her mouth shut," Sean said as they took off. "That's all I can say."

"She will," Samantha assured him. "I can guarantee it."

Sean didn't reply. There was nothing he could say that would be productive.

Chapter 26

Samantha pulled into the driveway of Ines's house and killed the engine. Sean had been here several years ago when the place had belonged to Mary Dottard, to tell her that her husband had been hit by a drunk bicyclist and was in the hospital with a fractured hip. Fortunately, Mary's husband had been all right. Sean had liked the looks of the place then and he liked it now.

The house was a small, neat, wood and quarried-rock bungalow set back off the street. It had diamond-paned windows and a large, welcoming front porch, a throwback to the days when people had time to visit. A couple of face cords of split firewood were neatly stacked along the porch's far wall.

Ropes of small white lights snaked around the two large stone pillars flanking the stairs. A trellis supported a clematis vine that Sean knew bloomed in the summer and early fall. The sounds of television floated out of the house. Sean smelled wood smoke, which made him think that Ines had a fire going inside. He heard Trudy barking as he rang the bell to the house. It made a nice jingly sound.

"What a pleasant surprise," Ines said when she opened the door a moment later. She nodded toward the presents he was holding. "If you were a Greek, I'd say something along the lines of . . . and bearing gifts no less . . . but since you're not Greek, you're Irish, I can't."

"Is this a bad time?" Sean asked. For some reason or another, he had a sneaking suspicion that he was not in Ines's good graces. Maybe it was the look on her face, which was not exactly welcoming. Or maybe it was the whole Greeks-bearing-gifts thing. If he remembered right, the saying Ines was alluding to was, "Beware of Greeks bearing gifts." "Would you like us to leave?" he offered.

"Don't be silly. Come on in." Then Ines turned to the little black pug that was standing beside her barking up a storm and wagging its tail so hard its little hindquarters were shaking. "Edna, stop that," she ordered. The pug barked louder. Ines threw up her hands. "What can you do?" she said to Sean and Samantha with a smile on her face as she beckoned them in. "She doesn't listen to me any better than my children did."

Sean stared at the pug. He was now thoroughly confused. "That's . . ."

"Edna," Ines said firmly. "We don't even use the 'T' word. At all. It's amazing how fast she got used to her new name."

"But she's black," Sean said.

"I know," Ines said. "I can see that."

"But how?"

Ines and Samantha looked at each other and laughed.

"Welcome to the world of hair dyes, Sean," Ines said as she took the dog biscuits and the flowers that he was holding. "And thank you for the presents. That was very sweet of you. And very wise."

Sean was about to ask Ines why she had said 'wise,' but Samantha spoke first.

"It was my idea," she said proudly. "I don't mean the presents," she said quickly.

"I know, dear," Ines replied. "You meant the hair dye, and I must say it was an excellent thought."

"But isn't that bad for . . . for . . . Edna?" Sean asked.

"Nope," Ines said. "I checked. The dye we're using on her is one hundred percent organic, one hundred percent nontoxic. You could use it on an infant if you wanted to—although I can't see why anyone would do something like that."

"Are you sure?" Sean persisted.

"Of course I'm sure," Ines said indignantly. She put Sean's presents on the hall table, then hung up his and Samantha's coats. Then, with Trudy hot on her heels, she picked up the presents and headed into the kitchen for a vase for the flowers. "Give me credit for some brains."

"But was it necessary?" Sean asked.

"Necessary?" Ines whirled and faced him. *"Necessary?"*

Sean took an involuntary step back and held up his hands against the onslaught of unleashed emotion. Obviously, he should have stayed off this topic.

"I was just asking," he said plaintively.

"Maybe it's necessary because I am harboring a kidnap victim in my house. You have made me into a felon."

"Well, I'd hardly go that far," Sean said.

"Well, I would," Ines retorted.

"Kidnapping implies a ransom," Sean said. "Unlawful possession is a more accurate designation for what we have here, and that's a misdemeanor."

"Wonderful. Now I can relax. Just think, I was worried when I saw that sign in the pet shop," Ines said. "Silly me."

"Oh, that thing . . ." Sean stammered.

"Yes, Sean. *That* thing. I walked into the shop and nearly had a heart attack. Thank God Edna wasn't with me."

He recognized the signs now. He had an angry, indignant female on his hands.

"I think you may be overreacting a tad," Sean observed gingerly.

"I don't," Ines snapped. She pulled the collar of her turtleneck sweater up. "Weren't you supposed to call and explain things to me? Tell me what was going on?"

"Yes, but . . ."

"Yes, but nothing. You didn't call. You didn't explain."

"You could have called me," Sean pointed out.

"I was afraid to. Fortunately, Samantha did call me."

Samantha smiled. Sean glared at her.

"I just wanted to make sure everyone was all right," Samantha said. "After all, I am kinda responsible for the situation."

"Kinda?" Sean repeated. "*Kinda* responsible?" He could hear his voice rising.

"All right," Samantha said. "I'm totally responsible for the situation. Does that make you happier?"

"Thank you," Sean said. "Yes, it does. Marginally."

"After all, I couldn't take the little darling out looking the way she did," Ines went on. "Someone might have spotted her."

"I think that may be overstating the case. . . ." Sean said. But before he could finish his sentence, Ines rode right over him.

"And I couldn't keep her in. She has to go for her walks. I was in a terrible quandary about what to do, which was when Samantha called. I asked her for suggestions and she asked Megan, who actually knows about dogs, and we came up with this." She pointed to Trudy/Edna, who was presently sitting on Ines's feet. "There are black pugs, you know."

"No, I didn't," Sean murmured. In truth, he knew not very much about dogs. They'd always been there when he was growing up, but he'd never interacted with them. He'd just given them an absentminded pat on their heads as he'd gone by.

"The whole hair dye thing has worked out really great," Ines continued enthusiastically. "I haven't worried since I did it. I even walked Edna past the police station yesterday. No one glanced at her twice. No thanks to you."

"You want us to go?" Sean asked.

Ines laughed. "Not at all. Now that I've had my little tantrum I'm fine. But you should have told me."

"I just . . ."

"I know. You just didn't want to put me at risk. I appreciate the sentiment, but you have to tell me what's going on and allow me to make my own decisions."

Sean nodded. That seemed like a fair request. He didn't know if it would work—his habits were longstanding—but he was willing to try.

Ines inspected his face. Sean decided she must have liked what she saw, because the next thing she said was, "Hot cider, tea, or coffee?"

Sean and Samantha both chose coffee. Ten minutes later, the four of them were seated around the coffee table in front of the fire. Sean, Ines, and Trudy/Edna were on the sofa, while Samantha was sitting cross-legged on the floor. The three humans were sipping coffee and everyone was eating pieces of cinnamon toast.

"Do you have the Longely High School yearbooks or the local community college ones at the Historical Society by any chance?" Sean asked.

Ines took a sip of coffee before answering. "I believe we do," she said as she put her cup down. "Is there a reason you're asking?"

Sean shrugged. "Samantha's friend Megan just told us that Richard and Annabel went to high school and college together. I was just curious to see what they looked like. No big deal."

"When we're done with our coffee we can go and look if you want to."

"Now?" Sean asked.

Ines laughed. "Why not?"

"But aren't you closed?"

"We are indeed. But since I have the key that shouldn't be a problem. After all, I am the person running the place."

Half an hour later, Ines, Samantha, Sean, and Edna were at the Historical Society. Ines's keys jingled as she opened the door. She flipped on the lights and the room sprang into view. It looked oddly forlorn, with its empty tables and chairs, and its neatly stacked reading materials. Sean had the feeling that the building was glad for the company. He shook his head to get those thoughts out of his mind. He had been hanging out with Samantha and Megan too long, he decided as he followed Ines, Edna, and Samantha into the back room. Weirdness was contagious. He'd always suspected as much and now he had proof positive.

"Here we are," Ines said as she turned on the lights.

As she did, it occurred to Sean that Ines hadn't turned off the burglar alarm. He squeezed his eyes shut for a moment as he pictured patrol cars squealing to a stop in front of the Historical Society and officers emerging with their guns drawn. And finding them. Not a good picture.

"Isn't the place alarmed?" Sean asked.

Ines grinned. "Nope. There's nothing here anyone would want to steal. No one comes here during the day. I can't imagine why they'd want to go to the trouble of breaking in here."

"But what about fire? Are you hooked up to the fire station?"

"We're not hooked up to anyone," Ines replied as she kept an eye on Edna, who was sniffing the table legs.

Sean gestured around the room. "But isn't that kind of risky with all this paper?" he asked.

"Obviously," Ines said as she went over to the shelves on the near right and began running her finger over the spines of the books stored there, "you have never dealt with my board of directors. They are a very tightfisted bunch. Ah. Here we go. The *Longely Lantern*." She stopped to do the math for a moment, then pulled out a volume, brought it over to the long table, and set it down. "This should be it," she said to Sean.

He sat down in front of it and began to flip through the pages. He passed the pictures of the hockey club, the football team, the school newspaper, the French club, and the notes from the Spanish club's trip to Barcelona. About halfway through he came to what he wanted—the class picture. He stared at it for a moment. Then he read the names underneath the picture. He reread them. And everything came together for him. He closed the book and pushed it away with the tips of his fingers.

"Well?" Ines said.

"I think I might know who killed Annabel," Sean said.

"Who?" Samantha and Ines cried.

"I think I might know the who, but I don't know the why." He turned to Samantha. "Do you think I can speak to Megan's parents?" Sean asked.

"I guess," Samantha said. "I don't see why not."

"Good," Sean said. "Because I need to ask them something."

Chapter 27

Brandon made a couple of calls before he found out where Rick Crouse was working. "The brotherhood always comes through," Brandon said to Bernie as he delivered the news.

She raised her eyebrows. "Do tell."

"You didn't say that the other night."

Bernie's eyebrows went higher. "Not everything is about sex."

"It is for any red-blooded American male."

"Leaving that topic aside for the moment."

"If you insist."

"I do."

Brandon pouted. "Hey," he said. "I got you your information, didn't I?"

Bernie leaned over and kissed him. "And in a very timely manner too."

"Which is why you love me."

"Yes, it is," Bernie said and she kissed him again.

Marvin cleared his throat, and Bernie and Brandon turned to look at him. "I'm not going to talk to him," Marvin said.

Libby patted him on the shoulder. She could tell just the idea upset him. "No one is asking you to talk to Rick."

"I'm afraid I'd hurt him if I did," Marvin said.

Bernie shot Brandon a warning glance. She could tell he was going to say something thoughtless like: *Ha. Ha. You're kidding me, right?*

"Yeah. Maybe you shouldn't go then," was the comment Brandon finally settled on after he was quiet for a second too long. "You don't want to hurt him too bad and send him to the hospital."

"I'm afraid I'd break his nose," Marvin said and he made what passed for a fist. "Or worse."

Libby nodded. "Why don't we go back to my place? We can watch a movie."

"I'd like that," Marvin said.

Bernie gave Libby the thumbs-up sign as Libby and Marvin headed for the door. After they left, Brandon called his boss to make sure it was all right to leave early if he could get coverage. Then he called one of the other guys who worked at R.J.'s.

"Fatty owes me," he explained to Bernie as he waited for Fatty to pick up. When he did, Brandon explained the situation. "He'll be here in twenty minutes," Brandon told Bernie once he clicked off.

Half an hour later, Fatty Armbruster walked through the door. He was five feet ten inches and weighed all of 120 pounds with his clothes on. Which, of course, was why everyone called him Fatty. He and Brandon talked for five minutes or so. Then he took Brandon's place behind the bar.

"See what I do for you," Brandon said to Bernie as they walked out of R.J.'s and toward Brandon's car. "I give up my livelihood to make sure you're safe."

"So, I take it this means your tank is on empty and you want me to pay for the gas," Bernie said as they got into Brandon's vehicle.

"That's why I love you," Brandon said, putting the key in the ignition. "You're so smart."

"No," Bernie said as they took off. "You admire me because I'm smart, but you love me because I'm a hottie and I do amazing things in bed."

"And because you're modest," Brandon said.

"That too," Bernie said. "And humble."

"Especially that," Brandon said.

Bernie didn't answer because she was too busy thinking about what she was going to say to Rick.

There was no traffic going down into the city, so it only took them about twenty minutes to drive in from Longely. The bar that Rick was working at was located on Third Avenue between Eighty-first and Eighty-second streets. Brandon found a parking space after driving around for ten minutes.

"Must be my lucky day," he commented as he maneuvered his car into the spot.

"Any day you're with me is your lucky day," Bernie said.

Brandon killed the engine. "That too," he said.

The plan was for Bernie to go in and talk to Rick while Brandon hung back and had a drink at the bar. Brandon was assuming nothing untoward was going to happen. After all, this was Rick's place of work, but he wanted to be there if it did. Or if Rick needed a little extra persuading to answer Bernie's questions. There were advantages to being big and strong and having a background in the martial arts, not to mention having some contacts on the darker side of life.

Brandon had parked the car two blocks away. He and Bernie huddled together as they walked over to Little Russia. It always seemed colder in the city, and the wind whipping down Third Avenue was strong enough to make their eyes tear. Both were glad when they finally got to the bar. Brandon pulled the door open, and he and Bernie walked inside.

The first thing that caught Bernie's eye was the big Russian flag hanging over the back of the bar. The second thing was a couple of posters of Moscow and St. Petersburg on the walls. But that was it in the Russian department. Whoever had decorated the place had run out of either money or interest and called it a day. Vestiges of Little Russia's former incarnation as an Irish pub were still visible in the form of Guinness and Harp signs. Looking around, Bernie couldn't help wondering who the next tenant would be, because except for three men watching the news on TV the place was empty.

Bernie watched Rick's head turn as he heard them come through the door. He definitely didn't look pleased to see them. But considering the way they'd left things, she hadn't expected that he would. His comment bore that out.

"You," he said.

"Yes," Bernie replied sweetly. "*C'est moi.* It is me." She supplied the translation in case he didn't know French, which she figured was probably the case.

Rick sniffed. He looked insulted. "I know what that means," he said. "I did *Camelot.*"

"Who were you?" Bernie asked.

"One of the extras. It was my first role on stage. Now get out of here."

Bernie wrinkled her nose. "But I just got here."

Rick put his two hands palm down on the counter and leaned forward. "And now you can leave," he said in what Bernie judged was his best threatening manner.

"I don't think I can do that yet," Bernie answered. "We need to talk."

"*We* don't need to do anything. *You* need to go." Rick nodded toward Brandon. "And take him with you."

Brandon grinned. "And deprive you of the pleasure of my company? No. I don't think so."

Rick's voice rose a little. "I mean it. Get out. Both of you. Or I'm calling the cops."

The three men down at the other end of the bar had stopped watching the television and were now watching Rick, Bernie, and Brandon, the promise of a fight being much more entertaining than anything that was on the screen at the moment.

Brandon stepped out in front of Bernie and started toward where Rick was standing.

"Before you do that, you might want to listen to why you're going to talk to Bernie."

"Really," Rick sneered.

"Yes, really," Brandon replied.

"I can't imagine anything you could say that would interest me," Rick said as he reached for his cell.

Brandon smiled. It was not, Bernie reflected, a nice smile. The corners of his mouth turned up, but his eyes remained steely.

"Then I'll tell you," Brandon said. "Ted. Ted should interest you."

"I don't know what you're talking about," Rick said. However, Bernie noticed he'd moved his hand off his cell and there was a very slight quaver in his voice.

"Sure you do," Brandon answered. "So tell the pretty lady what she wants to know. . . ."

Bernie kissed Brandon on the cheek. "Thank you. You're so sweet. . . ."

"I know I am," Brandon told her before turning back to Rick. "Nothing goes any further if you talk to her. And if you don't . . ." Brandon shrugged his shoulders. "Oh well. Then I'll call Ted and tell him that you're . . . how shall I put this . . . let's say reinvesting some of his funds. . . ."

"But I'm not," Rick protested. It was a weak protest.

Brandon smiled again. "Even if you're not . . . just the suggestion would be enough. Ted is a paranoid son of a bitch. Hey. In your line of work your face is your fortune."

Rick blanched.

"The choice is up to you," Brandon said.

Rick licked his lower lip. "How did you . . ."

Brandon held up his hand to stop him. "Find out? Let's just say you're not the only one with connections, not that it really matters. Now. Are you going to speak to Bernie or aren't you?"

Rick thought for a moment. Bernie could see the defeat in the slump of his shoulders. She almost—*almost* being the operative word—felt sorry for him. Then Rick straightened up and leaned over the counter. Bernie could see that he'd made his decision.

"Fine. Now what can I get for you folks?"

Brandon ordered an IPA and Bernie ordered a Brooklyn Brown. As they waited for their drinks to arrive, Bernie noticed that the three men down at the other end of the bar had turned back to watching television. The show was over.

"What do you want?" Rick said after he brought the beers over and placed them in front of Bernie and Brandon.

Bernie took a sip, then put her glass down. "Good," she said.

Rick started drumming his fingers on the counter. "Well?" he said.

"In a hurry?" Bernie asked, then took another sip. "First you didn't want to talk and now you can't wait."

"I'm curious," Rick replied.

Bernie raised an eyebrow. "Really?" she said.

"Yes. Really."

That was one word for what Rick must be feeling at this moment, but not the word Bernie would have chosen. She nodded. "All right. We want to know a good reason why you weren't the one who killed Annabel."

Rick blinked.

"Seriously," Bernie said. "You had the motive, you were there, so you had the opportunity, you know how to cork and recork a wine bottle, and you know how to take off the plastic cover without it being noticeable."

"Whoa," Rick said. "Stop right there. Anyone who's been around liquor knows that trick," he retorted. "Right, Brandon?"

"It's true," Brandon said. "It's a trick of the trade."

"And who else has worked around liquor in that group?" Bernie demanded. "No one."

"Not true," Rick cried. "For openers, Richard used to tend bar when he was in college, I know Ramona did a stint at R.J.'s when she was younger, and my ex worked at Hooters."

"Well, that figures," Bernie said.

"No. That was pre-surgery. That's what inspired Joanna to get them as large as she did."

"And you know all of this how?" Brandon asked.

"Because Joanna told me, of course."

"And how did she know?" Bernie asked.

Rick gave her a you've-got-to-be-kidding-me look. "Because Annabel told her. Remember, they used to be friends."

"Pre you," Bernie said.

"Yes. Pre me. And I had no reason to kill her. Absolutely none."

"And how do you figure that?" Bernie asked.

"Because once she died I didn't get any money. You can check if you want."

"We did," Bernie lied. "But you have a big ego. I'm figuring that you got really pissed that Annabel was cutting you loose, that your ego couldn't take it."

"And that's why I killed her," Rick scoffed. "You're going to have to do way better than that. I already have a new sponsor. . . ."

" 'Sponsor?' " Bernie mocked.

"Yes. Sponsor," Rick said firmly.

"What happened to Maggie the Cat?" Bernie asked.

"She's on the back burner for a while."

"So it's like the more the merrier," Brandon said.

"Something like that," Rick said.

"I admire your stamina," Brandon said.

"I try to live a healthy life," Rick said. "In fact, I met my newest sponsor in Whole Foods. She's hooking me up with a modeling gig, so no more bartending. I'm done with this. In a sense, Annabel did me a favor kicking me loose. Listen, I may have a large ego, I admit that—you can't be an actor and not have one—but I'm not a killer. A lover, yes. A killer, no."

"You have a bad temper," Bernie pointed out.

"So I'm a little reactive. So what? If everyone who was like me killed someone, there'd be no one left in the universe."

Bernie took another sip of her Brooklyn Brown and put the glass down. A fire engine went by, drowning out the sound of the television. She waited till it was past before she spoke.

"So who do you think the murderer is?" Bernie asked Rick.

"You know, I've been thinking about that a lot," Rick said.

"And?" Brandon said.

"I've been trying to decide who hated Annabel the most, and I gotta tell you it's a tough call, because they all go back a long way, you know?"

Bernie leaned forward. "Who is 'they'?" she asked.

"The whole bunch of them. Joyce, Melissa, Ramona. They were all really tight in high school."

"What about Joanna?" Bernie asked.

"She came in later. Annabel met her through Joyce, actually. My ex and Joyce were in a class together. Some sort of knitting or painting or crap like that. Anyway, as I was saying, they were all really tight. And then they got this hate going."

"Well, it couldn't have been that much of a hate," Bernie pointed out. "Because they all stuck together."

"See, that's what's so sick," Rick said. "Annabel told me she liked having them work for her, because they didn't like her. Or each other."

Bernie thought back to her afternoon at Annabel's place. That was certainly the sense she'd gotten.

"She said she got a real kick out of keeping them around," Rick said.

"Nice lady," Bernie said.

"Not really," Rick said. "Although she was not ungenerous."

"The car is nice," Bernie said.

"The car is very nice," Rick agreed. "What do they say? You can't beat German engineering? It's true." He grinned. "But I'm worth it. My mommy always said that you gotta pay if you want to play. Poor Annabel. She certainly wasn't getting anything from her husband."

"Okay," Brandon said. "I could see why you stayed, but why did the others stay?"

"The same reason I did—money. What else?" Rick said. His tone indicated you'd have to be an idiot not to recognize that fact. "No one else had much and Annabel did. None of that bunch could ever have made the kind of money they did anyplace else. I mean, Ramona was living rent free, she ate for nothing, and she had use of a car. Annabel gave Melissa expensive birthday presents and helped her out with her expenses from time to time. And Annabel didn't even like dogs. She sure as hell didn't like Trudy."

"So I gathered," Bernie said. Now that Rick was talking, he just kept on going.

"She was going to get rid of her, but then the Puggables hit big-time and she thought she had to keep her around for her image. The only person who really liked Trudy was that crazy kid Richard used to hire to do stuff around the house. The one with the weird hair."

"Samantha?" Bernie asked.

"Yeah," Rick said. "That's the one. She was always playing with her. No one else ever did. I mean, they took care of her. They fed her and walked her and even brushed her teeth, for God's sake. But no one ever was nice to her, if you know what I mean."

"I think I do. So why did everyone hate each other?" Bernie asked.

Rick shrugged. "Annabel."

"Annabel?" Bernie repeated.

"Yeah. She like"—Rick snapped his fingers—"what is that word . . . capitalized on the situation. She was like this queen. One day, one person would be her favorite. The next day another person would. She enjoyed watching everyone fight over the scraps. Then there was the whole sex thing. From what Annabel said, everyone was sleeping with everyone else. That's never good. It leads to all sorts of complications."

Bernie couldn't help it. She burst out laughing.

"What? What's so funny?" Rick demanded. "It's true."

"And who should know better than you," Bernie said.

Rick had the good grace to blush.

"Aren't you glad I was with you?" Brandon said as he and Bernie headed back to the car.

"I'm always glad you're with me," Bernie said.

"Not when you go shopping," Brandon said.

"That's true," Bernie said. "I like to go shopping by myself."

And she did. She didn't even like her friends along. It was too distracting. Shopping was serious business.

"So tell me," Bernie said, "how do you know all this Ted stuff and what is it anyway?"

Brandon grinned. "Well, I know Rick is dealing and I know his supplier is Ted."

"How do you know this?" Bernie asked.

"I can't tell you, and even if I could, I wouldn't."

"And why is that?"

"Because the less you know the better."

"You sound like my father."

"Well, there are occasions when he happens to be right."

"Are you involved?"

"If I say I'm not, would you believe me?"

"Yes, I would," Bernie told him.

"Good. Because I'm not."

"Okay. Moving on. How did you know that Rick was doing a little business on his own?"

"I didn't."

"You didn't?"

"No. I just guessed. Everyone does and I figured Rick was doing the same."

"You're a good guesser," Bernie said.

"Among other things," Brandon said.

Bernie laughed and snuggled closer. Neither one said anything else until they reached Brandon's car.

Chapter 28

Much to Sean's delight, it turned out that Megan's parents were willing to speak to him that evening. Ines wasn't going. She'd decided to stay home with Trudy after extracting a promise from Sean to call her as soon as he was done speaking with Mr. and Mrs. McKee and tell her what was going on. It was an easy thing for Sean to promise, because he would have done it anyway. So it was Samantha who drove Sean over to the McKee household, which was located one town over in Bolton, New York.

Bolton was a little less expensive, a little more down to earth than Longely, the town being peopled primarily by teachers, policemen, plumbers, and civil servants. As they drove to Megan's house, Sean noticed that Bolton's main street was missing the cutesy shop names and fancy lettering that had taken over Longely.

That was fine with him. He could have done with less of it in Longely. When he'd married Rose and she'd started the shop, there'd been none of it. But now the streets were infested with shops sporting catchy names, fancy signs, and overpriced merchandise. Looking at them made him cranky. But then, according to Libby, everything made him cranky. Too bad. He wasn't about to change. Someone had to uphold the standards. He was thinking about Stoddard's ice cream and how there had been five flavors of ice cream in the store—vanilla, chocolate, coffee, strawberry, and butter pecan, every single one a masterpiece—when Samantha roared into the McKees' driveway and slammed on the brakes.

Megan and her parents had to have been looking out the window because they had the door opened as Samantha and Sean came up the porch stairs. Sean liked the McKees on first sight. They exuded an air of comfort and competence. Both had short, black hair; both were a little stout around the middle; both were dressed in jeans, sweatshirts, and sneakers; both wore wire-rimmed glasses; and both were smiling at him.

He decided they were what his mother would have called salt-of-the-earth people. He'd be willing to wager that they went to church on Sunday, paid their taxes, and volunteered at the local soup kitchen. These were the kind of people who would tell the truth to the best of their ability. These were the kind of people who would not be prone to exaggeration. These were the kind of people who would not scream in horror when their daughter came home sporting a nose ring.

"This is so exciting," Megan's mother trilled as she welcomed Sean and Samantha inside. "I've never been involved in a police investigation before."

Megan gave an impatient snort. "I already told you, Ma. It's not a police investigation."

"Well, it's close enough for me," her mother retorted. "That poor woman," she said to Sean.

"Ma, Annabel was a bitch," Megan said.

Mrs. McKee stiffened slightly. "First of all, you shouldn't be saying things like that about someone. Secondly, even if it is true, no one deserves to die like that."

"My wife only sees the good in people," Mr. McKee said as he grasped Sean's hand and shook it.

Then he relieved Sean and Samantha of their coats and ushered them into the dining room. Sean instantly approved of the room as well. It was neat, but not overly so. A gray cat was curled up on top of the radiator cover. He didn't even open his eyes when everyone walked in.

"That's Otto," Megan said. "He sleeps the winter away."

Sean nodded as he took in the lace curtains on the windows and the beige carpet in a swirl pattern on the floor. Family photographs were hung on one wall, a collection of decorative spoons hung on the second, while a large breakfront that displayed the McKees' good china and glasses took care of the third wall. Sean felt as if he had time traveled back to his aunt's house.

"My wife not only likes to see the good in people, she likes to feed them as well," Mr. McKee said. He nodded at the dining room table, where a coffee cake, a platter of cookies, and a carafe of coffee were waiting.

"Here," Mrs. McKee said as she guided Sean to the table. She waited for him to sit down, cut him a large slab of Russian coffee cake, and plopped it down in front of him without asking him if he wanted any or not. "It probably isn't as good as your daughters', but it's not too bad either, if I do say so myself."

Sean had to agree that it certainly wasn't bad at all. Libby's was a little moister, this cake was a little more breadlike, a tad more austere, but it made up for that with a kick of . . . something. He took another bite and chewed carefully trying to figure out what the spices were.

"Cardamom?" he asked. "With a little bit of saffron and a touch of orange rind."

Mrs. McKee beamed at him as she poured him a cup of coffee and set it down in front of him.

"That's exactly right," she said. "It's a Swedish recipe. One of my neighbors gave it to me when Jim and I were stationed in Minnesota. I've been making it ever since."

"It's a definite keeper," Sean said.

"That it is," Mr. McKee said as he helped himself to a large piece of the cake.

"Cream?" Mrs. McKee asked Sean. "Sugar?"

"Both," Sean said. He expected the cream to be the real stuff, and much to his satisfaction, it was.

Mrs. McKee, Samantha, and Megan all helped themselves to cake and coffee. For the next ten minutes the only sounds were forks clinking on plates, coffee cups being refilled, and the ticking of the grandfather clock in the living room.

"Ma, I've already told Mr. Simmons what you told me about Richard and Annabel," Megan said once she'd finished her cake.

Mrs. McKee poured Sean a third cup of coffee. "I don't know that I have that much more to add," she said.

"Remember what you told me about Richard and that girl."

"Megan, that's all secondhand information," Mrs. McKee objected.

Sean smiled. "I'll take what I can get."

Mrs. McKee wiped her mouth with her napkin and set it back down on her lap. "Poor Missy."

"Missy?" Sean said.

"Well, back then she was Missy. Now she's Anna. I guess that's a lot more sophisticated."

Sean nodded. "Go on."

Mrs. McKee shook her head. "It was just very sad."

Sean took a sip of coffee and put his cup down on the red checked tablecloth. "Sad in what sense?" he asked.

"He ruined her life."

"He, being Richard?" Sean asked.

Mrs. McKee nodded. "She was this quiet mousey little thing who used to work in her family's liquor store, never dated or anything like that. She really didn't have lots of friends either, really just Annabel and Joyce. And they weren't tight. Not at all. Actually, I think they used Anna to get liquor from her parents' store."

"So Anna was kind of like Carrie," Megan said.

"Not that bad, dear," Mrs. McKee replied. She turned back to Sean. "Anyhow, then Richard came along and swept her off her feet."

"That's hard to believe," Samantha said. "He's such a dork. He looks like Ichabod Crane."

"It's true, dear," Mrs. McKee said. "Back then he was a lot heavier. He really was very good-looking. And he played basketball. He really owned the place. All the girls wanted to go out with him."

"And this was pre Annabel?" Sean asked.

"Oh yes." Mrs. McKee nodded. "Definitely. Then Annabel came along. I heard that Anna told Annabel she was pregnant and Annabel went right out and seduced Richard. I guess she saw it as her chance. In any case, Richard told Anna that she was on her own. And you know what? Annabel broke up with Richard shortly after that. Which was just like her. Of course, they got back together later, after Richard had divorced his first wife."

"What happened to the baby?" Sean asked. "Did Anna get an abortion?"

"No. Anna insisted on having it, but her parents made her get rid of it."

"That's terrible," Samantha cried.

"I'm sure it wasn't very nice for her," Mrs. McKee said. "But maybe it was best for the child."

"Maybe," Samantha said, but Sean could tell she wasn't convinced.

Mrs. McKee patted Samantha's hand. "These things usually happen for a reason," she told her before continuing on with her story. "The poor dear never went back to school after that. Just worked in the family store. She was getting home-bound instruction. And I think that's as much as I can tell you, because that's all I know."

"Did she stay here? Did she move?" Sean asked.

"Well, she went away for a number of years. But then

she came back and started her grooming business. And I guess she was able to move on," Mrs. McKee said.

"Why do you say that?"

"Well, the Colberts were her clients. If she hadn't forgiven them, she never would have worked for them."

"You wouldn't have worked for them," Mr. McKee said. "Not everyone feels the same way you do." He pushed the plate of cookies in front of Sean. "Have one," he urged Sean. "They're butterscotch oatmeal pecan."

Even though Sean was full, he took one anyway. After all, it would be rude to refuse. Mrs. McKee watched Sean take a bite. When she heard his sigh of pleasure she smiled.

"You can come anytime," her husband joked. "My wife is a sucker for a good eater."

Megan reached across the table and grabbed a cookie as well. "These are my favorites," she said. "Samantha, do you want one?"

Samantha shook her head. She looked as if she was deep in thought.

"Is there anything else you can tell me?" Sean asked Mrs. McKee after he'd finished his cookie and refused another.

Mrs. McKee shook her head. "I haven't been very helpful, have I?"

"On the contrary," Sean said. "You've been very helpful."

And it was true. She had been. As Sean got up to leave, Megan volunteered to walk him and Samantha out to the car.

"You know," Megan said once they were outside, "I don't know if this is important or not, but I think Melissa and Anna have a thing going."

"A thing going?" Sean said. He felt like an idiot. Either he was losing his marbles or Megan was unclear. Of course, he preferred to think it was the latter, but one never knew.

"You know—a thing," Megan repeated, giving him a meaningful look.

After a moment the light dawned for Sean. "Oh," he said. "You mean that kind of thing."

"Yeah. That kind of thing," Megan said. "What kind of thing did you think I was talking about?"

"I wasn't sure," Sean confessed. "Why didn't you tell me before?" he asked.

Megan bit her cuticle. "Well, it's like their private business," she explained. "I mean, who cares, right?"

"Right," Sean said.

"But then I thought, well maybe it has something to do with what happened, you know?"

"I know."

"Even though I don't like Annabel—I mean she was a total bitch—that doesn't give people the right to kill her."

"Yeah," Samantha said. "If we killed everyone who was bitchy, the world would be an empty place."

"But a better one," Megan said. "In fact, that's not a bad idea except the whole death thing skeeves me out."

"It's definitely gross," Samantha replied. "Once, I saw this cat that had gotten run over by a car." She shuddered at the memory.

"How sure are you about this, Megan?" Sean asked.

"I'm not sure, sure," Megan said. "But I'm pretty sure."

"What's pretty sure?" Sean asked.

"I saw them giggling together in the store."

"They could have been sharing a joke," Sean said.

"It wasn't that kind of giggle," Megan said.

"Then what kind of giggle was it?" Sean asked.

"It was a kind of sharing giggle."

"That's what I just said," Sean told her. He thought that given the circumstances he was doing an admirable job of retaining his patience.

"This was a different kind of sharing giggle," Megan told him.

"Maybe they're good friends," Sean suggested.

Megan shook her head. "That's not the kind of vibe I

got. I mean, I could be wrong. But I don't think I am. I'm usually not about that kind of thing." Megan rubbed her arms. "It's cold out here. I'm going back inside." And she turned and went up the steps.

"What do you think?" Samantha asked Sean as she pulled away from the curb.

"About what Megan just said?"

"Yes."

Sean closed his eyes so he wouldn't see how close they were to the cars parked on the side of the road. "Sure," he answered. "Why not? Anything is possible."

Samantha grunted. Sean decided she looked extremely distracted—not something he wanted to see when they were on the road together. To take his mind off of Samantha's driving, he called Ines and filled her in on the conversation he'd had with the McKees. Then he called Clyde and told him what he thought.

"But you can't prove anything," Clyde said.

"No, I can't," Sean said. "This is all speculation. But my gut tells me this is the way to go."

Clyde laughed. "Are you sure you're not having indigestion?"

"Maybe that too," Sean replied.

Clyde was quiet for a moment. He knew his old friend and he knew his hunches. Nine times out of ten they were correct. "All right," he said. "Let me nose around and see what I can come up with."

"That's all I'm asking," Sean said and hung up.

"So what's going to happen now?" Samantha asked.

"Nothing is going to happen."

"Nothing?" Samantha said.

"Not yet," Sean said firmly.

"That's ridiculous," Samantha said.

"No," Sean replied. "That's reality."

Five minutes later, Mrs. McKee called Sean and told

him the rest of the story. "I just didn't want to say any-thing in front of Samantha," she said.

"I can see why," Sean replied after he heard what she had to say.

"Who was that?" Samantha asked Sean when he was done.

"Megan's mom," Sean answered. "She just wanted to tell me she wanted to share her coffee cake recipe with Bernie and Libby," he lied.

"She's very nice," Samantha said.

"Yes, she is," Sean agreed.

Chapter 29

It was nine-thirty the next morning. Bernie was in the kitchen of A Little Taste of Heaven putting a pumpkin pie in the oven. She was wondering if they should invest in one of those fancy new cash registers instead of sticking with their old basic ninety-nine-dollar model when her cell rang. She slid the pie in, closed the oven door, and picked up her phone. Megan was on the line.

"You've got to come over to the pet shop," she cried. "Samantha is flipping out."

"Flipping out as in how?" Bernie asked while she wiped her hands on the towel lying on the counter.

"Just please come," Megan replied. Then she hung up.

"Great," Bernie said.

"What's wrong?" Libby asked.

Bernie told her. "It's probably nothing," she added.

"Probably," Libby agreed.

The sisters were silent for a moment. The sounds of their early morning customers seeped in over the soundtrack of *My Fair Lady* that Libby was playing.

"On the other hand, it could be something," Libby finally said.

Bernie nodded. Given the circumstances, there was no doubt about that.

"You'd better go," Libby told her sister.

"I know. What about the cranberry bars?"

"I'll take care of them," Libby replied.

They had an order for five dozen cranberry nut bars for three o'clock that afternoon for a fund-raising event at the local high school.

"I'll say one thing about Samantha," Bernie said as she went to get her coat. "She definitely is a pain in the ass."

Libby didn't disagree.

Ten minutes later Bernie arrived at the pet store. She could see Samantha through the window. She was sitting on the floor with her back to the counter clutching a sheepskin lamb to her chest. The moment Bernie parked the van, Megan, who had been anxiously hovering by the shop door, ran out and dragged her inside.

"It's her dad," Megan whispered nervously to Bernie as they came through the door.

The door closed behind them. "What about him?" Bernie whispered back.

Megan swallowed. "They just had a fight and he's kicking her out. He just told her he's not her dad, so there's no reason he has to put up with her nonsense anymore."

Then she stopped talking, because they were four feet away from Samantha. "Here she is," Megan said unnecessarily.

"I told you not to call her," Samantha hiccupped between sobs.

"Well, I'm glad she did," Bernie told her.

Samantha looked up at Bernie. Her nose was red. Tears were pouring out of her eyes. "All I said was that he should teach his brat to respect other people's property—one of the spawn took my iPod and dropped it in the toilet—and he told me he was fed up with my attitude and he'd just taken me in as a favor anyway after my mom died. He said he wasn't my real dad—Richard was.

"So I could go and live with him and see if I liked it better. I hate my dad, but I hate Richard even more. He's a total control freak. I mean, you can't take a breath without his counting it. He spies on people. It's really creepy.

"I never even want to go to the bathroom in that place. I mean, what if he's one of those sickos who likes watching people pee? And now I'm supposed to live there. I'll have to go in a bucket outside. I'll live in a homeless shelter before I'll live with him." And she started sobbing again.

"I'm sorry," Megan said to Bernie as she was looking down at Samantha. "I'm really, really sorry. I didn't know who else to call. I mean, I don't know what to do. Sam can't stay here."

"That's right. Kick me out into the cold," Samantha cried.

"I already told you that if my boss comes in and sees you like this, I'll get fired. I told you that you could stay at my place—my mom won't mind." Megan turned to Bernie. "But she doesn't want to."

"Don't you see?" Samantha wailed. "It will make me feel worse. Your mom and dad are nice. If anyone is nice to me I'll die."

"Spoken like a true drama queen," Bernie said.

Samantha's head shot up. She glared at her.

"This is not the end of the world," Bernie said.

"Yes, it is," Samantha cried. "How can you say that it isn't? Have you no heart? No soul?"

Bernie crouched down next to Samantha. "Look at me," she instructed. "Okay," she said to her when she had. "We're going to go back to the shop and go upstairs. You're going to clean up and have something to eat. Then you're going to tell me what happened, all right?"

"I told you," Samantha protested.

"Well, you're going to tell me again," Bernie informed her.

Samantha nodded.

"And then we're going to see what we can do about it."

"There's nothing you can do," Samantha protested. "I always thought I wanted to know who my real parents were. Talk about being unclear on the concept," she said as Bernie led her out of the shop and into the van.

By the time they'd reached A Little Taste of Heaven, Samantha's sobs had subsided into the occasional muffled sniveling and Bernie had a pretty good idea of what was what. Evidently Samantha's dad had caught her taking some of his wife's clothes to donate to the Salvation Army. The fact that one of the dresses that Samantha had chosen was a two thousand–dollar Missoni probably had something to do with her stepmother's wrath.

Bernie was listening to her dad tell her what Mrs. McKee told him.

"This is very complicated," Bernie said when her dad was done.

Sean laughed. "Tell me about it."

Bernie could hear that. The water in the bathroom was still running. Which was good. She wanted to finish this discussion before Samantha came out.

"Let me repeat this," Bernie said. "Anna, Trudy's groomer, had something going on with Richard when she was going to Hampshire Community College. He knocked her up. Then Annabel came along and seduced him. Richard left Anna for Annabel. Anna went off and had Samantha. Samantha was adopted by Richard's friend Robert Barron and his first wife. All four of the parties involved signed a nondisclosure document."

Sean took a sip of his hot chocolate. "Go on," he said. "You're doing great."

"Barron and his first wife got divorced after a year of

marriage. She took Samantha and headed down to New York, where she stayed. Meanwhile, Barron remarried a woman with two young children. Or maybe she had them by him. I don't remember."

Sean shook his head. "It doesn't matter."

"Okay. When Samantha's mom died, Sam had nowhere else to go, so she came up here and moved in with Barron. Barron wasn't exactly pleased to see her, having his hands full with his second family and all. And Samantha wasn't pleased because he's a big-deal hunter—you know, one of those people who fly to Africa to kill inedible animals so he can mount their heads on the wall—a displeasure she was not shy sharing with him." Bernie took a deep breath and said, "And now we come to the present. She started fighting with everyone and then came the final straw. Samantha decided to take it upon herself to reallocate resources." Bernie explained about the dress. "And her stepmom hit the roof."

"Understandably so," Sean said. "She has a habit of relocating things," he said, thinking about Trudy. "Always with the best of motives, of course. Actually, she reminds me a little of you when you were younger. Remember when you donated a freezerful of steaks to a homeless man . . ."

". . . who turned out to be wanted on a bank robbery charge?" Bernie groaned. "Yes. I remember," she said.

"Fortunately, we got the meat back in the freezer before your mom returned from her aunt's." Sean chuckled and shook his head at the memory.

"Anyway," Bernie continued, "according to Samantha, her stepmom told Barron he had to make a choice. Either Samantha went or she went. So he kicked Samantha out. That's what we know."

Sean took another sip of his hot chocolate, sat back in his armchair, and thought about the yearbook pictures he'd seen at Joyce's house, the one of Annabel and Joyce and Anna at Rockefeller Center.

"So," he hypothesized, "maybe one day Anna comes into the Colbert house and sees Samantha working there. She looks at Samantha and she knows that this is her kid."

"How does she know?" Bernie asked.

Sean shook his head. "Maybe there's a family feature that stands out. Maybe Anna's been in touch with the dad. I'm not sure. But let's just say for the moment that she knows."

Bernie nodded. "All right. Go on."

"Everything comes back in a rush to her. All the hurt. All the angst. The betrayal. And she decides she wants to punish Richard and Annabel by killing Annabel and laying the blame on Richard."

"That would explain the time frame," Bernie said.

Sean nodded his agreement.

Bernie went on. "So Anna steals a bottle of the wine Annabel drinks, doctors it up, and makes sure that it's the one on the sideboard the day of the party—which would be easy enough for her to do because she was there that day. After which she leaves, figuring that everything will go as planned. But it doesn't."

"That's the problem with poison," Sean said. "It's unpredictable."

"Very. That's why most people use guns or knives. Unfortunately, those didn't fit in with her scenario," Bernie said. "So instead of Annabel falling over dead, thereby rendering the site a crime scene, Annabel passes out. Since everyone told the police she was having a heart attack—which in a sense she was, never mind that it was brought on by the insecticides—the cops didn't secure the scene. That allowed Richard to engage in a bit of housecleaning, thereby throwing a major monkey wrench into Anna's plans and leaving Richard free and clear and unarrested."

"That must have pissed her off to no end," Sean said.

"I would guess so." Bernie fingered a button on her

cardigan. It was coming loose and she needed to resew it. "About Samantha," she said, changing the topic.

"You're thinking that it's going to be tough on her if what we think is true really is true?" her dad asked.

Bernie nodded.

"I know. That occurred to me as well."

They were both silent for a moment.

"So what can we do?" Bernie asked.

"It may be irrelevant."

"Meaning?"

"Meaning that it might never get to that point. What we're talking about is still circumstantial—at best. Certainly there isn't enough evidence to make a case against anyone with what we've got."

"I'm aware of that," Bernie said.

"Good," Sean said. He leaned forward in his chair. "Do not—and I mean do *not*—go talking to Anna."

"And why would I do that?" Bernie asked, hiding her dismay. Was she really that easy to read?

"To get her to do something she might not do otherwise," Sean snapped. "And don't bother denying it. I know how your mind works."

"Just like yours."

Sean opened his mouth to say something, but before he could Samantha emerged from the bathroom.

She'd washed her hair and scrubbed her face. When she sat down on the sofa, Bernie noted that though there was a slight redness around Samantha's eyes, she looked as if she hadn't cried at all. Bernie felt a moment of intense envy—when she cried, her eyes swelled up like a puffer fish—but she managed to suppress it.

"I guess I overreacted," Samantha said after she'd had a glass of milk and two chocolate walnut brownies. "I mean, so what if I get thrown out? Right?"

"Right," Bernie agreed.

"Now I don't have to look at all those disgusting heads mounted on the wall. Just seeing them is such bad karma." Samantha wiped off the top of her upper lip with the back of her hand. "I was going to move to Brooklyn in a couple of months anyway and be a waitress. Or maybe I can do voice-overs. Do you think Richard will give me some money?" Samantha asked. "You know, to kind of get me started."

"Well," Sean began but Samantha cut him off.

"Because I'm going to ask him. I'm going to ask him right now. Either he will or he won't. And if he won't, I can sue him for child support."

Sean didn't point out that Samantha was past the age where that would apply. He could see from the set of Samantha's jaw that nothing he could say was going to register. She'd made up her mind and that was that.

Samantha turned to Bernie. "Can you give me a lift back to the pet shop? That's where I left my car."

"Bernie will take you to the Colberts' house," Sean said before Bernie had a chance to answer.

"You will?" Samantha asked.

"She will," Sean said.

"By all means," Bernie said, intuiting that her dad didn't want Samantha wandering around in the state she was in. Of course, given the way she and Richard had parted company she wasn't sure she was going to be a helpful presence, but it would still probably be better if she went along. "We could always hold Trudy up for ransom if Richard doesn't agree to your demands," she said as she crossed her arms over her chest and turned her gaze on her father. "That is, if we knew where she was."

"Which we don't," Sean pointed out.

"Evidently," Bernie said. She was about to add something to the effect of asking what she'd find if she dropped in on Ines when Samantha spoke up.

"You wouldn't! You couldn't!" she cried.

"Bad joke. I was just kidding," Bernie said.

"No. You weren't."

Bernie held up her hand. "I swear I was."

Sean sighed. Sometimes he wondered if Bernie had any common sense at all. She should never have brought Trudy up. Or maybe she just delighted in stirring things up. He couldn't decide which one was true. At this point he didn't want to waste mental energy trying to figure it out either.

"Let's solve one problem at a time, shall we?" he said to Samantha.

Samantha didn't reply. Sean didn't think she'd heard him because she was heading toward the door when he'd spoken. Either that or she was practicing willfull deafness, a talent both his children excelled at.

"Good luck," he said to Bernie as she got ready to follow Samantha out the door and down the stairs.

He didn't envy Bernie at the moment. He didn't envy her one bit.

Chapter 30

Bernie didn't envy herself either. She was not happy. Put that in capital letters. She was thinking about how she'd much rather be back at the shop rolling out pie dough and waiting on customers instead of dealing with the upcoming Richard and Samantha fiasco. At the very least, it wasn't going to be pleasant. At the very most, it might involve a police presence. But then everything could turn out fine too, which was about as likely as a millipede walking on crutches.

Of course, if the drive over there was any harbinger of things to come, the meeting was going to be irritating at best. A tractor trailer had jackknifed on the ice on Bernard Street. That meant Bernie had had to take Questview instead, a street Bernie usually avoided because of the cars that always spilled out from the big-box shops lining the road. They'd been stuck in traffic for the last ten minutes.

Samantha was looking out the window and uncharacteristically not saying much of anything. As they came up to the first entrance to the Hudson Mall, Bernie was wondering what Richard was going to do.

"Stop!" Samantha cried.

Bernie startled. "Why? What's wrong? Are you sick?"

"Nothing is wrong. I need to go in there." And Samantha pointed to Dick's Sporting Goods.

"Now?" Bernie asked, wondering what on earth Samantha could possibly want in a store like that. She couldn't imagine someone who was more at odds with the store's aesthetic. Her dad and Libby would mock her for using those words, but it was true.

"Definitely now."

"But why? Do you want to get a rifle and shoot someone?"

"Ha. Ha. You're a funny lady. No. I promised Megan I'd get these camo T-shirts for her. She wants to use them for a project she's working on. She's going to sew them into a dress. Then she's going to paint dead animals dripping blood on them and stand by the hunting section of Dick's, which is why I want to get them for her here."

"Kind of a karma thing," Bernie said.

Samantha beamed. "Exactly. And it'll also be like a thank-you for this morning. Please," she said. "It'll just take a second. Then we'll go see dickhead."

"I take it you mean Richard?"

"Whatever," Samantha said.

Bernie sighed. But she turned into the mall anyway. Given the situation, she was willing to cater to Samantha for a little while. After all, even though Samantha was putting on a brave front, she must have been feeling positively wretched inside.

"How long do you think Megan will last before the security guards come and throw her out?" Bernie asked as she pulled into a parking space next to the mall's main entrance.

"Megan's not going to be the only one there," Samantha said.

"Do you think this will do something?" Bernie asked.

"I don't know," Samantha said. "But you have to keep trying. You can't just turn a blind eye to stuff. That's wrong."

"No. I suppose you can't," Bernie said. Suddenly, she felt incredibly old.

She and Samantha got out of the van and scurried into the mall. It had gotten colder again and smelled as if it was going to snow.

"This place is huge," Bernie commented as she and Samantha paused at the entrance of Dick's.

She'd never been in the place. Why would she? But she knew that Brandon shopped here for his camping gear. She knew this because he'd suggested she come here and buy a sleeping bag. That way she could go camping with him. She'd declined the offer. Her idea of roughing it was staying in a motel without a swimming pool.

Now she was thinking she should have said yes. It might be fun. As they went through the aisles of the shop, Bernie stopped now and then to assess the merchandise. By the time they reached the hunting section, she was fairly certain that aside from some yoga pants, water bottles, and hand warmers there wasn't too much in the store that she wanted to buy.

Looking at the crossbows hanging on the walls and the rifles lined up like sentinels, Bernie felt as if she'd wandered into another country, one where everyone was wearing ugly clothes manufactured out of cheap fabrics. She was contemplating a particularly unlovely hat when she became aware that Samantha was staring at something in one of the display cases.

"Can I help you?" the man behind the counter asked her.

It was clear from the look on his face that he disapproved of Samantha's bright blue hair. Or maybe, Bernie thought, he was merely puzzled by Samantha's choice of hair color.

Samantha tapped her finger on the glass. "How much are those?" she asked.

"You mean the stealth cams?" he asked in turn.

Samantha nodded.

"They range in price from one hundred and fifty to over one thousand dollars, but most run about two hundred and fifty, and there are really low-end ones for one hundred dollars. The resolution isn't as good, but they still do the job. Are you interested in buying one?"

"I'm thinking about it," Samantha said as Bernie came up beside her.

"What are they?" Bernie asked.

"My downfall," Samantha said.

"Hunting cameras," the man behind the counter explained. "You mount them on a tree and they take pictures of deer and such."

"Or people," Samantha said bitterly.

"Well, I suppose you could use them that way. Most people who want to do that kind of thing would use something like a nanny cam. These just take stills, while a nanny cam uses video technology."

"But these are cheaper," Samantha said.

The clerk nodded. "They are indeed."

"And easy to hide."

"I suppose they are," the clerk said. "I mean, that's the whole point. Can I show you one?" he asked Samantha. "Do you see a model you're interested in?"

"Do I look like someone who hunts?" Samantha asked. Then she turned and walked off.

"You want to tell me what that's about?" Bernie asked when she caught up with her over by the rack of hunting clothes.

Samantha held up two T-shirts. One was in varying shades of green, while the other was in browns. "Which do you think Megan will like better?" she asked Bernie.

"The green. It's marginally less ugly. But it's huge."

"It'll be fine," Samantha said. "She's going to make a dress out of it, remember?"

"Tell me about the stealth cams."

"There's nothing to tell," Samantha replied.

"Obviously, there is."

"Why do you care?"

"I'm not sure," Bernie said. "I just . . . I want to know."

"It's not very complicated. The man I thought was my father, the moron, set one up in his bedroom, so he could see who came in there—the putz."

"So that's how he knew you'd taken the clothes from your stepmother's closet?"

"She's not even my stepmother. She's this personage in the house."

Bernie threw up her hands. "Fine. Let's call her the Wicked Witch."

Samantha giggled. "That's how he knew I took some money from his drawer. It was only ten dollars, for Pete's sake. I was giving it to that old guy who lives on Spenser— the one who collects the cans. . . ."

Bernie nodded. Sam's list of crimes was getting longer by the minute.

"And I was going to return the money as soon as I got paid. It's not as if Barron can't afford it. He said it was the principle of the thing. Ha." Samantha fell silent for a moment. "People shouldn't be allowed to spy on people."

Bernie declined to point out that taking things without asking permission was also not a good thing.

"Barron's like a disease. That's what my mom always said, and she was right," Samantha continued. "He infects everyone he's around. He even has the dickhead—"

"Richard Colbert?"

"Yeah. Him. Using those stupid cams. I heard Barron talking to him over the phone one day and telling him that if he wanted to protect his wine collection—like who would ever take any of that crap; it tastes horrible—he just needed one of those stupid things."

"Stealth cams?"

"Yeah. That's what I just said."

"And they take pictures?"

"Absolutely. You heard what the guy behind the counter said."

"And you can look at the pictures?"

"Duh. Of course you can. Why else would you take them? What would be the point?"

"Why else indeed," Bernie replied.

Samantha gave her an odd look. "Is everything okay?" she asked. "Because you seem a little out of it."

Bernie pulled herself together. "I'm just thinking."

"About what?"

"About the camera in Richard Colbert's wine room. About seeing what's on it."

Samantha's eyes lit up.

Bernie felt a stab of guilt. "I'm not sure that would be a good thing for you," she said gently, and she explained about Anna.

"No. That's fine," Samantha told Bernie when she was done. "My *real* mom was the person who raised me. I don't care about Anna. Especially if what your dad thinks is right. That means she knew who I was, and well . . . anyway . . . I don't want to go there."

"You're sure?" Bernie asked.

"I'm positive," Samantha said. "And do I have an idea for you."

"It could work," Bernie said when Samantha was done talking.

"It will work," Samantha said. She scrunched up her nose. "But I don't think we should tell your dad, do you?"

"Absolutely not," Bernie said.

"I mean, it's not like what we're going to do is danger-ous," Samantha said. "It's just deeply weird and I don't think your dad does weird well."

That's an understatement, Bernie thought. "You know

what," she said. "Let's just surprise him with the stealth cam if we get it."

"*When* we get it," Samantha said.

"Yes. You're right. *When* we get it." Bernie rubbed her hands together. This was going to be fun. Even if they didn't succeed, it was still going to be fun.

Chapter 31

It took three phone calls—one to Brandon and the other to Megan, who in turn called her mother—and an hour to organize everything.

"This is going to work," Samantha said.

Mrs. McKee bounced up and down on the soles of her feet and clapped her hands. "This is so exciting."

Brandon just looked bemused. He understood the concept well enough; he just couldn't decide what he thought about actually doing it.

Bernie gazed at her coconspirators in crime. She couldn't help smiling. They were such an unlikely bunch, especially Holly, the potbellied pig that Mrs. McKee had recruited from her neighbor for the occasion, and Otto, the McKees' cat, who was securely if not happily sitting in his cat carrier. Megan had wanted to add one of the parrots in the store to the mix, but saner heads, and the observation that it was too cold for a parrot to be outside even for a short time, had prevailed.

Bernie was only sorry that Trudy couldn't have joined them. But that would have put her back in the Colbert household. And then there was the fact that Ines would probably have called her dad to let him know what was going on.

"Are we ready to get the show on the road?" Bernie asked everyone.

Brandon gave a thumbs-up, Holly snuffled, Samantha and Mrs. McKee both flashed V-for-victory signs, while the cat remained quiet. He was not pleased, a fact he made abundantly clear by trying to scratch anyone who came near his carrying case.

"Then let's get going," Samantha said.

Mrs. McKee, Samantha, and Holly jumped into Mrs. McKee's Ford Explorer, while Bernie, Otto, and Brandon got into Brandon's vehicle.

As they pulled out of Mrs. McKee's driveway, Brandon said, "You know, this is so silly I think it's going to work."

"It will work," Bernie said. "I just prefer you let me get the stealth cam."

"Four eyes are better than two," Brandon told her.

"If we can get in there," Bernie said. She'd been assailed by a moment of doubt.

"We will," Brandon assured her. "And even if we don't, this will be very amusing."

Bernie brightened. "That it will be."

Including the potty stop for Holly—"just to be on the safe side," Mrs. McKee explained—it took twenty minutes to get to the Colbert house. Richard Colbert answered the door in his typically gracious manner.

"What do you want?" he demanded of the crowd of people in front of him.

Samantha came forward. "Daddy!" she cried, throwing her arms around him.

Richard tried to take a step back, but Samantha held on fast.

"It's all right. I've always loved you and Anna better," Samantha said. "I've always sensed a mysterious connection between us."

"What are you talking about?" Richard demanded.

He has a look of horror on his face, Bernie thought. She was surprised at the amount of satisfaction that gave her.

"Well, Anna's my real mommy and you're my real daddy. Barron told me everything."

"And we're here to help her move in," Mrs. McKee said. "We've brought Samantha's clothes, her family Bible, and her pets."

Brandon and Bernie put down the boxes and suitcases they were holding and stepped aside to reveal Holly. Richard's jaw dropped.

"This is Holly, Samantha's potbellied pig," said Mrs. McKee, who seemed to have taken charge of the proceedings. "And this is Otto, the cat. He's a tad hostile right now, but I'm sure he'll be fine once he settles down. It only took him four months to stop scratching the furniture in my house."

"Pets? What pets? Samantha doesn't have any pets," Richard squeaked. He seemed to have trouble assimilating the situation.

"I have to confess she was boarding them at my house," Mrs. McKee confided. "She thought Barron would be upset if she arrived with them. Poor child. First her mother, then her animals. It would have been too much. And anyway, my child has allergies." Mrs. McKee beamed. "But now she can be together with them. Thank you. Thank you so much. I can't tell you how nice this is of you. Samantha is so lucky."

Holly gave a polite oink. Richard looked as if he was going to choke. Mrs. McKee led the charge inside, with the pig, the cat, Bernie, and Brandon following in her wake. Richard was too stunned to say or do anything.

"My, my," Mrs. McKee said when they were all safely in the house and Brandon had closed the door behind them. "This certainly is a large house. Holly will have lots of room to roam." And with that she unleashed Holly and let the cat out of his carrier.

"What are you doing?!" Richard screamed.

"Why, getting them used to their surroundings, of course," Mrs. McKee said in a tone that made clear the stupidity of the question. "Now, where do you want us to put Samantha's belongings? We have lots more of her stuff in the car."

"Yes, Daddy," Samantha said. "Where do you want me to put my saxophone? I'm trying to get at least two hours of practice in a day. Usually, I try to do it between five and seven in the morning. That way I get it done and over with."

But Richard didn't reply. He was watching in horror as Holly took off down the hall. The cat was close at her heels.

"Oh dear," Mrs. McKee said. "Maybe we should follow. Holly does have a habit of eating things she shouldn't. She's especially fond of Oriental rugs."

"Oh my God," Richard said. He grabbed his chest. "The Shiraz."

He took off after the pig, along with Mrs. McKee and Samantha. That left Brandon and Bernie by themselves.

"Shall we?" Bernie said. She bowed and extended her hand.

"Lead on, McDuff," Brandon said, "and your loyal henchman will follow."

As Bernie and Brandon hurried toward the room where Richard Colbert stored his wine, they could hear assorted screeches, oinks, and yells coming from the other wing of the house.

"How long do you think we've got?" Brandon asked.

"Not a clue," Bernie said as they entered Richard's wine room. "I have a feeling Holly's pretty hard to get when she doesn't want to be got."

"Nice place," Brandon observed, looking around.

Bernie had to agree that it was. The room itself was on the smallish side. There were two leather chairs and a small round table in the center. A few feet from that was a bar made out of copper and oak. A variety of wineglasses hung from an overhead wire rack. A wine rack made out of crisscrossed pieces of polished golden oak and filled with bottles of wine sat in the back. The shelves on the opposing two walls were filled with bottles of wine as well.

"He's got enough wine in here to open a liquor store," Brandon observed.

Bernie nodded and pointed to a metal rectangular box butting up against the far wall. "I'm betting that's the wine safe," she said.

"Yup. Here be vintages," Brandon said. "Which means that the camera has to have a view of that."

"Which would put it right behind the bar."

"Exactamundo, Sherlock."

Brandon and Bernie scrutinized the wall in back of the bar. There was a rather large, badly executed picture of three fat men sitting at a table smoking cigars and drinking brandy. Similar pictures decorated the other walls.

"Are you thinking what I'm thinking?" Brandon asked.

"That Richard Colbert has terrible taste in art?" Bernie held up her hand. "Just kidding," she said to Brandon as she moved toward the picture.

Brandon did the same. In the background, they could hear the sounds of running footsteps, Mrs. McKee saying, "Oh, I'm so dreadfully sorry. Holly has never pooped on a rug before," and Richard screaming, "Get out! I want you out!"

"We'd better hurry," Bernie said as she and Brandon lifted the picture off the wall and propped it against the bar.

The stealth cam was right there, nestled in the cavity that Richard Colbert had made for it. Bernie lifted it out and put it in her bag. Then she and Brandon picked the picture back up and carefully put it back in its place. As she did Bernie could see the small hole in the cigar tip that lined up with the stealth cam's lens. They stepped out from behind the bar.

"I wonder if there are any more cams in here," Brandon said. "I think we should check."

Bernie was about to answer when Richard appeared at the door. He was panting. His hair was a mess. His clothes were disheveled. "What are you doing in here?!" he screamed.

"You don't have to yell," Bernie said. "We were looking for the cat."

"The cat went in the other direction," Richard cried.

"I guess that explains why we couldn't find him," Bernie said as she started edging around him.

"I want you out of here! I want you out of here now!" Richard screamed as he pointed to the door.

Samantha appeared behind him. "Daddy, don't throw me out into the street," she begged.

He turned. She got down on her knees and embraced his legs. "Please," she sobbed.

"Now, now," Bernie said as she got past Richard. "Samantha, it's time to go."

"Don't make me leave my father," Samantha moaned, playing the scene for all it was worth.

Bernie had to look down so she wouldn't laugh. Samantha continued to sob. Brandon went over and lifted her up. *Maybe the kid will make it as an actress,* Bernie thought as she watched her. She was certainly good at improv.

"Sorry," Brandon said to Richard. "She tends to get a little emotional."

By the time all of them got to the front door, Mrs. McKee was standing there with Holly and Otto. Bernie gave a slight nod to Mrs. McKee. She gathered up Holly's leash and picked up the cat carrier, where Otto was safely ensconced.

"Come, children," Mrs. McKee said. "This is not a nice man after all."

She hurried out the door, with everyone else right behind her.

*   *   *

Sean and Libby looked more than a little surprised when everyone, animals included, came trooping into the Simmons's flat twenty minutes later. Sean was even more surprised after he'd looked at the pictures on the stealth cam.

"Don't tell me how you got this," he said to Bernie and her gang before he called Clyde. "I don't want to know."

After Clyde had had a chance to see the pictures, he said the same thing to them. Then he took a drive out to the Colbert house. Richard and Joanna were packing up when he arrived.

Chapter 32

Three days later, Sean, Libby, Bernie, Samantha, Brandon, and Trudy reconvened at Mrs. McKee's house to go over the events that had transpired at the Colbert estate. They, plus Mr. and Mrs. McKee and Megan, were sitting around the dining room table eating cupcakes supplied by Bernie, drinking tea supplied by Mrs. McKee, and sipping champagne that Brandon had relocated from the Colbert estate. The only notables absent were Otto, who was sleeping on the upstairs radiator, and Holly, who had a prior engagement at the Longely Elementary School.

Sean, who had already had one glass of The Widow, was reading the headlines of the local paper for the second time.

"I still can't believe it," Mr. McKee said as he sat down next to Trudy, who was busy licking the frosting off a cupcake wrapper.

Sean tapped the paper with his thumb. "Give me a straightforward criminal any day. That's all I can say."

"So it wasn't Anna?" Mr. McKee said.

"We told you that already, dear," Mrs. McKee said. "It was Joanna."

"The names sound alike," he complained as he fed Trudy a piece of cupcake.

"Only to you," Mrs. McKee said.

Samantha came in from the kitchen with a glass of water and sat back down at the table. "Well, I'm glad it wasn't Anna."

"You said you didn't care," Bernie pointed out.

Samantha twirled a strand of her hair, which was now pink, around her finger. "Well, I don't. But I do."

Mrs. McKee got up, walked over, and patted Samantha on the shoulder. "Maybe we should invite her over for dinner one night? What do you think?"

Samantha wrinkled her nose at the thought.

"Maybe it's too soon," Mrs. McKee said. "Let me know when you're ready."

"It was very nice of you to let Samantha move in with you," Sean told her.

Mrs. McKee looked truly offended. "And let this poor child and her dog live out on the street, when we have a perfectly good empty bedroom and backyard going to waste? She and Trudy can stay as long as they want."

Megan nodded. "I think she has a great acting career in front of her, don't you, Mom?"

"Indeed I do," Mrs. McKee replied.

Brandon nodded his agreement. "Considering the performance she put on at the Colberts, I'd say so."

Libby took a sip of her tea. "I don't understand how you ended up with Trudy," she said to Samantha.

"It's simple," Samantha said. "Annabel is dead and Richard is in jail . . . so I decided to keep her. Nobody's said anything."

"That's because no one knows," Sean said.

"Everyone knows," Bernie said. "No one is talking about it."

Sean put the paper down. "I think Ines was sorry to see her go."

"That's not what she said to me when we went to pick her up," Bernie retorted.

"She didn't mean it," Sean said.

"Yes, she did," Bernie told him.

"Why isn't she here?" Samantha asked.

"Because she's out in California visiting her daughter," Sean explained.

Mr. McKee interrupted. "Can someone please explain this to me again?" he asked.

"I did," Mrs. McKee said. "Twice."

"I still don't get it," Mr. McKee said.

"It's simple," Mrs. McKee told him.

"Not the way you're telling it," Mr. McKee retorted.

Sean interrupted. "Well, it took me a little while to figure it out too, but I can give it a try if you want."

"I'd be grateful," Mr. McKee said.

"To put it in its simplest terms, Richard and Annabel Colbert were not getting along. They were not getting along for a number of reasons, one of them being Richard's habit of sleeping with every available female he could find. For some reason, Richard's relationship with Joanna was particularly irritating to Annabel, or maybe it was just the excuse she was looking for to untangle herself from Richard. I don't know. In short, she'd had enough and was going to divorce him.

"Now this presented a problem for Richard. For business purposes, Annabel had all the assets—meaning everything was in her name—and he had all the liabilities."

"Meaning he would lose everything," Mr. McKee said.

Sean nodded. "Indeed he would. While she was at it, Annabel decided to make a clean sweep and get rid of all the dead wood"—Sean bracketed the last phrase with his fingers—"around her. That meant that Joanna would be out on her ass, as well as Ramona, Joyce, and Melissa.

"Somehow or other Joanna found out what Annabel was planning to do. She told Richard. He, in turn, had learned from Barron that his daughter . . ."

Samantha raised her hand. "He means me."

"We know that, dear," Mrs. McKee said.

Sean coughed and everyone fell silent. "As I was saying," he continued, "he found out that Samantha was back in town. The wheels began to turn. Then one day when he saw Anna coming down the stairs, something clicked. He had the solution to his problem. He was going to kill Annabel in such a way as to make the blame fall on Anna, whom he disliked anyway.

"So he suggested to Joanna that she doctor up the bottle of wine—Trudy's birthday party being a perfect opportunity, in his mind, to shove suspicion onto Anna, which it did. It's certainly what Bernie, Libby, and I thought. And if that didn't work, he had a backup plan. Joanna. She didn't know about the stealth cam. She had no idea. So after Annabel was dead, Richard wasn't going to have to worry about his partner in crime. He could blow her in whenever he wanted. The stealth cam was added insurance. And it would have worked too."

"Except we stole the stealth cam," Brandon said.

"Exactly," Sean said.

"What's going to happen now?" Samantha asked.

"According to Clyde, Richard and Joanna are going to be brought up on murder one charges," Sean said. "Evidently they both ratted each other out. Joanna was particularly incensed when the ADA showed her the pictures."

"So everything worked out fine," Mr. McKee said.

Samantha took a cupcake and plopped it on her plate. "Or as Bill says . . ."

"Bill?" Bernie asked.

"Duh. As in Bill Shakespeare."

"Naturally," Bernie said.

"What does he say?" Brandon asked.

"All's well that ends well," Bernie and Samantha chorused together.

"A toast," Libby said. "A toast to happy endings."

And they all drank to that. Even Trudy, who had a sip of champagne from Samantha's glass.

RECIPES

These two recipes come from Renee Crandell, who runs a dog-grooming place called Best Paw Forward. She is a wonderful lady who does dog rescue work. The appetizer and the birthday cake would be ideal for a dog birthday party. They certainly are a hit with my dogs. The recipes are dedicated to Renee's basset hound, Edna Jean.

Cheesy Roll Appetizers

¼ cup grated cheddar cheese
¼ cup grated Swiss cheese
½ teaspoon brewer's yeast
2 tablespoons vegetable shortening
½ cup toasted oatmeal

Combine the cheeses, brewer's yeast, and shortening. Using plastic wrap, shape the mixture into a log about 1 inch in diameter and 8 inches long. Roll the log in toasted oatmeal. Refrigerate. Slice into half-inch rounds and serve.

A Doggy Birthday Cake

½ pound liver
13-ounce can dog food
2 eggs separated
1 cup flour
1 ½ teaspoons baking powder
12 ounces low-fat cream cheese
Cheez Whiz
dog treats

Preheat oven to 300 degrees and generously grease a 9-inch cake pan. Simmer the liver in a small amount of water until cooked, then cool, and grind in a blender until it's a smooth, soft paste. Mix thoroughly with the canned dog food. Beat the egg whites until stiff and fold into the liver mixture. Add the yolks. Gently fold in the flour and baking powder.

Bake for 35 to 45 minutes until a toothpick comes out clean. Cool and frost with cream cheese. Decorate with Cheez Whiz and dog treats.

Not to be evil or anything, but if you really don't like someone you could serve him or her this as a birthday cake. Just frost with whipped cream and leave off the dog treats and Cheez Whiz.

The next recipe is my son, Noah's, favorite birthday cake. He's been eating it since he was six. The genoise recipe comes from Paula Peck's *Art of Baking*.

Noah's Strawberry Shortcake

6 large eggs
1 cup sugar
1 cup sifted flour
½ cup sweet butter melted and clarified
1 teaspoon vanilla extract

Topping

2 pints strawberries
Powdered sugar
Lemon juice
2 pints heavy cream
1 teaspoon vanilla extract
Strawberry jam or Grand Marnier
Finely chopped pistachios

Preheat oven to 350 degrees. Butter and lightly flour two 9-inch layer-cake pans.

Put the eggs and sugar in a large bowl. Stir until they are combined. Set the bowl over a saucepan containing 1 to 2 inches of hot water. Water in the saucepan should not touch the bowl, nor should it be allowed to boil. Place the saucepan over heat for 5 to 10 minutes or until the eggs are lukewarm. Stir four or five times to prevent them from cooking at the bottom of the bowl.

When the eggs feel lukewarm to your finger and look like a bright yellow syrup, remove the bowl from the heat. Begin to beat, preferably with an electric mixer. Beat at high speed for 10 to 15 minutes, scraping the sides of the bowl with a rubber spatula when necessary, until the mixture becomes light and fluffy and has increased in volume to almost three times its bulk. The mixture will look like whipped cream.

Sprinkle a little flour at a time on top of the egg mixture and fold in with a rubber spatula. Use a gentle motion. Then add the butter and vanilla using the same technique. Be careful not to overmix.

Pour the batter into pans and place in the oven. Bake for 25 minutes or until the tops spring back when touched. Cool on racks.

Rinse and hull 2 pints of strawberries. Put 10 large ones aside for the top of the cake. Take the others, slice, and put in a bowl. Add powdered sugar according to taste—probably 1 or 2 tablespoons—and add about 1 tablespoon of lemon juice. Allow to macerate.

Whip 2 pints of heavy cream. Then add 3 tablespoons of powdered sugar (or more if desired) and 1 teaspoon of vanilla.

Remove the first cake layer from the pan and put on a serving plate. Thinly spread 2 teaspoons of melted strawberry jam on the cake or sprinkle 2 tablespoons of Grand Marnier on the cake or do the same with the juice that has accumulated at the bottom of the bowl of strawberries. Spread a thick layer of whipped cream on the cake and put the strawberries over that. Then add the top layer. Frost with the rest of the whipped cream. Take the reserve strawberries, dehull, glaze them with melted strawberry jam, and arrange on top of the cake. Decorate the sides of the cake with finely chopped pistachios. Serve and enjoy.

The following recipe comes from my good friend and neighbor April Grover. It was her daughter Rachel's favorite birthday cake. She believes it originally came from the back of the package of Baker's German Sweet Chocolate.

Ten-Minute German Sweet Chocolate Cream Pie

4 ounces Baker's German Sweet Chocolate
⅓ cup milk
2 tablespoons sugar (optional)
3-ounce package softened cream cheese
8 ounces Cool Whip
Chocolate wafers

For the crust, place chocolate wafers in an 8-inch pie tin.

Over low heat, heat the chocolate in 2 tablespoons of milk until the chocolate is melted. Beat the sugar into the cream cheese. Add the remaining milk and chocolate. Beat until smooth. Fold the chocolate mixture into the Cool Whip. Stir until combined. Spoon into the crust. Freeze for 4 hours or until firm. Garnish with chocolate curls, strawberries, or whatever you desire.

This cake comes from another good friend and neighbor, Sarah Saulson. It was her favorite birthday cake when she was growing up.

Mother's Milk Chocolate Cake

2 ¼ cups sugar
3 tablespoons water
2 squares melted unsweetened chocolate
¾ cup softened butter or margarine
1 teaspoon vanilla extract
4 eggs separated
2 ¼ cups sifted cake flour
1 teaspoon cream of tartar
½ teaspoon baking soda
½ teaspoon salt
1 cup milk
Standard thickened custard filling from *Joy of Cooking*

Chocolate Cream-Cheese Frosting

¼ cup softened butter or margarine
8 ounces softened cream cheese
3 squares melted unsweetened chocolate
Dash salt
3 cups confectioners' sugar
⅓ cup light cream
1 teaspoon vanilla extract

Cream butter or margarine. Add the next three ingredients and blend. Add the sugar mixture alternately with the cream, beating thoroughly. Add the vanilla. Set aside.

Add ¼ cup of the sugar and the water to the chocolate. Cream the butter or margarine well. Add the remaining 2 cups of sugar gradually, beating until light and fluffy. Add the vanilla, then the egg yolks one at a time, beating well after each addition. Add the chocolate mixture and blend. Add the sifted dry ingredients alternately with the milk, beating until smooth. Fold in egg whites, beaten until stiff but not dry. Pour into three round 9-inch or four round 8-inch layer pans lined on the bottom with greased waxed paper. Bake at 350 degrees for about 40 to 50 minutes. Let stand 5 minutes. Then turn out onto racks to cool. Remove the paper. Put the custard filling between the layers and spread top and sides with the chocolate cream-cheese frosting.